Lyndon Mallet is a B   l
cartoonist with film, TV   e
learnt his way around th   :r
became Road Manager ⸜   ıg
on a career in advertising. He lives in Buckıngнаш   ıd
writes full time.

TAFFIN ON BALANCE

LYNDON MALLET

Matador
9 Priory Business Park,
Wistow Road, Kibworth Beauchamp,
Leicestershire. LE8 0RX
Tel: 0116 279 2299
Email: books@troubador.co.uk
Web: www.troubador.co.uk/matador
Twitter: @matadorbooks

ISBN 978 1788039 093

British Library Cataloguing in Publication Data.
A catalogue record for this book is available from the British Library.

Printed and bound in the UK by TJ International, Padstow, Cornwall
Typeset in 12pt Bembo by Troubador Publishing Ltd, Leicester, UK
Cover, Steven Amos

Matador is an imprint of Troubador Publishing Ltd

My thanks to Austin Legon for wise words: Be Lucky. And in memory of Brian Lecomber, for a lifetime's friendship and inspiration. God's speed, Old Chum.

ONE

SOUNDS LIKE THE OLD TROUBLE starting up again. A knock on the door: a couple of locals with a problem they can't fix themselves. Harry Hawkins from the Rookwood estate and Ivy Lewis, who may or may not be his girlfriend. They stand in the doorway like lost souls. He tells them, those days are over, but they won't have any of it. He's got a reputation and they've got long memories. You could fix it, they say, no questions asked. And they fidget like resentful children when he shakes his head.

From the office window, Charlotte watches as Harry and Ivy walk away across the forecourt, looking back, discussing their disappointment, past a restored '78 Corvette Stingray, past a Dodge Charger of uncertain vintage, past the sign that says *Muscle Motors.*

There hasn't been a visit like this in a while but Charlotte knew what was coming by the way the couple approached – uncertain, trying to look confident, wishing it didn't have to be them doing the asking. She heard fragments of the conversation, could picture their faces without having to look, knew the man they came to see wouldn't say much.

He never says much.

THE TOLLGATE BOOKSHOP occupies all available space in a red brick house that once had five bedrooms on two floors. The upstairs rooms have windows with leaded lights that filter the morning sun, casting shadow patterns on floor to ceiling shelves packed with volumes on every imaginable subject, carefully sorted, offering their squashed-up spines for perusal. Inside, you can lose yourself in a dusty wooden maze where floorboards creak and people stand aside to let each other pass. It's a browsers' catacomb where book-lovers lose all sense of time: a place of peace and learning.

The two windows facing the road show racks of books facing outwards: a taste of what's inside. Nothing new: all well-thumbed. Anything you might be looking for, from historical romance to higher mathematics, drama to economics, comic books, Si-Fi, suspense, theology and everything in between. The bookshop is an open secret; you need to know it's here, and those who do pass the word around.

Viewed from the main street, the building looks like many others in the village, hemmed in by centuries of rural architecture, overgrown with wisteria, set about with pots, stone and ironwork. The difference is it stands on the edge, overlooking ten acres of its own land. By any standards, this property is worth owning.

Lorna Moorcroft works here Tuesdays and Thursdays to alleviate the boredom of retirement forced on her when the library closed. Somewhere to go and be useful, but not for long, if the rumours are true. The owner is under pressure to sell. Control of the bookshop has passed from a benign eighty-seven-year-old to an entrepreneurial nephew who has used a certain disingenuous charm to get into government.

Gordon Glennan MP is well aware of the site's commercial potential and the word is out that he is open to suggestion. There's a prospective buyer in the background who knows a good thing when he sees it and won't let anyone's sensibilities stand in the way.

Mrs. Royce, in charge of day-to-day management, reports recent visits from men in well-cut suits who say nothing, take measurements, make notes, fill up space, exude disregard for their surroundings and wander among the shelves without buying. She doubts they're book-lovers, says they make her feel uneasy and, more to the point, they deter regular customers.

Lorna was hoping no one answering that description would come in on either of her days, but it seems her luck has run out. Someone is at the door. A bulky shadow blocks the sunlight. Hard angles shift, the bell *dings* as the door opens and closes.

Slow footsteps on the boards and the room seems to close in. Expecting more sound, Lorna feels a prickling in her ears. Unaccustomed stillness. She looks up from the catalogue she was reading and feels a sudden contraction of the scalp.

This space was designed for smaller people.

The face now turned to her occupies its own shadow and conveys no readable expression. Dark hair, dark glasses, no sound; no reaction required.

On a normal day, Lorna would establish contact, ask if she could help in any way. Not this morning. The stranger is making slow progress down an aisle of obscure titles, browsing, pausing to hook a volume from a shelf, flipping through the pages and becoming engrossed.

Lorna allows herself to relax. This one at least pretends to show an interest.

She looks around. He was there a moment ago. Curious, she peers into the shadows and catches her breath. He is here, beside her. Without apparently having moved. Not what you expect from a heavily-built man.

'I'm sorry, you startled me.' Lorna exhales slowly and attempts a smile. Dark glasses nod once in reply. The man sets a book down on the counter: *Debt, Debit and the Economics of Mismanagement* by Warren Palmer. Lorna knows the author's name, looks at the flyleaf where the price is written in pencil.

'That's five pounds.' She meets his gaze. 'Warren Palmer. I've tried to read him but this stuff is way beyond me. He says if people didn't delay paying for things no one could charge interest, so the bankers would have to rethink everything. He's the one who quoined the term *Miseconomics*, isn't he?'

Dark glasses incline slightly. That's confirmation, she thinks. Five pounds in change has appeared on the counter and she puts it in the till, deciding, at the same moment, not to be passed over by this stranger.

'Is he British, do you thing, or American? I like to hear a voice in my head when I'm reading. It helps to know something about the author.'

A hint of amusement brushes the blank face for a moment. 'Scottish.'

'Thank you. I probably won't try him again, but if I ever do, I can imagine a Scottish voice.' She hands him the book. 'Enjoy.'

Dark glasses dip once more. Floorboards creak. The doorbell *dings* and the shop is empty again.

And long after this customer has left, Lorna tries to imagine what use a man like that could possibly have for the ramblings of an obscure professor of economics.

'WHAT ARE YOU READING?' Charlotte tips the book up to see the title and makes a gargoyle face. 'Economics? Your idea of economy would be a V8 motor with less than six litres of Alfa Male grunt. Who are you kidding?'

Taffin sits back in the bulky armchair and watches her face. 'So?'

'What's *so* s'posed to mean? I worry about you.'

'What's the problem, girl?'

'Your reading matter. You're getting too serious.'

'Broadens the mind.' A twitch at the corner of the mouth. A scolding from her never fails to lighten his mood.

'Broadens the mind,' she mimics the flatness of his voice. 'What did those buggers want this morning?'

'A favour.'

'And you said?'

'I don't do favours.'

'Except for me.' She poses, slim hand planted on a delectable curve of thigh.

He nods, peacefully.

'Yeah...' her face is serious now. 'I get twitchy when people ask you for favours. You haven't told me what they wanted.'

Taffin lays the book aside and gazes at her. 'They wanted me to have a word with someone.'

'They wanted you to scare someone fartless. Who?'

'Some politician.'

'Local?'

'Lives locally. This one's a minister.'

'Give me strength.' Charlotte settles down on the arm of his chair. 'You mean...'

'A junior minister.'

'They want you pressuring the Government now.'

'I decided against it.'

'Good call. Who is it?'

'It don't matter. They're all the same.'

'I might've heard of him. You're not the only celebrity round here.'

'I ain't a celeb.'

'Of course you are. They made a movie about you, didn't they? Your name is known, Mark Twill Taffin.'

'Gordon Glennan Em Pee. The Right Honourable.'

'And you're not interested.'

'That's what I said.'

'Yeah...' she leans in close to his face. 'You're broody – I know that look. You get involved in anything heavy, young man, and you'll have me to answer to.'

FIRST LIGHT. Fresh, clean air. A whisper of wind stirs the treetops over the sprawl of workshop buildings.

Taffin leaves the Jeep under the sign that says *Muscle Motors* and wanders among the oversize monsters on the forecourt: automotive junk or classics, depending on your point of view; for Taffin, they're a living, nothing more or less.

Ed Pentecost is waiting in the office and turns the lights on as he approaches. Taffin thinks Ed has aged since they've been in business, but then, who hasn't? Ed thinks Taffin looks the same as ever: broad, solid in the timeless dark suit and white shirt, and definitely not inclined to move any faster than suits him.

Ed is always in by eight but it's been a while since he was summoned at first light. He breaks the silence.

'Three geezers in a Mercedes turned up here yesterday looking for you. Didn't leave their names. Said they'd be back.'

'Is that so? I had a visit too.'

'They found you then.' Ed plugs the kettle in and spoons coffee into mugs.

'No.' Taffin folds his arms. 'I was approached by two worried villagers who I know from way back. You say your fellas didn't leave their names.'

'Not the same people then?'

'No way. Listen to the music, Ed – I'm hearing different tunes.'

Ed brews the coffee and leans against the counter where the day's worksheets are already laid out in order of priority from left to right. Charlotte's system, established when they first set up the business. Ten years ago, or is it twelve?

'What did your worried villagers want?'

'A favour, Ed. It happens now and then.' Taffin ambles to the counter and takes a mug, nursing the warmth in his hands.

'Like old times?'

'Like old times.'

'I'm guessing Charlotte ain't happy then.'

'Your guesswork is accurate, Ed, as always.'

'And you're considering it – or we wouldn't be here. At six in the A.M.'

'I turned them down flat.'

'But you're thinking about it.' Ed addresses the remark to his coffee cup, aware of Taffin's stillness. 'Tell me it's not the big one.'

'What would the big one be, Ed?'

'StarTrack – that's all anyone talks about.'

Taffin nods thoughtfully. StarTrack is the company running a proposed high-speed rail link in a Westward loop from London. The favoured route cuts through the landscape brushing up against ancient towns and villages, uprooting households and slashing property values. The name is a dirty word locally.

'I'm flattered.'

'It's possible.' Ed meets the blank stare. 'There's always going to be some clown who thinks you can wave a wand. I've been waiting for someone to come to you about StarTrack.'

'Not my business.' A hint of amusement touches Taffin's face. 'No Ed, that ain't it. There's a second-hand bookshop that might have to close, and a few people feel a word in the right ear might get a speculator to think twice.'

Ed nods, relieved. 'And you're thinking about it.'

'I set a high value on this bookshop. I'm tempted.'

'Like old times?' Ed frowns with the realization that his long time mentor and boss is asking for an opinion. 'Those days are over. You don't want to go back there.'

'That's what Charlotte says.'

'Well –' Ed turns over a job sheet ready for the morning's work – 'she's right – and I'm in. But you knew that.'

'That's all I wanted to hear.'

'Reckon the same goes for Rick. You want me to mention it to him?'

'I'll talk to Rick.'

'And the three fellas in the Mercedes – what kind of favour d'you reckon they want?'

'We can only guess, Ed.'

TWO

RICK BISHOP brings the flatbed truck to a halt outside the workshop at *Muscle Motors*. An early start today. There's a 1966 Ford Mustang quietly decomposing in a lock-up somewhere near Derby, waiting to be collected. Taffin has done the deal with the owner, Ed has directions to the place and Rick is ready to go but there's no light in the office yet, so he has to wait.

On the other hand, three men he doesn't know are leaning against a gunmetal grey Mercedes outside the office. The Mercedes is this year's model and the windows are dark – a feature Rick has always found irritating: nonentities pretending you might recognize them.

Something not right here. Rick steps out of his cab and approaches, limbs hanging loose, no hurry.

'Can I help you gentlemen?' – a phrase he learnt from Taffin way back when he and Ed were learning the art of persuasion.

One of the three eases himself away from the car to face him.

'Mister Taffin?'

'And you are?'

The other two amble forward to flank the first.

'You don't look like Taffin. They say he's a big fella. Where would Mister Taffin be, do you think?'

'Who wants him?' Rick Bishop stands very still, inwardly alert. *Never show what you're thinking; never answer a question.*

The first speaker moves closer, the other two keeping pace on either side.

'I asked you a question. I haven't heard an answer.'

'I'll answer yours when you answer mine.'

It took years of patient training to get Rick's aggressive nature under control. Even now, every instinct is telling him to lash out to left and right – get the first blow in while they're still thinking about it.

He turns away from the speaker to size up the opposition on his right. In the same instant a fist smashes into his midriff, a kick sweeps his legs from under him and he hits the ground face first, tasting the diesel-soaked soil.

Should've swung first. Roll away fast but it doesn't help. A well swung foot takes him in the ribs knocking the breath out of him.

Pain feeds fury and Rick drags himself upright as a heavy boot takes him on the shoulder and bowls him over, clawing at the earth.

Hands hauling him to his feet. The first speaker looks him over, reaches out to wipe the mud from his face: a concerned onlooker.

'That was a nasty fall. You have to watch where you put your feet on this rough surface.'

Rick says nothing.

The speaker's eyeline shifts. A beam of headlight flashes

along the trees, a track bike weaves among the parked cars, grumbles towards them and comes to a halt beside the Mercedes.

Ed Pentecost dismounts slowly, removes his helmet, places it carefully on the saddle and wanders across to the group where Rick stands, propped up between his attackers. The speaker turns to watch him – a bystander, expressing idle curiosity.

Ed looks Rick over. 'You alright, mate?'

'He had a fall.' The speaker brushes damp earth from the front of Rick's jacket. 'Took a swing at my colleague and tripped.'

'Yeah?' Ed speaks quietly. 'Not like him to trip.'

'These things happen.'

Ed Pentecost looks over the three unfamiliar faces and nods, agreeably. 'Don't piss down my back and tell me it's raining. Tell your pal not to stand behind me.'

'That's not very friendly. We're waiting for Mister Taffin. You don't mind if we wait inside.'

'You can tell me who wants him.'

Take them to the point where they have to act now or back off. Watch their faces.

The speaker shows disappointment with a shake of the head. A glance, and the other two release Rick, who lurches but remains standing.

The moment has passed but Ed doesn't relax yet. Push a bit further to see what these people are made of.

'I'll need a name from one of you.'

'Seems reasonable.' The speaker makes a slow turn, inspecting the forecourt, then: 'This is a business. We could be customers. You can call me Sir.'

Rick Bishop shakes off the hands restraining him and takes a step towards the speaker.

'Leave it, Rick – not worth it.' Ed takes his arm and leads him to the huddle of buildings.

In the washroom behind the office Rick splashes water on his face, wipes the grime off with a sheet of kitchen towel and examines his ribs for damage.

'I'm glad you pitched up when you did. One of those bastards had a heavy boot on 'im.'

'You did well, Rick. I thought you were about to give them some back.'

'Maybe I'll get a chance later. Are they still there?'

'Sitting in their car.' Ed leans for a view through the window. 'They can sit there all day if they like. I'm here. You better get off to Derby if you're fit.'

'I'll do.' Rick flexes his shoulders and winces. 'You don't want me to stick around? There's three of them.'

'They won't give me any trouble. I'll be in the workshop minding my own business.'

'Give me the directions and I'll be on my way.'

Five minutes later, Rick Bishop swings the flatbed truck through an elegant U-turn missing the Mercedes by inches and heads out along the main road.

'LET ME EXPLAIN, MISTER TAFFIN.' The speaker props himself on the edge of a desk. 'I represent the interests of a serious collector. He likes cars. You're known to share his enthusiasm for high capacity engines. He believes you can help him.'

The sharp stutter of an air wrench lets him know the workshop is active. Dust drifts in the partial light. The speaker pauses, watching the silhouette framed in rays from the sunlit window.

In the absence of any reaction, he continues: 'My client wants a late 'thirties Cord – the 812 supercharged model, with a Lycoming V8 engine, pop-up headlights, front wheel drive, state of the art in its day – an immaculate example, of course. He thinks you're a man who would know where to find one.'

Taffin stands by the window, looking out, partially obscuring the only source of light.

The speaker continues. 'My client knows you by reputation. He regards you as a man of influence – a celebrity. I should add that he knows what he wants and can smell a fake without even having to look at it.'

'What does your client call himself?'

'I address him as Mister Adams.'

'And you are...?'

'I'm just the messenger.'

The sky brightens beyond the window, creating an aura around Taffin's silhouette. Rays of light shift as he turns.

'We like to know names around here. My colleague asked yours. He got a kicking instead.'

'We got off on the wrong foot.'

'So I hear. Your pals were lucky to catch him in a good mood.'

'He misread the situation. I'm sure there won't be any hard feelings.'

'Let's hope not. You're on my premises. You know who I am. I'll ask once more – who are you?'

'My friends call me Silver. That won't mean anything to you.'

'And Mister Adams – what's his real name?'

Silver folds his arms and shows a row of china-white teeth. 'They said you were smart. Let's talk business.'

Taffin moves from the window, shedding light on Silver, forcing him to recoil in the glare. 'I'll talk. You listen.' The voice is just above a whisper. 'First, whatever Mister Adams wants, he can ask me himself.'

'I'm authorized to speak for him.'

'Not by me. Next, the two gentlemen with you can get themselves in here now.'

'Mister Rott and Mister Weiler we call them. They're high-spirited lads, I warn you.'

Taffin lets the stillness settle. Silver shrugs: 'By all means, call them in.'

'You call them.'

Silver allows himself an insolent pause, crosses to the door, opens it with a flourish and summons the two men with a jerk of the head.

Greg Dupree and Michael Wyatt don't expect to explain themselves: their work doesn't call for it. They enter the office in the easy way of speculators looking over a new acquisition. Wyatt closes the door and leans against it, arms folded. Dupree becomes absorbed in a wall poster featuring a 1971 Pontiac GTO. Silver perches against a desk, radiating benevolent calm.

Taffin stands at the window with his back to them. Metallic sounds from the workshop; the air wrench stutters again.

'You gentlemen owe my colleague an apology.'

By the door, Wyatt unfolds his arms.

Dupree turns from the poster, face beefy with triumphant scorn. 'Excuse me?'

'You heard.'

'In your dreams.'

On the instant the room is full of light and Dupree finds himself staring into an expressionless face.

'We ain't got many rules here, son.' Taffin looks past him as if he, too, were studying the GTO poster. 'Just one – we insist on good manners.'

'You cute old-fashioned thing.' Dupree hesitates for a moment and his face hardens to compensate. Taffin's dark stare settles on him.

Wyatt takes a step forward. Silver signals him to stay still.

'It's all about balance.' Taffin addresses Dupree earnestly like a lecturer outlining a vital principle. 'We have here a delicate situation, so the balance needs to be precise. Treat people right, they'll treat you right. Mister Silver has understood he needs to keep still. Your pal hasn't grasped that yet.'

Wyatt has edged closer. Taffin raises his head. A fractional flexing of the shoulders and Wyatt folds up behind him like a roll of old carpet.

Dupree freezes, eyes fixed on the impassive face in front of him.

'Balance...' Taffin remarks, as if summing up after his demonstration.

Wyatt is working his way up from a kneeling position. Silver remains calm. Taffin turns to face him.

'Upset the balance and people become unreasonable. That's why it's important. Now we have a gentleman on the floor, and the one behind me wants to make the same mistake. Set him straight.'

Silver nods, showing an icy spread of teeth. 'They said you were smart, Taffin. Let's move on – I've still got business to attend to.'

'Not with me.' Taffin ambles to the window, darkening the room. 'Not until we discuss the small matter of an apology. You gentlemen will need to show me you're in earnest before we get to business. Listen carefully – here's how it's going to be.'

Wyatt is on his feet now, jaw slack with fury. He glances at Silver for direction. Silver makes a slow arc with his hand as if wiping the slate clean. Three faces turn to the silhouette at the window.

RICK BISHOP has been watching the broad grille in his mirror all the way from Derby. He manhandled the old Ford Mustang onto the flatbed truck with the aid of chains and pulleys, slightly impeded by the previous owner, whose idea of helping was to stand in the way and offer advice. Rick got away eventually with the car firmly strapped down behind him, the running Mustang badge inches from the rear window of his cab.

His day started with unexpected violence, he has been on the road for nearly six hours and now he could do with a rest – which he's not going to get until he's unloaded the Mustang. He hopes Ed Pentecost is still around to give him a hand.

As he swings the truck into the lane that leads to *Muscle Motors*, he has a glimpse through the trees of the gunmetal grey Mercedes on the forecourt. From Rick's point of view this is a good thing and a bad thing. On the plus side, he would relish a moment with the man who gave him bruised ribs; on the other hand, all he really wants is Kath, a beer and somewhere to put his feet up.

He parks the truck beside the workshop and is relieved to see Ed Pentecost in the doorway, wiping his hands on a rag. A bit of help never comes amiss when the odds are out of balance. And the odds are not looking good. The three from the Mercedes are walking towards him and there is purpose in their stride.

The man with unnaturally bright teeth is in the middle, the one with the heavy boot to his right, the third hanging back to watch their rear. Professional, but something in their collective posture tells Rick there is no threat for the moment. As they come closer he tries to read their faces but can't see beyond those teeth.

He climbs down from the cab and at the same moment the office door opens and Taffin is standing there, hands behind his back. Rick knows that posture well: stay still – do nothing.

He watches with mounting surprise as the two men who would have been happy to make a stretcher-case of him this morning set themselves to unstrapping the Mustang and carefully easing it off the flatbed truck, the man with the teeth supervising. Weird but welcome, Rick thinks. He wasn't looking forward to this job, so he is happy to stand back and watch someone else do it. Ed Pentecost, framed in the entrance to the workshop, makes no effort to help. Taffin watches from a peaceful distance.

When the Mustang is on the ground, Taffin strolls out and inspects the bodywork.

'Thank you, gentlemen.' He addresses Silver, including Dupree and Wyatt with a glance. 'You've restored the balance. You can go now.'

As the gunmetal grey Mercedes disappears down the track towards the main road, Ed and Rick follow Taffin into the office. Over the years, they have trained themselves not to show surprise at anything that happens when Taffin's face, never expressive, assumes that disturbing stillness.

At this moment, both are wondering how he transformed their visitors – men with an aptitude for casual violence – into silent, obliging automatons.

'What did I miss?' Rick turns a questioning stare on Ed.

'You tell me. They've been here since you left. I've been in the workshop minding my own business.'

'They decided to be polite.' Taffin turns to them, hands in pockets. 'The geezer with the teeth was the messenger – the other clowns were a sideshow. Their employer wants something he thinks I can arrange, I explained he ain't going to get it by upsetting us, so they unloaded the truck for you as a goodwill gesture. The tooth fairy had the wit to understand that.' He wanders out to the forecourt. 'Let's have a look at this Mustang.'

THREE

AT SEVEN O'CLOCK this morning, Ashley Gunn phoned the police to report his car stolen. It's a brand new Jaguar XE in Odyssey Red with black leather interior. He parked it in front of his house in Rookwood a few minutes after midnight and it was gone by six forty-five. All he knows is it was there when he went to bed and it's not there now. He didn't hear a thing.

Ashley is quite relaxed about it. His insurance covers theft, he has a Landrover as well so he's not stuck for transport and he reported the Jaguar missing in good time. There's not much more he can do.

The desk sergeant at Stoleworth Central (Dave Walls – they were at school together) took his mobile number and promised to get back to him with any developments. Ashley has every reason to think his car will be returned to him before long.

Time to think of the day's schedule. His company's current project is a barn conversion on the hill above Little Lasherham. Pleasant work: an opportunity for fine craftsmanship and considerable job satisfaction in an idyllic location. He will be on site by eight and drive down to Lasherham for lunch in the White Lion at about twelve-thirty. Life is good.

'STICK YOUR FACE IN THE HOLE and get comfortable.' Tessa Van Hagen, slim and crisp in clinical white, moves round the massage table rubbing her hands to warm them up. The waft of good oils.

Taffin settles down, face in the hole as instructed. The hands on his back are cool, perfect, understanding. Tessa is the only other woman Charlotte allows to touch him: the trust between friends.

'Sorry if they're cold.' Tessa always says that.

Taffin makes an approving sound that might be a grunt or just a way of giving in to the magic hands.

Sometimes they talk. Sometimes he just lets what will be will be. This morning he is picking up on something in her touch.

'What's on your mind, girl?'

The hands pause for a moment. 'How do you do that?'

A non-committal grunt answers her and she resumes a swirling hand movement, wondering, at the same time, whether he really wants to know.

'Is it telepathy? Are you a mind-reader? Or am I that transparent?'

'Nothing transparent about you, girl.'

'Alright –' she frowns, thumbs on vertebrae, one by one – 'I was thinking about my brother.'

Another grunt. Taffin knows a bit about Tessa's family through Charlotte. The brother is a wistful, drifting figure, occasionally seen around in a long coat. Charlotte describes him as 'alternative' because he lives outdoors a lot and rejects anything he regards as commercial. He has changed his name from Allan to Pierre for reasons no one has been able to fathom.

'What about him?'

'He wants to take the railway on single-handed. Did I tell you he's an old Trekkie. Star Trek is still his world. He regards StarTrack as an insult to the name.'

'Fair enough.'

'He says future generations are going to look at the scarred up landscape and wonder what the – pardon my French – we thought we were doing. Why don't we just enjoy the world as it is, he says, and stop buzzing about like blue-arsed flies.'

Another grunt from the buried face. Tessa lets her hands swim on Taffin's back.

'You could lose a bit of weight.'

'I'll give it some thought. What's *Pierre* done to upset you?'

'He's built himself a makeshift camp up in Chalkpit Woods. Says he'll go and live in it when the construction starts, right where the track's going. Silly boy.' Tessa concentrates on a knotted muscle in Taffin's shoulder.

'They'll move him on.'

'That's what I'm worried about. He'll get hurt.'

Taffin watches Tessa's feet – all he can see of her in this position. She isn't asking him to get involved – he knows her better than that – but there is anxiety in her fingertips.

Later, fully clothed, limbs and muscles freshly loose, he pauses in the doorway.

'You worry too much.'

'About my brother? He's got no sense. Who wouldn't worry?'

'No need –' surprisingly light touch of a huge hand on her shoulder – 'some have got principles, some have got sense. The trick is getting the balance right.'

Taffin leaves her to wonder what that meant and walks down the steps, raising a hand in farewell. The Jeep sinks slightly under his weight as he climbs in. The V8 mutters to itself as he reverses out of the drive – and the phrase, 'Like old times' runs through his mind again. Charlotte used it, with a resigned look on her face. Ed Pentecost used it several times, trying not to let his enthusiasm show.

Old times don't seem so remote today.

'HAVE YOU SEEN THE MOVIE?' Perry Butt swivels on his stool to challenge the person who spoke.

Heads turn in the bar at the White Lion. Butt, the veteran journalist, is always good value when he decides to join battle. Mostyn, ever the middle-aged schoolboy, is the protagonist, always open to humiliation at Butt's hands.

'I have not seen the *movie*, as you call it –' Mostyn sips his half of bitter and locks horns without fear – 'I don't need to. From what I've heard, it's the story of an honourable man, who may or may not live locally – perhaps drawn from real life, perhaps not – showing him up in a favourable light. If it does indeed draw on events that took place here – I emphasise *if* – the man in question is justly lionized for services rendered to the community, not least because it caused him to be alienated at the time, which must have been galling.'

'Galling?' Butt snorts the word with weary scorn. 'Our man was lucky to survive – and having done so it's remarkable he didn't emigrate.'

'He did indeed leave the country for a while –' Mostyn takes another sip – 'you know that as well as I do, Perry – we were all here at the time, all guilty in a sense. Taffin's celebrity status is fully merited, whether the *movie* is about him or not.'

'Once again you've missed the point with unerring inaccuracy.' The old fighting cock's plume of white hair rises like a battle standard. 'No one's disputing our man's sterling qualities. My quibble is with those who seek to glamourize the tragic truth that violence inevitably breeds more violence.'

'All I'm saying is that heroism should be presented as a virtue.'

'You astound me, Mostyn. By your own admission you haven't bothered to watch the movie and yet you shamelessly peddle an opinion – and don't even think of complaining about that split infinitive.'

'So long as you acknowledge it.'

'I acknowledge without apology. Now – no one who knows Our Hero could possibly credit him with the poise, agility and good-looks of the excellent man who played him in the movie. It's fiction – far removed from real life – romantic stuff for people who believe in Robin Hood.'

'I choose to believe in Robin Hood.'

'Describe to us the object of your belief, Mostyn: an athletic fellow, I suppose, in Lincoln Green tights – a master of unarmed combat, never so happy as when he's championing the poor and needy.'

'A romantic hero, yes.'

'Indeed. My own version, I'm bound to say, is a more realistic figure, with all the fashion-sense of a compost heap, who lurks in the forest, being careful not to stray downwind of habitation because in those romantic days you could smell a settlement a mile away. Which is it, Mostyn?'

'A mixture of the two.'

'Well, it doesn't matter much which. You choose to believe the movie is based on the real live gentleman who occasionally drinks in this very pub.'

'Most people do. The similarities are inescapable.'

'Of course most people do, MOSTYN.' The old journalist sends one eyebrow soaring. 'Everybody needs heroes. And invariably those heroes are exemplary in every way – the embodiment of physical perfection, endowed with flawless integrity, endearing roguishness, stunning good looks – and that most elusive quality, PRESENCE.' Butt pauses to reflect before adding, as if to himself: 'This last does indeed square with our Mister Taffin.'

'So you agree, the film was about him?'

'In that respect. Whether by design or happenstance is open to debate.'

'Of course it's about him, Perry.' Ivy Lewis, standing by, waiting for her chance to slip into the argument, won't stand for criticism of her hero.

Harry Hawkins, next to her, nods agreement and Ivy continues: 'The problem is he seems to have retired – doesn't want to know anymore. Harry and I went to ask a small favour and he turned us down, didn't he Harry?'

'Turned us down. Didn't want to know.'

'Has it occurred to you –' Perry Butt gives his empty glass a nudge – 'that none of us are as young as we used to be?'

'He doesn't change. He's got ways...' Ivy's adoring eyes

settle on some far distant place for a moment. 'Just a quiet word in the right ear – that's all it used to take.'

Harry Hawkins turns away, snorting. Ivy rounds on him. 'What's that for?'

'It took a bit more than that sometimes.' Harry's face splits in a huge smile. 'Remember the bloke who tried to get you into that pyramid selling scam? You wouldn't want a *quiet word* like what he got.'

'That's true enough.' Ivy's face becomes solemn. 'But that bloke had it coming. Nasty bit of work.'

'What did you want with Taffin this time?' Mostyn gets his question in before anyone else can speak.

'Should I talk about it?' Ivy glances at Harry Hawkins, who is still chuckling over what happened to the *nasty bit of work*.

'About the bookshop? Yeah, why not?'

'Gordon Glennan's got control of it now. His uncle used to have it but from what I hear Glennan's got Enduring Power of Attorney and the rumour is he's negotiating with a developer. There's ten acres of land with that property, to say nothing of the house, which must be worth a tidy sum by itself.'

'That's if they leave it standing,' Harry Hawkins remarks.

Perry Butt does something with his eyebrows and Meg, behind the bar, pours him a double shot of gin adding a splash of Angostura Bitters without a thought.

'D'you mean that odious politician?' Butt's eyebrows resume full battle formation. 'What kind of perverse fate puts a sub-literate gobshite like Gordon Glennan in control of a bookshop – especially *that* bookshop? If true, this is appalling. Can you vouch for it?'

'Debi Royce told me. She runs the business side of it and she's right pissed off because she's going to be out of a job if the sale happens. That's why I had a word with Taffin – or tried to.'

'And Robin Hood turned you down...' Perry Butt holds his pink gin up to the light, savours the first sip and purses his lips. 'The Folk Lore Police should be notified at once. Established heroes have a mystic obligation to us all, especially where revered bookshops are concerned. This matter must be addressed with all speed.'

'If you're going to address it, you'd better work out what you're going to say... with all speed.' Harry Hawkins has noticed an elderly Chevrolet Corvette edging its way into the White Lion's car park with a noise like a giant gargling. 'He's here.'

GORDON GLENNAN is confused. The two police officers who arrived at his door this morning failed, in his view, to show the respect due to a member of Parliament. Their manner was casually intrusive and, he felt, judgmental of the opulence they saw around them as they walked in.

He has no idea who owns the Jaguar XE now parked in the barn behind his house, or how it got there. The officers are skeptical. The Jaguar was reported stolen and here it is, on his property, tucked away out of sight. Would Mister Glennan like to comment on that? No? Perhaps he would come to the station and help them by answering some questions. Yes, they know he is an MP, which is every reason why he should set an example by cooperating with the police. Like any good citizen with nothing to hide.

Glancing in a wall mirror a moment ago, Glennan

witnessed the officers' murmured conversation and thought he lip-read the word *wanker*.

'What's going on?' Janice Glennan has taken a few minutes to fix her hair and make up and now sweeps down the stairs to confront the officers.

'God knows.' Her husband shrugs. 'They say we've got a stolen car in the barn.'

'A stolen car? How did it get there?'

'That's the question.' The taller of the two officers – PC Bailey – answers without looking at her. 'It's here, so this is where we start.'

'Yes, of course – our property is full to the brim with stolen goods. Anyone can see we're major criminals.' As a politician's wife, Janice has found sarcasm more effective and accessible than reasoned argument and uses it with practiced ease.

'You'd be well advised to take this seriously, Mrs Glennan.' Bailey turns a disappointed stare on her.

Janice is having none of it. 'I'll treat this as I see fit. And anyway, how is it our problem?'

'We have to investigate, Madam. That's our job.'

'Shouldn't you be out looking for whoever stole it?'

'That's what we're trying to do. The first step is to find out how the car comes to be on your property.'

'I hope you're not suggesting we're involved...'

'Leave it, Janice.' Glennan decides to take control. 'I'll go with them and get this over with.' Then, to the officers: 'I suppose forensics will be all over the car.'

'They'll be here any time now.' Bailey lets his gaze sweep the room, settling on Janice. 'Quite a little crime scene you've got here, Mrs Glennan.'

MEG MOPS IMAGINARY BEER from the bar noting, with mild amusement, that none of the group around Perry Butt said anything to Taffin when he walked in through the door marked *Gents*.

He is not alone today. Mo, his larger, elder brother, is with him. This is a welcome rarity: Mo is a mountain of goodwill; soft benevolence rests in his pumpkin features and his presence always lightens the atmosphere that prevails when Taffin is by himself.

The brothers have settled down with their beer at the corner table by the window and no one – not even Ivy Lewis – cares to disturb them.

The door swings again and Ashley Gunn finds a place at the bar. He, too, is glad to see Mo and acknowledges the brothers with a casually raised forefinger. Apart from being friends since their teens, he and Mo share the bond of countrymen and regularly shoot together.

Taffin respects Ashley as his brother's best mate; by the same token, Ashley is immune to the unease some locals feel when Taffin is around.

Now is the moment to make eye contact. Ashley directs his gaze towards Taffin and receives in response the briefest inclination of dark glasses: a question asked; confirmation given.

He has every confidence that the temporary loss of his car was in a good cause.

FOUR

ERICA LYLE Knows where all the local dignitaries live: it's her job.

As a journalist, she wouldn't think of revealing her sources, but a great many of hers are local and not hard to trace. They include Dave Walls, currently a sergeant at Stoleworth Central, who is also her brother-in-law.

No one would challenge Dave's discretion but he's fond of Erica, sometimes forgets what she does for a living and has yet to grasp the breadth of her ambition. She's done three years on the Stoleworth Observer and is ready to move on to a national daily at the first opportunity. She is not inclined to waste any story involving a Member of Parliament.

Janice Glennan doesn't recognize the stylish young woman on her doorstep but assumes she is collecting for some charity or other.

'Can I help you?'

'Mrs Glennan?' Erica knows better than to ask this woman if her husband is at home; a question like that, from a youthful blond, can put a wife on the defensive. 'Have you got a moment? I hear you had a surprise this morning and I'd like to hear what you think happened...'

'Who are you, exactly?'

'Erica Lyle –' Erica offers a smile laced with a touch of apology – 'Stoleworth Observer. We like to give maximum coverage to car crime...'

'You're a reporter. You people think my husband is a target for any local tittle-tattle and let me tell you that doesn't make a politician's life any easier.'

'I was hoping – is your husband available?'

'No he isn't. And neither am I.'

The heavy door judders in its frame and Erica is left staring at the brass lion's head knocker.

In the absence of anything else to share the thought with, she murmurs: 'Unavailable for comment – never reads well.'

PIERRE – formerly Allan – Van Hagen doesn't enjoy sleeping in the woods but he does it occasionally to acclimatize himself in case it becomes necessary. Come that day, there will be a point to be made and he is determined to be the one to make it.

Some time ago, when StarTrack announced the route for its proposed western loop, Pierre built himself a shelter in Chalkpit Wood, right in the path of it. This structure of corrugated iron and tarpaulin, with a hammock slung underneath, represents his opposition to the hurtling, superfast trains that will pass over this very spot if the project goes ahead as planned.

The novelty has worn off but the resolve is as strong as ever. Rather than ruin his health for the final confrontation, Pierre spends his nights in a camper van and either goes for a bacon sandwich at the station or to his sister's place for breakfast.

This morning he has read all the national and local papers and lets himself into his sister's treatment room without pausing to think there might already be a client on the massage table.

'Have a look at this, Tess...' he brandishes the paper, quoting the front page headline... 'STOLEN CAR HIDDEN ON MP'S PROPERTY. That's Gordon Glennan, Emm Pee – the Right Honourable. Don't know what he's been up to but it looks like he's in deep doo-doo. Couldn't happen to a nicer bloke.'

'Not now, Allan.' Tessa waves him out but Pierre is on a roll:

'The guy's a Cabinet Minister or some such thing. These people think they're above it all – bent as corkscrews, the lot of them.'

A low growl reaches him from the massage table and Tessa turns anxiously to her client, whose face is buried in the hole.

'Excuse my brother,' she remarks.

'This is important...' Pierre is bubbling over... 'Glennan is one of the bastards who proposed the StarTrack abomination in the first place – and get this – apparently he tried to sell his house when he thought the track might run too close to his gracious property. Now they're saying the route's going to change again, and guess who's behind that. One rule for them and another rule for us underlings.'

'OUT.' Tessa gives him her hard-eyed look.

'Junior Minister,' a muffled remark from the couch.

'What?'

'Junior.' Taffin raises his head to stare at Pierre. 'Get your facts right, son. And here's a tip – if you don't want to catch pneumonia – that hammock of yours needs hanging up to dry, or burning. The tyres are bald on that camper van by the way.'

Tessa pauses to blink at her client then rounds on her brother again.

'Now perhaps you'll have some consideration for my client and let me get on with my work. OUT.'

Pierre leaves the room closing the door behind him. It takes a moment for him to register what Tessa's client said and a longer moment to wonder who the fuck this bloke is who knows about his woodland shelter and the camper van.

He would like to go back and ask, but instinct tells him the conversation is over.

JANICE GLENNAN doesn't care for the slur on her husband in the Stoleworth Observer. She is even less impressed by insinuations in the *Mail* and the *Mirror*, both of which have picked up on the story.

'You can't let this go, Gordon. They're twisting things as usual, nibbling away at your reputation.'

'Let them nibble. There's nothing in it, and they know that very well.'

'And you've got to say so.'

'Which is exactly what they want.' Glennan lowers his paper wearily. 'You know the press. They'll goad you into a denial and then ask why you felt it necessary. It all makes column inches. Dignified silence is the trick.'

'So you come out as aloof and disconnected – the classic voters' definition of successful people in government. That bitch reporter will be back for sure, then what are you going to say?'

'I might ask her to shift focus – concentrate on who might have stolen the car in the first place.'

'You don't get it, do you?' Janice speaks slowly and clearly, as if to a child. 'You've been framed, Gordon – and next time anyone mentions it, that's exactly what I'm going to say.'

Gordon Glennan eases himself out of his chair and looks his wife in the eye. 'You'll do no such thing, Janice. Until the alteration to the StarTrack route is finalised, you and I will be keeping as low a profile as possible. My name is linked with the StarTrack project and I won't have it said that I manipulated the findings of the Parliamentary Select Committee, which I chair, incidentally, to suit my personal interests.' He pauses, gauging his wife's reaction before continuing. 'There are other, more complex reasons why this is a bad time for me to attract attention but I'm not going into that now – it would mean a breach of confidence among other things, so... no discussion. I hope you can grasp that.'

Janice Glennan understands. Her husband, so willing to take centre stage in public life, is always evasive when it comes to private business. She tells herself he likes to surprise her with success rather than disappoint her with failure.

Fine – let him enjoy his fantasies.

PIERRE IS UNDECIDED. Should he burn his hammock, as the large man on his sister's massage table advised? Should he worry about bald tyres on the camper van? It's not his anyway – he has it on permanent loan from a mate who's gone abroad – so probably not.

The sky is lightly overcast, the way he likes it: warm grey

with a gentle wind that laps at your hair as you walk. Good for wandering and getting your brain in tune. He skirts Chalkpit Wood, trying to imagine the mentality that could contemplate ripping it up to give the world another high-speed rail route. Where's everybody going? How important can it be... to get us all from A to B? That had a pleasant meter.

His shelter is in there among the trees, not visible unless you're looking for it. No more nights in there, though. The large man was right; the hammock is crap and to be truthful there is something unnerving about woodland when darkness falls. The camper van is comfortable but cold. Time to swallow pride and go back to his mother's semi in Rookwood.

Mesmerized by his own footsteps he reaches the fork where the path leads up to Rookwood or down through the woods towards Lasherham. He heads downhill without conscious decision *plod plod*.

Having no ties is one thing; having no money is something else. In reflective moments Pierre puts his lack of clear purpose down to a profound sense of social responsibility, *plod plod*; someone's got to make a stand, carry a spotless banner in a corrupt world. But what's the point if no one's taking any notice?

All you can do is improve your mind *plod plod* and keep yourself as well-informed as possible. Pierre takes education seriously and has vague thoughts of teaching some day. Politics should be the answer *plod plod* but that's where the rot begins. So teaching it must be – which means getting qualified.

'Talking to yourself, son – you want to watch that.'

The voice close to his ear shocks Pierre into the present, wide-eyed and spluttering.

A deep breath to cover his sense of outrage, then he turns to see who spoke. Dark hair, dark clothes, dark glasses – no readable expression.

'What...?

'Pierre, isn't it?'

'Yes...' realization: the voice, last heard in his sister's treatment room.

'Settle down, son. You look like you just stuck your finger in the light socket.'

'You gave me a shock.'

'Here's another – I need to borrow your van.'

'It's not mine to lend.'

'I know, son. The owner ain't traceable. You'll get it back with a new set of tyres.'

'I don't know where the keys are.'

'They're under the front seat. Listen carefully now, I've got a job for you. Time to make yourself useful.'

FIVE

'YOUR PROBLEM, not mine.' Daniel Frey-Morton uses words sparingly, giving full value to every syllable. English is not his first language, or even his second, but he uses it with fluent precision.

Gordon Glennan is never comfortable in this man's presence; all he knows about Frey-Morton is that he was a self-made billionaire by the age of forty and conducts business from hotel suites. During their meetings he offers no hospitality other than mineral water, ignores any attempt at small talk and concludes the day's business by simply getting up and leaving.

'It'll probably blow over –' Glennan is anxious not to be dismissed so easily this time – 'but I need to soft-pedal until it does. Right now, however ludicrous it may sound, I'm the subject of a police investigation. I'd rather not make any further statements about StarTrack while the spotlight is on me. Christ man, there's too much at stake.'

'You must get your priorities straight.' Frey-Morton remains perfectly still as he speaks: no body language.

Glennan takes his time phrasing an answer.

He thinks: *Don't you dare lecture me on priorities.*

You're an obscenely wealthy man who's lucky enough to have a Minister of the Crown in his corner. My priority, as I'm uncomfortably aware, is to manipulate the StarTrack inquiry to keep the public baffled – so the route swings north one minute, south the next, the future remains uncertain, property values decay, people move out – and finally, when you give me the nod, a grateful public hears StarTrack is cancelled... and the way is clear for you to swoop in with your crazy micro-city development.'

He says: 'The long-term plan is my priority, as always.'

'I hope so.' Frey-Morton's flint eyes turn on the politician. 'A stolen car on your property is nothing. Ignore it. And for all our sakes, my friend, don't think out loud.'

ED PENTECOST gives the Mustang a final polish and stands back to admire it.

'Very tasty.' Rick Bishop climbs out of the inspection pit and strolls round the car to take it in from all angles. 'Better than the first time I saw it.'

He and Ed have worked on the engine, drive-train, suspension and bodywork day and night for two solid weeks and the result is a spectacular example of a classic. The chrome is dazzling. The engine note is music: a burbling baritone that calls out to lovers of fine tuning.

'No orange-peel then.' Charlotte moves gracefully round the car, running a light finger over the surface.

'Just a showroom shine, Charl – nothing fancy.' Ed Pentecost flicks at the bodywork with a duster. 'You ain't never seen orange-peel in any paint job of mine.'

This is true. Ed has applied five fine coats, each one rubbed down and prepared before the next, and the surface gleams like glass: no chance of the orange-peel effect of a hasty spray-over.

'It'll just have to do, then.' Charlotte shakes her head in mock reproof.

During this exchange, Rick Bishop stands off to one side wondering if Ed is going to mention the job offer. By agreement, neither is going to say anything unless the other does and neither of them can decide whether to take it seriously.

The offer arrived two mornings ago in a Ferrari driven by a man who looked like a retired schoolmaster.

This person, who introduced himself as Eric McDermott, spent half an hour admiring the craftsmanship displayed on the forecourt and asked to speak to whoever did it.

When Ed told him the Boss wasn't around today, Eric explained that he was only interested in the people who did the real work of restoration – the boys with the magic touch – who could bring automotive classics back to life. Forget the Management – this was all about Craftsmanship with a capital C and he, Eric McDermott, was offering top dollar for the skills he could see displayed here, on this forecourt.

He expected to pay a high price for results like this, he said. He outlined an eye-watering financial package and wished to point out that it was a lot better than anything Ed or Rick could dream of in a backwater like this.

Would they be interested? The money was on the table: they could let him know in a day or two.

He left in a leisurely cloud of dust, leaving Ed and Rick to stare at each other in disbelief.

Neither has ever worked for anyone but Taffin and

Charlotte. Their lives have been intertwined for as far back as either cares to remember. But this is crazy money.

They both have responsibilities now. Ed thinks of himself as a family man these days: he met Julia in the course of a job for Taffin, eventually set up house with her and they're still together after ten years. At the same time, Rick moved in as lodger and caretaker with the Brewer family, whose lives had been shattered when their younger daughter was found murdered on Rookwood Hill. Kath, the elder daughter, took over the running of the household at seventeen, and Rick was there for her. He's been there ever since.

'Where is the Boss today?' Ed is still flicking at the Mustang with his duster.

'He's probably at Tess's place getting a massage.' Charlotte plants a hand on her hip in mock outrage. 'He's addicted to it – or her – I dunno which.'

'I need to have a word –' Ed glances from Charlotte to Rick – 'we both do.'

'THAT'S A LOT OF MONEY.' Taffin stands with his back to them, looking out over the car lot. 'Dare say you was tempted.'

Ed nods, aware that Taffin can see him reflected in the window.

Rick leans against the wall beside the Pontiac GTO poster. Eric McDermott's money, if it's real, would set him and Kath Brewer up in their own place, or give them the option of extending the Brewer family home to give everyone more privacy.

Ed has done the sums as well. Julia has put herself through a photography course and is now taking wedding commissions. The money McDermott was talking about would equip a studio and give her the freedom to branch out. Ed would like to be a part of that.

He also knows – and is aware that Rick feels the same – that Eric McDermott's offer is too good to be true. There's got to be a catch, but curiosity is powerful. Instinct says look at the choices, even one involving the inconceivable step of leaving Taffin, *Muscle Motors* and all the history that goes with both.

'What would you say –' Ed searches for the words – 'if we told you right now we was going to leave?'

'Be lucky.'

'You make your own luck. You always said that.'

'True, Ed.' Taffin turns from the window and ambles, hands in pockets. 'Luck... judgement... it's all about balance.'

'You wouldn't try to talk us out of it?' Rick shifts slightly as Taffin moves past.

'No point, Rick. What can I tell you? If you mean it, you'll stick by it.'

'That's a compliment, by the way.' Charlotte turns her patient look on Rick.

Rick nods. 'I know.'

'What do you mean by balance?' Ed watches Taffin's profile, aware of mild amusement on Charlotte's face at the same time.

'He's been using that word a lot,' she remarks. 'He keeps going mystic on me. It's all the weird stuff he reads, Ed. I worry about him.'

The ghost of a smile brushes Taffin's face.

'Everything you do, every decision you make, is in the balance until the split second you commit to it, then it's irreversible – the moving finger writes.'

Ed glances at Charlotte, mystified. Rick does the same. Taffin continues:

'Chance against judgment – come to a fork in the road, which way do you go?' He turns to face the three of them. 'You weigh what's in reach against what you want, then you weigh that against what you've got. When they balance out, it means you're doing something right.'

'Where did that come from?' Charlotte goggles at him.

'Russell Chambers Gates – a wise man who writes stuff you should read. Start with *'Dynamics of Balance'* – you can all borrow it. Read, absorb, enjoy.'

Charlotte murmurs, 'Yeah, good luck with that.'

Rick shrugs: 'I don't read a lot.'

Ed wags a finger at Taffin. 'I knew you was brewing something. There's stuff you're not telling us.'

'True enough. What's happened recently? I've had a decoy project dangled under my nose – a mystery man wants a rare Yank motor from the Thirties – something he could probably find without help from me. At the same time, you and Rick have been offered a lot of money to go elsewhere.'

'We're all being tempted.' Ed leans to flip open a file on the desk, revealing a stack of black and white prints of classic cars in various stages of disrepair. 'Take a look at this.'

Taffin spreads the prints out and studies them.

'These are what your man McDermott left?'

'That's right. He wants some classy motors restored – or whoever he works for does. He left these pictures to give us a taste.'

'And you don't know who's pulling his strings.'

'He didn't say. Maybe he's independent.'

'The Tooth Fairy don't want to say who he works for either. What does that tell you?'

'Got to be a connection.'

'Looks likely.' Taffin nods slowly and thumbs through the pictures again. 'Do you see what I see?'

'A lot of tasty machinery.' Rick turns one of the prints for a better look. 'There's Jag corner – an XK120 and an SS100. That there's a De Tomaso Pantera, I'll swear that's a Chrysler Imperial under them cobwebs, there's a Hudson Super Six – and what's that behind them?'

'Don't know.' Ed hunches over the print. 'Half hidden... don't recognize it.'

'I'll tell you.' Taffin strolls to the door and pauses. 'It's a Cord from the late nineteen-thirties – an 812 if it's supercharged – just what the Tooth Fairy wanted me to find.'

'There it is again from another angle but still half hidden.' Charlotte fans the pictures out on the desk. 'That's no coincidence.'

'Too right, girl. I'm being led right to it. Looks like we're all being tempted.'

'What are you going to do?' Ed straightens up.

'A bit of thinking, Ed. Here's a tale to be going on with: there's a fork in the road; one way leads to the desert, the other way leads to the town. Two brothers live in a house where the road forks. They're identical twins, but one always lies, the other always tells the truth. Everybody knows that, but no one can tell them apart, so... A traveller comes to the door asking which way he should take to get to the town. He doesn't know which brother he's talking to. What question should he ask to get the right direction?'

'He's stuffed, isn't he?' Rick looks to Ed for guidance and

gets a blank frown in return. Charlotte folds her arms and looks skywards.

Taffin continues: 'Someone's trying to break up the business. I want to know who and why. The question is, who should I ask?'

He steps outside and wanders among the extravagant machinery on the forecourt, pausing to appreciate the red Mustang.

Charlotte watches him through the open door and turns to Ed and Rick. 'Get the picture? You'll let him know what you decide, won't you?'

'I've decided.' Ed takes a quick step to the open door and calls out to Taffin's retreating figure. 'Here's the question – which way would your brother tell me to go?'

'Why?'

'The liar would say his brother would point him to the desert. The truthful one would say the same.'

'So?'

'Whatever answer he gets, he goes the other way.'

'There you go, Ed.'

THE TOLLGATE BOOKSHOP dreams in the afternoon. The Mustang barks a greeting and falls silent. Taffin steps out of the left hand driving seat and strolls to inspect the books displayed in the window through a reflected image of the Mustang and screen of trees in the background.

Sandwiched between a collection of *Sempé* cartoons and a book of mediaeval maps is a plain grey volume with the title set in bold white capitals: *WALKING DISTANCE – from the author of STILL LIFE – Russell Chambers Gates*.

Lorna Moorecroft looks up as the doorbell *Dings*. Debi

Royce is with her today, helping her sort through the latest pile of books to be bought for pennies or pulped, depending on rarity or second-hand worth. She straightens up and steps aside as her space darkens, noting Lorna's fleeting alarm.

Dark glasses turn to her for a moment, then to Lorna.

'There's a book in the window – *Walking Distance*.'

Lorna says 'Yes', but nothing comes out and she clears her throat. 'Yes... you're the man who reads Warren Palmer, I remember.'

'I'll get it out for you.' Debi Royce picks her way through stacks of reading matter to the back of the window.

Lorna decides this customer needs drawing out. 'You certainly have specialized tastes. Russell...?'

'Russell Chambers Gates.'

'I don't know him. What's his subject?'

Before her question is answered, Debi Royce is back, dusting the grey cover with her sleeve. 'Russell Chambers Gates. I nearly let it go but we don't see many of his. What's this about?'

'Ideas.'

'Big subject.' Debi Royce turns the book over in her hand, then looks up. 'I know you. You're Mister Taffin. My friend Ivy Lewis talks about you a lot.' Then, to Lorna, 'They made a film about him, you know.'

Lorna's face lights up.

Dark glasses betray a hint of amusement.

Debi tries to engage Taffin's eyeline as she continues: 'You're Ivy's hero. She says you help people.'

'How much?' Barely more than a whisper.

'Well, not so much now – she says you've retired.'

'How much for the book?'

'This one's seven pounds.'

Taffin digs in his pocket for cash and hands it to Lorna, who is determined not to let this man off the hook a second time.

'We need some help here. There's talk of shutting us down. Where will you find Warren Palmer or Russell Chambers Gates then?'

She hands the book over to Taffin. He takes his time leafing through it, then: 'This fella says no one with a brain ever retires.'

SIX

'YOU HAVE NO IDEA what a gun like this can do.' Daniel Frey-Morton weighs the Colt Python in his hand, runs a finger over its bright nickel finish and holds it out by the barrel. 'Feel the way it fits in your palm.'

Gordon Glennan was beginning to relax until the revolver appeared. Now he feels a sharp contraction of the scalp and shifts uneasily in his seat. Frey-Morton watches without looking directly at him.

'What you need to understand about this gun, Gordon, is that I myself will never be connected with it in any way. I never have to touch it or be anywhere near it in order to direct its fire. No bullet from it will be traceable because the gun that fired it doesn't exist. Quite a remarkable weapon. Take hold of it.'

Glennan would like to say: *'You're a fucking maniac. You think you're above the law. You probably are. Is this how you people do it? What have I got myself into?'*

He says: 'I'd rather not.'

The revolver hangs briefly in the air and Glennan catches it by instinct. Heavier than expected.

'Does it repel you?'

'I'm not really a gun enthusiast. It's not loaded, is it?'

'Open it and find out.'

'These things are illegal in this country. I can't imagine it's licensed.'

'How could it be? It doesn't exist.'

Glennan nods, humouring the game. 'What has this to do with the matter in hand?'

'I want you to understand that business is not always what it seems. And you are most definitely in business.'

Glennan affects a light laugh and lays the gun aside. 'To use your own words – I, too, will never be connected with this in any way.'

'If it makes you comfortable to think so. Tell me, how is the property market looking in your part of the world?'

'Slow at the moment.'

'Let's be sure to keep it that way. Time for another change of route for StarTrack.'

Glennan thinks: *'Who are you to give me orders, you freak? I have the upper hand here. The property I control may be a dot on the map but it happens to be central to your lunatic scheme. I'm the one who has to steer the StarTrack Inquiry and manage the land sale – and I have to achieve that without attracting attention if I want to stay in politics.'*

He phrases a careful answer, aware of the flint eyes watching him and the industrial bluntness of the gun on the table beside him.

'I need time. Another revision to the route has been proposed. As for the land, I have Enduring Power of Attorney over the estate, so releasing it for development won't be a problem if it's done discreetly, a piece at a time – but it's going to take tact and patience.' He pauses, reaching for his glass of mineral water, finds it empty and continues. 'One of the buildings is occupied by a business – a bookshop – nothing in itself, but local support is strong and I am known to be connected. You see the need for subtlety.'

'Subtlety never achieved anything. Forget your reputation, stop prevaricating and arrange for the business to close. If necessary get someone to condemn the building on safety grounds. Try to remember what you're being paid for.'

Glennan sits forward, sets his empty glass down, trying to distance himself from the revolver on the table. 'Please remember I am a public figure – a target for local discontent. Someone is trying to put the spotlight on me – I mentioned the stolen car on my property...'

'Planted, of course – but you don't know who by.'

'No idea.'

'I could make an educated guess.'

'Really? That would surprise me. I wouldn't doubt you keep yourself well-informed where the big picture's concerned, but detailed local knowledge – that's something else again...'

'There's a man called Taffin.'

Glennan takes a moment to absorb this. 'There is, now you mention it. Something of a celebrity in the area. Of course – there was a movie, wasn't there.'

'The man emerges as a hero.'

'Just a local wide boy. Why do you mention him?'

'The area, as you put it, is familiar to me.'

'I didn't realize.'

'By chance it was the scene of my first commercial opportunity when I arrived in this country. We all need luck when we start out. I had the good fortune to work for a man named Arch Sprawley. He taught me how to build and expand and think without constraints. He was my mentor and his patronage at a crucial time has stood me in good stead. The company he built up foundered and he died a broken man. This bastard Taffin was responsible for his downfall.'

'Are you saying Taffin put him out of business?'

'If you mean, was he responsible for Sprawley's early death, the answer is yes.'

'So you think this man's going to be a problem.'

'I don't expect him to get the opportunity. When you face intimidation, from him or anyone else who stands in the way, close your mind to it – you can afford that luxury. You understand? Good – you know as much as you need to. Get to work.'

Glennan is still phrasing a response when the room comes alive, the door closes and Frey-Morton has gone.

The revolver that didn't exist has vanished too.

A RUSTLE OF RAIN stirs the trees around the forecourt at *Muscle Motors*.

Two men and two women stand in the open. Ed Pentecost puts a protective arm round Julia's shoulders. She doesn't mind getting wet; not much bothers Julia.

Rick Bishop and Kath Brewer wander to the shelter of a sycamore and prop themselves against the elderly Dodge Charger.

From the office doorway, Charlotte looks down the rough track leading to the road and nudges Taffin's elbow: 'This'll be him.'

Taffin, hands in pockets, watches as a white Range Rover powers up the lane and stops a few inches short of the Dodge. The driver addresses Rick Bishop through his open window.

'Didn't expect a reception committee.'

Kath answers him: 'Nobody here but us chickens.'

'I meant them.' Eric McDermott nods towards the office doorway.

'That's the Boss and the other Boss.'

'Good enough.' McDermott gets out, breathes the fresh, damp air and beckons Ed and Julia to join him. 'We're not bothered about the Boss, or the other Boss. You're the people I came to speak to – and I see you both have charming partners.' He acknowledges the women with a nod. 'Can I assume you've done some thinking?'

'We have.' Ed glances at Julia to include her in any agreement. 'We're impressed by your offer.'

'Does that go for you too?'

Rick nods. 'Very impressed.'

'No problems with management?' McDermott indicates the distant figures of Taffin and Charlotte in the doorway.

Ed allows a momentary pause. 'They just want what's best for us.'

'That's good news, lads. When can you start?'

'You haven't said where these cars are.'

'They're all in one place, you'll be happy to hear. It's a collection housed on a farm estate not far from Northampton. We can provide accommodation close by if you don't fancy the commute, but I expect you'll be wanting to move up there in due course.'

'In due course?' Rick Bishop studies his fingernails.

'That sounds permanent. How long's this job going to take?'

'There's a lot of work waiting for you,' McDermott tells him, 'and more when that's done. This is an open ended deal – I'm tempted to say a job for life – or at least as long as the classic car market stays healthy.'

Ed moves to stand beside McDermott, arms folded. 'Who's paying us?'

'As manager of the collection, you'll be dealing with me.'

'Not your money though, is it?'

'OK, listen up.' McDermott gathers the four of them in with a gesture. 'The collection is worth many millions and maintaining it is going to be an ongoing expense like you wouldn't believe. I'm talking about a clean, dry, temperature-controlled environment, specialist materials, ultra-violet lighting, museum conditions – because that's what this project is all about. We'll be building a museum of automotive classics. You're damn right it's not my money.'

'So whose is it?'

'A finance-based company. There's a board of directors somewhere, a load of boring accountants, but they won't be in our way.' McDermott holds a hand out to Julia and Kath. 'We haven't been introduced.'

In the doorway, Charlotte murmurs in Taffin's ear: 'Ooooh, he's a slimey one. Do you know him?'

'I ain't seen him before.'

'Looks like a librarian... or a scoutmaster.'

'He ain't either of those, girl.'

'Who's he working for, I wonder.' Charlotte gazes across the forecourt at the group gathered round McDermott.

'That's what we're aiming to find out. Time to put our word in.'

Taffin takes his time strolling over to the group, not making eye contact with McDermott until he's close enough to speak softly.

'You're hiring my lads, then.'

'No hard feelings, I hope.' McDermott pauses, watchful in spite of the quiet manner. 'They've got the skills – I'm in the market.'

'Are you a wealthy man, Mister McDermott?'

'I represent wealth.'

'Get this clear then, my lads are the best.'

'That's the conclusion I came to.'

'What makes you think they're for sale?'

'They seem happy enough with my offer.'

'I'm not.'

'What can I say?' McDermott keeps his face neutral. 'It's their choice – I'm doing business with them, not you.'

Dark glasses study the man for a moment, then turn slowly to Ed and Rick.

'You want to work for this clown?'

Julia feels Ed's arm tighten across her shoulders. Ed says, 'That's what we've decided.'

'And you?' Taffin's blank stare settles on Rick.

'Same. You pay us fair but we've had a better offer.'

Charlotte has moved up to stand by Taffin, sweeping Rick and Ed with her *fuck you* face. 'Ever heard of loyalty?'

'Forget it, girl.' Taffin takes a leisurely pace towards Ed and Rick. 'Be clear about this – you two are finished. Don't come whining back to me if it don't work out. When you leave this forecourt you're gone for good.'

It's raining harder now but no one seems to notice. Taffin turns his back and walks away towards the workshop.

SEVEN

'HE'S NOT HERE.' Charlotte's normally easy manner seems strained.

'Up at the garage?'

'No, I've just been there.'

'We was supposed to go for a drink. Where's he got to?' Mo Taffin's benign pudding face reflects Charlotte's concern.

'You tell me. I haven't seen him for three days. He hasn't been home and I haven't heard a word. It's not like him.'

'No, it isn't. He ain't left a note at the workshop?'

'Not a dickey-bird.'

'What about his lads – Ed and Rick?'

'Gone. They left.'

'You're joking.' Mo stares at her as he struggles to take this in. 'They can't leave. They've been with him since... well, they've always been around.'

'Not any more.'

'I don't believe it. What happened?'

'I wish I could tell you, Maurice. There's some weird stuff going on, that's all I know.' Charlotte hangs in the doorway of the house in Mitres Well Lane where she and Taffin have lived for... ten years? – where Taffin has lived most of his life.

And all this time, Mo and Shirley have lived next door, separated from them by the width of a few bricks.

'He didn't give you no clue?' Mo is having trouble reading Charlotte's mood. He shifts his stance, unwilling to walk away with uncertainty in the air. 'Something ain't right – you can tell me anything, you know.'

'I trust you, Maurice – we're almost family – but all I can do is be patient and see what turns up.'

'Fair enough.' Mo fumbles in a pocket for his pipe and matches. 'I ain't got my brother's brains, anyone'll tell you that. All I know is a bit of country craft, how to clean a shotgun and how to keep a pipe lit...'

'Yeah,' Charlotte tries a smile, 'He says a match will light anywhere for you, even in a howling gale, because you spend half your life in the open. It's one of the things he admires about you.'

'...and I know when there's something people ain't telling me.' Mo strikes a match and nurses the pipe's bowl with the flame. 'Me and Shirley are just through the wall when you want us.'

OPEN COUNTRY as far as you can see in every direction. A building that might once have been an imposing manor house stands among barns and outbuildings on rough, neglected ground. A faded sign saying *Linklater Farm* hangs on the fence.

A white Range Rover and two motor cycles pull up beside a large mobile home inside the enclosure. Three men and two women leave their vehicles and stretch their limbs.

'This is the best we can do for you for the moment.' Eric McDermott throws open the door of the mobile home releasing a waft of damp blankets and old sweat. 'It sleeps four in comfort with a certain amount of privacy. 'We'll be able to move you into the main building when it's been fixed up.'

Ed Pentecost casts a critical eye over the surroundings. 'What's wrong with the main building?'

'You wouldn't like it in its present condition. This is much better in the short term.'

'We're not squeamish.' Julia eases her rucksack off her shoulders and looks to Kath for confirmation. 'What is this place? The house looks like something out of a horror movie.'

'Some toff's country estate originally.' McDermott is full of fresh air bonhomie. 'It's got all the space we're going to need for a world class museum and no shortage of parking space, as you can see. This place is going to be jumping by the time we've finished.'

'In the meantime, we live in a caravan.' Ed runs a hand over the bodywork and peers inside.

'The ladies don't seem to mind.' McDermott rubs his hands – eager host and master of ceremonies. 'Let's get you installed.'

Rick turns to survey the main building. 'That place is empty, you say?'

'Locked up. It's definitely unsafe – half the joists and floorboards are rotten.'

'So who does it belong to now?'

'There's an owner around somewhere – an old man, product of Old Money, if you know what I mean – and none too bright from generations of inbreeding.'

'What's his name?'

'Bob Sherman. The motor collection was in his family, put together by one of his relatives who had the money and the enthusiasm to do it. Old Bob didn't know what he was sitting on 'till we came along.'

'When do we get to see the collection?' Ed chucks his and Julia's packs into the caravan.

'Right now. Meet me in that barn over there when you're settled in. I'll go and open it up.'

He marches off towards the cluster of outbuildings surrounding the main house. Ed turns to Rick.

'If my guess is right, we're about to be shown a pile of old crap.'

Rick shrugs. 'Maybe it'll be just like those pictures.'

'Yeah? I'll give you ten to one against.'

'What d'you want to do then?'

'I guess we just work with what there is and see what happens.'

'Not a lot of choice, is there?' Julia climbs into the caravan and looks around. 'I hope you boys know what you're getting us into.'

'Not really.' Ed follows her in. 'Never lived at close quarters with Rick, so I can't answer for his personal hygiene.'

'I'll make sure he behaves.' Kath makes a face and inspects the sleeping arrangements – bunks at each end, each compartment separated by a folding partition. 'I hope we're not going to hear you going at it hammer and tongs all night.'

'We're quiet as mice,' says Julia, fitting a lens to her camera. 'Let's go and see this load of old wrecks you're going to restore.'

The four of them make their way across the rough

ground to the largest outbuilding. McDermott is standing in the entrance, sweeping them in with a gesture. Strip lights on low-slung beams reveal what they've come to see and for a moment no one says a word.

The first impression is that some giant child has tossed rusted, neglected toys at random over the floor. In every recess of the barn, steel wings curve over corroded wheels; headlamps droop from once-proud grilles; elegant bodies, some with running boards, others streamlined like tin fish, lie rotting in harsh-cut shadows, all in paintless, cobweb monotone.

McDermott watches their reaction in silence.

Ed Pentecost makes a slow, thoughtful tour of the nearest specimens – an SS Jaguar beside a Ford Thunderbird parked nose to nose with something he doesn't recognize. He turns to McDermott.

'What's this?'

'You won't have seen one of those before. That's a Kaiser Darrin – great American flop from the fifties. Worth serious money now.'

'And this?' Ed pauses by a sleek monster, part concealed in shadow.

'That's a Facel Vega. This particular car was once owned by Mel Kinnear – you know who he is?'

'Mel Kinnear –' Kath moves up for a closer look at the car – 'he's an old rock star. Lead guitar with Lucifer's Oven-Glove. My brother's into 70s heavy metal bands. That's got to be worth a fortune.'

'You get the idea?' McDermott smiles benignly.

'Fucking hell...' Rick Bishop looks around, dazed.

'That's one way of putting it.' McDermott turns to Julia. 'First, I'll take that camera off you.'

'You will not.'

'Don't worry, it'll be in safe keeping.'

'No way. That's a state of the art Olympus and it stays where I can see it.'

'I'll have to insist.'

'You won't be insisting on anything.' Ed speaks quietly without looking at McDermott.'

'Alright, but no cameras in here – in fact no photographs anywhere on this property. Security is crucial and you need to respect that.'

'Fair enough.' Julia lowers her camera. 'You just had to ask.'

Kath says, 'We've all got smart phones anyway. You want to take those off us?'

'Like I say, security is of the utmost importance. We can't afford for any record of this collection to get out until we're good and ready – you understand?'

'Sure, we understand.' Ed remarks. 'No photos. You'll just have to trust us.'

'Right –' McDermott is back in team-leader mode. 'Next, we make a list of everything you need and I'll get it delivered in the morning. Tools, compressors, cleaning materials, abrasives, primers, masking and grinding equipment, compounds, paints, polishes – anything you're likely to need or think you might need in the future. When we've done that, you can give me your orders for dinner and I'll get it sent to the caravan. Then I suggest you get some sleep, you're going to need it.'

EIGHT

NIGHT. Julia sits up and moves the blind aside to look out the window by her bunk. Ed has stopped snoring and she senses that he is awake.

'I don't like Eric.' She speaks softly. A snort from Ed tells her he hears.

'I don't either.'

'I don't trust him. You don't demand somebody's camera unless you've got something to hide.'

'That's been gnawing at you. I could tell.'

'He just demanded it, like he has the right to order me around – like some fucking Nazi.'

'He's no saint, that's for sure.'

'And I'll tell you something else –' she shakes Ed's shoulder – 'there's someone in that house. There's a light in the top window.'

'Yeah?' Ed props himself on an elbow to look past her. 'Where?'

'It's gone out. I saw it though.'

Ed sits up. 'What's the time? – bloody hell Julia, it's twenty to three. Go back to sleep.'

'I'm not tired. This place spooks me. There was definitely a light.'

'You're not tired? I'm awake now and I've just thought of a way to take your mind off it.'

'Get off...' She resists, but without conviction. He takes her suppressed giggle as submission and for a moment the cramped space is filled with the rustle of coverings thrown aside.

Some time later they lie back and contemplate the pre-dawn glow.

Julia says, 'It's not so spooky now. D'you want to get up and have a look around while we've got the place to ourselves?'

'Why not?' Ed reaches for T-shirt and jeans. 'If there is someone in that house, I wouldn't mind knowing.'

There's no sound from Kath and Rick's end of the caravan as they let themselves out to the Neutral light, huddling against the chill, breathing the flinty, damp earth smell.

The house looms in front of them, featureless.

'Where did you say the light was?'

'Up the top,' Julia points, 'where that gable is.'

'You up for a bit of breaking and entering?'

'Not really. If the floors are all rotten the place is a death trap.'

'We met in a place like that, I seem to remember.' Ed gives her a nudge. 'You were hanging out in the attic.'

'Don't remind me. Those were my commune-dwelling, rebel days.'

'Why don't we try the door? If it's locked, we'll forget it.'

'Here's the thing –' Julia slows the pace – 'I get pissed off in scary movies because the suspense is all fake – incredibly stupid people wandering into horrible places where you can tell something gruesome's going to happen to them, and we're supposed to be shocked when they trip over a corpse or bump into a zombie. You'd think the music would've warned them anyway.'

'So we'll just go for a walk then.'

'I'm not scared of the dark.'

'I never said you were.'

'I just think we should leave the place alone.'

'Woah...' Ed's eye-line shifts. 'There's the light. You weren't hallucinating.'

'So we're definitely going to try the door now, aren't we?'

'If it's locked...'

'Yeah, yeah – get on with it.'

The door is locked but it's loose in the frame and yields to Ed's shoulder.

RICK BISHOP always sleeps well. Kath sleeps lightly, sometimes not at all. She heard the door open and close as Ed and Julia went out. She has no particular wish to go with them but gets out of bed anyway because what she really wants right now is a cup of tea.

She spends a moment fumbling for the gas tap and strikes a match before noticing the kettle is electric.

Not really awake. She gazes out of the window and it takes some seconds to register there's a light on high up in the main house.

Rick's day starts with a pillow crashing against his ear. He has no control over his first remarks but he surfaces to the certain knowledge that Kath doesn't appreciate language like that. Moments later he is outside the caravan, fully dressed, without having consciously made the effort to get there.

Kath rubs her fingers against his temples. 'Wake up – we're needed.'

'What?'

'Julia and Ed are in the house. They might fall through the floor and need help.'

Rick struggles to comprehend as she leads him to the dark mass of the main building. No light is showing now but the door is open.

BOB SHERMAN closes the internal shutters and walks carefully to his wing-back armchair. Three paces, but it takes effort and a balancing act on ninety-year-old legs. It's worth it though; an occasional trip to the window and a breath of night air restores him.

Bob is used to visitors: he has several every day. Doctor Morley looks in regularly to see how he's doing and although he looks too young to be qualified he seems to know his business. Doctor Morley is relatively new on the scene, having replaced Bob's original doctor for reasons that were never explained. There's also a nurse called Kitty who helps him bath and shave a couple of times a week.

Bob can't complain; as the youngest son of a landowning family he grew up on the estate and never had to think seriously about making a living. He is used to service and expects to have a jocular relationship with those who look after him.

A tall, mild man who wears tweed jackets and cravats, Bob has very little sense of time. One day moves seamlessly into the next and he spends his waking hours in his chair, reading old copies of *Country Life* and *Punch* or Churchill's *History of the English Speaking Peoples.*

There have already been several visitors tonight. Most are regulars. One in particular, who he calls 'Geronimo', put in an appearance around midnight. Geronimo has shoulder-length hair, a bandana round his head and elaborate pendants round his neck. He wanders in and out without a word, grinning broadly.

There is also a lady in early-Victorian dress who carries a lantern; he knows her as Florence Nightingale. Sometimes the room fills with Sixteenth Century courtiers who mingle for a while and leave without ceremony. There have been others, but Geronimo and Florence are occupying his thoughts at the moment.

Bob knows they are hallucinations but enjoys them anyway. They seem to have substance and are undeniably present, even if only to him.

He was diagnosed, years ago, with *Charles Bonnet Syndrome*, a condition sometimes associated with poor eyesight, in which people and things appear in apparently tangible form. The illusions are powerful and can last for a few minutes at a time, or all day. Medical advice to sufferers is to stay home, out of harm's way. Sudden reaction to perceived danger could be fatal, and rather than risk side-stepping an imaginary stagecoach and going under a real bus, Bob complies.

Staying indoors is no problem; he enjoys the comfort of his room and looks forward to whatever the day may bring.

And here, without warning, are two new visitors – a man and a woman, both in modern dress – T-shirts and jeans – which marks them as real.

Definitely real.

'Well good morning, or good evening, whichever it is.' Bob peers at them over his glasses.

Ed Pentecost blinks at him. 'We saw the light...'

'Was it a heavenly experience?'

'Pardon?'

'We're sorry to walk in on you,' Julia stays in the doorway. 'We thought the house was unoccupied.'

'It is, apart from me. And the doctor, from time to time. And other people who pop in. And now you, of course.'

'We didn't mean to disturb you.' Julia includes Ed with a glance.

'You're not disturbing me. What are you doing here?'

'We're here to work,' Ed tells him.

'What kind of work?'

'Restoring some motors.'

'Mechanics, are you?'

'Kind of. Who are you?'

'I live here. I think courtesy requires you to tell me your names before enquiring after mine.'

'He means –' Julia interrupts – 'I'm Julia, this is Ed. Are you Mister Sherman?'

'I am indeed.'

'I'll tell you what –' Ed steps forward – 'That's a seriously valuable collection you've got down there in the barn.'

'Is it? I never go down there. The new people have taken it off my hands.'

'The new people – do you mean Eric McDermott?' Julia leans to the old man's face.

'I don't know all their names. There's young Doctor Morley – he's new – and a couple of others. You must be working with them.'

'Not really. Have they bought the collection from you?'

'They've tried flashing paperwork in front of me.' Bob Sherwood flips a hand to dismiss it. 'I can't get excited about legal documents so I keep disappointing them. Too much paper in the world.'

'Never sign anything,' Ed remarks. 'An old mate taught me that.'

'Sound advice.'

'I think we should leave you.' Julia takes Ed's arm and steps back. 'Is there anything you need?'

'Can't think of anything. Bit of peace and quiet never goes amiss.' The old man pauses. 'I'd like some sherbet lemons, but I don't think you can get them any more.'

'YOU SAID THERE WAS A LIGHT.' Rick stumbles after Kath, hands thrust deep in pockets.

'It's gone out. I saw it though.'

'This is too early for me, Kath – I need my beauty sleep.'

'Stop griping you miserable sod.' Ed's voice, out of the darkness ahead.

Two dark forms emerge from the shadow of the house.

Julia speaks softly. 'There's an old man in there. He doesn't want to be disturbed.'

'Fine. Let's get some breakfast.' Rick turns to the caravan and at the same moment a glow of headlights moves along the hedgerow in the lane and a white Transit Van swings into the enclosure.

'This'll be our toys,' Rick remarks.

'Stay close –' Ed holds him back – 'No reason to let them see us.'

The Transit sweeps past them and parks outside the

barn. Two men get out: one in overalls, the other in a pale overcoat. They move quickly to the barn door, haul it open and the strip lights cut a square glow in the dull morning.

Four silent figures watch from the shadows as the two men haul heavy boxes into the barn. After a while the lights go out, steel doors close with a clash, the Transit sweeps past them and twin ruby tail-lights lurch away along the lane.

A moment later the pale overcoat moves in the half-light, and they hear the main door of the house being eased open. A moment's pause, then the door closes again and slow footsteps climb the staircase inside.

NINE

THE SUN COMES UP and low clouds send shadows scudding across the landscape. The smell of bacon lingers on the air. Ed steps down from the caravan nursing a warm coffee cup in his hands. The others follow.

After a while the sound of an engine disturbs the stillness and the white Range Rover pulls up beside them. McDermott climbs out and stands square, facing them, hands on hips.

'I thought I made it clear the main building is off limits.'

Julia offers him a chilly smile. 'You said we wouldn't fancy staying there in its present condition. Those were your words.'

'I should have put it more plainly, the place has been condemned, so if you're tempted to go exploring, don't.'

'Well, yes SIR!'

'You need to take this seriously,' McDermott turns to the other three. 'My colleague tells me the door had been forced when he arrived this morning.'

'Sure – I tried the door.' Ed looks him in the eye. 'The lock's knackered. If the house is dangerous you ought to do something about that.'

'I expected you to take the hint and leave well alone, so now I'm warning you for your own good – the place is a death trap and I don't want to be the one who has to explain a fatal accident. Are we all clear on that?'

They're all clear.

'Alright then.' McDermott's stance eases. 'I don't want to speak harshly to you any more than you want to hear it, but we're going to need some discipline here. We've got a mountain to climb and no one said it was going to be easy. I'm paying big money so there are no tea breaks, no early nights – just sweat and more sweat – no let-up until we get some results.'

'Where did you learn to talk like that?' Ed tosses coffee dregs aside.

'That's just my way – you'll get used to it. Your equipment's here now so what are you standing around for? And by the way, I'm glad to see you're early risers. That's a bonus.'

'Couldn't sleep.' Julia, ready to provoke him by any means possible.

'Sorry to hear that. You can catch forty winks while the lads get to work.'

'We all work.' Kath studies him with distaste.

'You ladies are engineers and bodywork specialists as well?'

'We get by.'

'So be it. I hope you don't expect to bill me for extra man-hours. We've agreed a deal and that stands, so let's get on with it.' McDermott leads them to the barn, heaves the door open and flicks on the lights.

Ed makes a slow tour of inspection. 'You mentioned a colleague. Where is he?'

'There'll be people here from time to time but they won't be in anybody's way. Their work needn't concern you.'

'I like to know who's around. Whoever it is doesn't mind going in the 'death trap' house then?'

'They're experts – surveyors.'

'Well, that's a comfort. Next question: There's a Cord eight-twelve in the pictures you showed us. I don't see it here.'

'Ah yes, beautiful car, beautiful example. It's no longer available – sold to a very persistent collector.'

'That don't make sense. Why would you sell a Cord when you're trying to put a motor museum together?'

'Not my decision.' McDermott goes to the pile of newly delivered boxes.' Let's get your supplies unpacked and start climbing that mountain!'

TAFFIN LIES ON THE BED looking up at the dark beams straddling the high pitch of the ceiling.

A key scrapes in the lock and a latch opens with a *clack*.

'Bloody'ell, it's freezing in here.' Charlotte, hands full of carrier bags, forces the door open with her knee and walks across the bare, polished parquet floor. Taffin watches her peacefully as she unloads thermos, chicken drumsticks, a pork pie and a Tupperware box of potato salad.

'The place ain't finished yet,' he remarks. 'Has that pie got jelly in it?'

'You think I'd get you a pork pie without jelly? Never in this world.' Charlotte unrolls a napkin of cutlery. 'I saw Ashley. He reckons he'll be putting the heating in next week. How long are we going to stay here?'

'Until I hear from Ed.'

'Then what?'

'You'll be here by yourself for a bit.'

'How long? How long is a bit?'

'Depends. When we know who's behind our present troubles we can make plans. Until then, we both stay away from the business and let them wonder where we might be.'

'You can almost see the business from here.' Charlotte wanders to the window. 'About a mile and a half I reckon, beyond those trees.'

'Near enough.'

Charlotte crosses the room and looks out of the window on the far side. 'There's the church tower, so Lasherham's down there to the left, Mitres Well Lane starts at the top of the hill on the other side, so our place is about a mile that way.' She leans to look left. 'See? I'm getting orientated now.

'You've got it.'

'How are you doing with that gadget?'

The gadget is an iPad that Taffin keeps beside him. It has a link to night vision security cameras at Muscle Motors, allowing him to monitor any activity there, day and night. There is a similar connection to their house in Mitres Well Lane. Kath Brewer supplied and set up the system at Taffin's request, then spent hours patiently trying to teach him to use it. In the end she gave up and showed Charlotte.

'Alright.' Taffin glances at the iPad. 'It's smarter than me. I get a nice view of empty rooms without having to be there.'

'That's what you call luxury.'

'She's a good girl, that Kath.'

'Yeah, Rick got himself a good one there. Well, come on, has Big Brother shown you anything yet?'

'I've watched you in the shower.'

'No you haven't. There's only cameras downstairs and on the outside wall at our place.' Charlotte picks up the iPad and peers at the screen. 'Not really you, is it? Kath says you're not at one with technology.'

'Better off with a book.'

'So I see.' Charlotte puts the iPad aside and picks up the copy of *Walking Distance* propped against the bed. 'Russell Chambers Gates again. You can't get enough of this fella. Looks a bit dry to me.'

Taffin watches her with mild amusement. 'I'll read to you if you like.'

'Later.' Charlotte peels off her jacket and top. 'Not doing anything else today, are we?'

IF THE TASK is to clean a large area strewn with antique machinery, you start high and work downwards to floor level, then clear away the debris, raising as little dust as possible.

By midday, the part of the barn closest to the door is clean and free from obstruction and several venerable motors have been unveiled as the cobwebs were swept away. The SS Jaguar and the Facel Vega have been put on blocks, the wheels have been removed and the brake drums cleaned.

Looking at progress so far, Ed Pentecost reckons they have two weeks work ahead of them before any kind of restoration can start.

McDermott stayed to satisfy himself they knew what they were doing and left them to it.

'Not a man for manual labour.' Rick's voice from a far corner as the Range Rover disappears along the lane.

'Yeah,' Ed wipes grease from his hands. 'He thinks we

paddled up the Thames in a coracle. 'If the old geezer in that house owns this lot, he's being conned out of a fortune.'

'We can't get involved in that.' Julia straightens up from the Jaguar's front suspension. 'He's a real old gent but he doesn't know what day it is. Maybe all this belongs to him, maybe not – maybe he's signed it away without knowing what he was doing – we don't know.'

Ed shakes his head. 'I want to know what happened to that Cord.'

'Kath reckons the Cord was never here.' Rick picks his way towards them.

'It was in two of the photos. We all saw it.'

'We've found the place where it was, but there's no room for it there. Kath thinks the pic was faked. There's no way you could fit a thing that size into the space.'

'Time to make a call.' Ed fishes in his overall pocket for his phone. 'Someone's messing with the Boss.'

'I HATE TO BE the bearer of bad news, but I felt I should be the one to tell you.' Gordon Glennan shifts his weight deliberately to make the floorboards creak. 'This building isn't safe, so we have no choice but to close it up pending extensive renovation, which will mean gutting it first.'

'What d'you mean *we*?' Debi Royce faces him across the bookshop's ground floor counter. 'Who else is involved in this farce? You've been wanting to shut us down for ages and now you've found a way that sounds official. I'd like to know who *we* is. It's pathetic...'

'It's a local authority matter...'

'You're an MP – you're also the owner.'

'Not technically –' Glennan tries his knowing smile –

'but I am legally responsible for health and safety where the public is concerned.'

'How do people like you get into power?' Lorna Moorcroft has stayed out of the conversation so far and now surprises herself. 'Does this shop mean anything to you? I doubt it. I've never seen you browsing the shelves in here, never mind buying a book.'

'I regret this as much as you do...' Glennan makes a helpless gesture. Unexpected fury on the faces of two middle-aged women has him at a loss.

'Bollocks.'

'I'm sorry?' He is not sure which of these prim ladies said it, but senses it's time to wrap up the conversation. 'Let's not be too downcast. Perhaps the business can find a new home. All I can tell you for certain is that public safety comes first, so the bookshop can't trade from these premises any longer.'

Debi Royce comes out from behind the counter and stares him in the face, close up.

'You know what makes me sick? People put their trust in the likes of you. Most of the time you can hide behind your inflated egos and delusions of public service, but now and again you show yourselves for what you really are – greedy, self-serving windbags, with an extra dose of smugness that comes from a privileged education.'

'I'm sorry you feel like that...'

'And while I have your attention, you're running the StarTrack fiasco, aren't you? What's happening there – which way's it going? You're not thinking of running high speed rail through Lasherham, I hope. These things had better not be connected.'

'Mrs Royce – Debi...'

'Make that Mrs Royce, you were right first time.'

'Mrs Royce, we're straying off the subject and I can't discuss...'

'Don't smirk at me – you're killing an irreplaceable facility, putting us out of business and for all I know flattening the whole area as well. You're going to regret this, Mister Glennan. There are better men than you who know how to look after us everyday, ordinary people. Don't ask me how I know, but you can bet on it. Now get out.'

Glennan leaves without a word, having to force his way past Harry Hawkins and two others, who couldn't have helped overhearing Debi's tirade.

TEN

PIERRE IS READY, in principle, to support any cause he considers worthy of protest, but he is not used to being organized. His sister tries it from time to time, but not with the level of conviction he is experiencing now.

He has just arrived, as requested, at a house overlooking Lasherham, and introduced himself to the occupant. The house is a barn conversion, the kind of rural hideaway that appeals to people who didn't grow up in the country, and is clearly work in progress. There is no furniture other than a workbench, a trestle table, a couple of kitchen chairs and two camp beds pushed together. The interior smells of plaster and fresh wood shavings.

Pierre recognizes the slim, dark lady who let him in as Tessa's good friend, but has only just connected her with the large, quietly-spoken man who nearly gave him a seizure on the path from Chalkpit Wood.

Charlotte looks him over. 'You need to relax. Love.'

'I'm cool, but I'd like to know what's going on.'

'That's what my ol' man's trying to find out. He's one of your sister's clients, you know – big fella with not much to say.'

'I know him. Mister Taffin. My sister reckons he's the bloke they made a film about some time ago – quite a local celebrity.'

'That's what they say.'

'What does he want my old camper van for?'

'He wants to tidy it up a bit for a job – and it ain't your van, love.'

'So what's this job he wants me to do? "Time to make myself useful", he said. What's that supposed to mean?'

'He probably thinks you're a bit of a waste of space, love. Your sister thinks so, and she talks to him a lot while she's torturing his knotted muscles.'

'Well, here I am.' Pierre makes a wide-arm gesture and props himself against the trestle table, which promptly folds up under his weight.

Charlotte helps him to his feet, flicking wood shavings from his jacket. Pierre regains his composure.

'Like I said, I'm here, wasting space. What do you want me to do, and whatever it is, why me?'

'My ol' man reckons you're about right for an unusual sort of job that's coming up.'

'So I'm in demand, all of a sudden.'

'The job's going to mean spending time by yourself, mostly at night, but that's fine because you're happy with your own company, aren't you, and you don't mind being out at all hours. I talk to your sister as well, you know.'

'Well, that's tough. I'm not available right now.' Pierre dusts himself down. 'It so happens I've just taken a life-changing decision to get qualified for something.'

'Oh, what are you going to do?'

'I haven't decided yet.'

'You've taken a life-changing decision but you haven't worked out what it is yet.'

'I'm thinking it through.'

'That's alright, love – you'll have plenty of time to think about it while you're doing this little job for us. My ol' man's a very good employer. He doesn't expect anybody to work for free.'

Charlotte stands back and looks him over, then crosses the room and comes back with a heavy rucksack.

'This is for you. It's full of interesting toys, so settle yourself down and I'll tell you what you're going to do with them.'

'That's if I agree to whatever it is.'

'You will, love. You'll have the camper van back for this job, too, all done up and running sweetly, so that should cheer you up. Life just goes on getting better and better, doesn't it?'

'HE SHUT US DOWN.' Debi Royce moves through the Friday evening crush in the White Lion and accepts Mostyn's offered bar stool next to Ivy Lewis. 'That's Lorna and me on the scrapheap. He wanted to pay us up to the end of the week, cheap scumbag – we had to push him for a month in lieu of notice.'

'Where on Earth did you acquire a word like... *scumbag*?' Perry Butt chomps on loose dentures and studies his empty glass.

'I read a lot – and it's the only repeatable word that comes to mind.'

'You should've heard the mouthful she gave him.' Harry Hawkins signals Meg for refills, accidentally including Butt's glass. 'I caught the tail end of it. The little creep couldn't get out the door fast enough. There's your classic Member of Parliament, I thought – public servant, my arse. Proud of you, girl.'

Debi takes a moment to relish the compliment, then turns to Ivy Lewis. 'I thought we were going to get some help from that mate of yours – Mister Taffin.'

'I told you, he's retired. Me and Harry went to see him and he turned us down flat.'

'Yes, but he came in the shop after that and said something like, people with brains never retire. Very – what's the word? – enigmatic, our Mister Taffin.'

'Maybe he's away.' Meg pauses in the act of mopping the bar. 'We usually see him once or twice a week, but not lately.'

'The garage is all locked up.' Harry Hawkins tries to catch Meg's eye a second time. 'I passed by there today – no sign of anybody. Ashley, where's that mate of yours disappeared to?'

Ashley Gunn has just walked in and the question catches him off balance. 'Who's disappeared?'

'Your mate Taffin.'

'I don't know. Ask Mo – he's right behind me.'

Mo Taffin is stooping through the doorway and now looks up to see every face in the room turned to him. He has never been comfortable as the center of attention and the idea of making a public pronouncement strikes him dumb. Ashley Gunn rescues him.

'They want to know what's happened to that brother of yours.'

'Don't know.' Mo's massive, shy shrug.

'That's right,' Ashley continues. 'I've seen Charlotte and she doesn't know either. Looks like the lad's gone walkabout for a while.'

'He don't go walkabout.' Mo's pumpkin face is clearly troubled. 'I know when there's something people ain't telling me.'

Ashley Gunn, friend and ally of the Taffin family, says nothing.

A long moment passes before Ivy Lewis raises a triumphant finger. 'I'll bet I know –' she challenges them all with a look – 'he's gone off to figure out some way to deal with Glennan.'

'The heart-warming thing is, you really believe it.' Perry Butt's plume of white hair rises like a battle standard. 'I love you dearly, Ivy. You are indeed Marion to Robin Hood, who is at this very moment holed up in Sherwood Forest devising a plan to rescue us all from oppression, confound the tyrannical Sherriff, save the bookshop and deliver us from the abominable StarTrack, all in one brilliant, courageous stroke. That's a pink gin please, Meg.'

'You miserable old cynic.' Ashley Gunn pushes Butt's empty glass in Meg's direction. 'How d'you know Ivy's not right? Maybe that's just what he's up to. Think about it – all he's got to do is get Glennan dancing to his tune. It wouldn't be the first time he's surprised us.'

'THAT'S THE NEW ROUTE, IS IT?' Janice Glennan leans over her husband's shoulder.

Glennan folds up the map he was studying. 'It's a viable alternative. We're looking at it.'

'Oh, come on –' Janice takes the map from him and

flattens it out on his desk – 'you can't flash something like that under my nose and expect me not to take an interest.'

'I didn't flash it under your nose and why would you assume there's a new route anyway? That sort of information is supposed to be confidential.'

'It won't be confidential when the work starts, will it?' She peers hard at the map. 'Is that black line the new route? Bloody hell, you're joking – it goes straight through Lasherham.'

'Not through – under.'

'A tunnel?'

'That's right. This proposal goes underground into the hillside just outside Stoleworth and comes to the surface... here.' He stabs a finger at a green area.

'What's that?'

'Don't worry, it misses the village by about two hundred meters.'

'That's the field beside the old bookshop.'

'Correct.'

'I hope you're going to declare an interest.'

'I've already done so. If anything, being involved with the property shows my commitment to the StarTrack project without regard for my own interests.'

'Very noble.'

'If this turns out to be the preferred route, no one can accuse me of Not-In-My-Back-Yard.'

'What a servant of the people you are.'

'A little uxorial support wouldn't go amiss, Janice. This is the fourth proposed alternative. There's no guarantee it'll be the final one.'

'I hope you know what you're doing.' Janice Glennan

takes another look at the map and straightens up. 'I'm out tonight, by the way. There's food in the fridge or you might want to go to The King's Arms.'

'Where are you going?'

'Do I ever ask where you're going?' She pauses in the doorway. 'When I do, you can ask me.'

Gordon Glennan sits at his desk staring at nothing, listening to his wife moving about upstairs, hears drawers and cupboards opening and closing, imagines her at her dressing table, wonders what's going through her mind while she makes herself ready for whatever her night may hold.

He is still there an hour later when she closes the front door on her way out.

THE TOLLGATE BOOKSHOP presents a dark frontage tonight. No lights; no sign of life. Charlotte parks the Jeep on the opposite side of the street, close to the trees.

In the back seat, Pierre gathers his kit – a bulging rucksack and a second bundle almost twice the size – and opens the door.

'Not yet.' Charlotte has caught a glimpse of lights in the wing mirror; headlights approaching. 'I'll tell you when it's clear.'

A Volvo whisks by, close and fast. Charlotte waits until the tail-lights have disappeared.

'Why are people in such a hurry?' Pierre grumbles. 'A second later, that car would've taken the door off.'

'That's why I said to wait, love. Now, have you got everything?'

'I have everything: sleeping bag, thermos, toolkit and all

the electronic wizardry I've spent my life trying to avoid. I could be charged with breaking and entering just for being in possession of this lot, so you'd better hope nobody comes snooping around.'

'No one's going to come snooping, love. And if they do, you're here to record birdsong, the dawn chorus, all the nocturnal sounds of nature. You look like the kind of weirdo who'd do that, so don't fret.'

'Thanks. Now all I've got to do is remember what plugs into what and how to turn it all on.'

'You'll be alright, love. You managed it back at the house.'

'Yeah, that was in daylight, with the instructions. Inanimate objects don't like me.'

'They love you. Now get going. 'The camper van's parked in a secluded corner of the field behind the bookshop. It's your home for the next few days.'

Pierre struggles out of the Jeep, hefts his kit and sets off across the road. Charlotte watches him force his way through a gap in the hedge and melt into the shadows behind the bookshop.

At the same time, a mile away, a speeding Volvo heads into the night. Janice Glennan drives with her window open, relishing the rush of air. Hardly any traffic this evening. She wonders, idly, what the couple in the parked Jeep were up to. It's always a pleasure to witness other people's clandestine pleasures, if only briefly.

ELEVEN

AT DAWN, lace-black trees cut hard edges on a flint silver sky with a glow beyond, as warm as frost can get. Ed Pentecost has found that a mug of coffee can be made to last from first glimmer to full sunrise. This has become a daily ritual.

When the first long shadows reach out across the yard to the barn he walks over and hauls the doors open, revealing four partially restored cars under tarpaulins. They have achieved a lot in two weeks.

The Hudson is next. Rick has dubbed this monster 'The Whale' for its curvaceous lines and the fact that it measures just over 17 feet from front to back. They left it uncovered last night ready for an early start this morning.

Ed runs a hand over the front wing where the paint has faded to a dull moss green. This massive body will call for a marathon clean up job and they can't think about that until the guts have been restored to running order. Rick's conclusion last night was that suspension parts were going to be the problem; they would probably end up making components and rebuilding the whole assembly from scratch.

Finally they would get to the interior. Ed opens the left hand driver's door releasing the dust of ages from threadbare cloth upholstery. The huge, bone-white steering wheel presents the Hudson badge at its center, with the chrome horn ring around it. The rear seats are in deep shadow; Ed leans in for a look, then peers more intently and freezes.

'You're up early, Ed.' The voice is just above a whisper.

Ed takes a moment to focus on the dark shape in the back. The rear door creaks open and Taffin steps out, flipping dust from his jacket.

Ed shrugs. 'You know me. Crack of dawn, every day.'

'Interesting place, this.' Taffin wanders among the tarpaulins. 'They've got stuff here I've never seen.'

'But no 1938 Cord.' Ed watches him. 'We don't think it was ever here.'

'I agree, that was bait. The question is, who wants me here and why? Who else is around, Ed, apart from the four of you?'

'We've only seen McDermott to talk to. There's a geezer who turns up with him now and again but he keeps his distance – a surveyor, McDermott says. And there's the old fella who lives in the main house, but he never comes down here.'

'So how do you know about him?'

'Me and Julia had a look around the house when McDermott wasn't here. Nice fella, very polite – Old School, don't y'know? Are you going to stick around?'

'I won't be far away.'

'Fair enough –' Ed makes no attempt to hide his relief – 'so who's minding the shop back home?'

'Muscle Motors is closed for refurbishment. Charlotte

will let the specialist press know when we're back in business.'

'Can't happen soon enough. Rick wants to string Eric McDermott up from one of them beams. So do the girls.'

'I'm asking you all to be patient a while longer.' Taffin casts an eye over the exotic collection of cars. 'One more thing, Ed. Have you seen any paperwork for this lot – logbooks, service sheets, registration?'

'Nothing.' Ed shrugs.

'Stuff like this needs provenance – something to show where it was before it wound up here. There's got to be paperwork, and I'm guessing it ain't far away.'

'I've got my work cut out for me here, Boss, without looking for bits of paper.'

'I wouldn't ask you. Just keep your ears open.'

'Yeah – all in the line of duty. Where are you staying?'

'Like I said, not far away. Look after yourself.'

Taffin wanders into the daylight, turns the corner and is gone.

'I THOUGHT THE BOOKSHOP WAS CLOSED.' Ivy Lewis calls through the open window of the White Lion to Debi Royce, who is perched on a stool at the bar.

'That's right, it's closed,' Debi calls back. 'What d'you think I'm doing in here on a weekday?'

'I've got news for you then...' Ivy is in the bar in a breathless moment... 'Harry's just been past it and he says the place is buzzing.'

'It's probably Glennan's architect measuring up.'

'No, there's a sign on the door saying *Business as Usual*.'

'That doesn't make any sense.'

'It's what Harry said and he isn't making it up.'

'So who's running it? I've got to see this.' Debi Royce heads for the door, walks into Ashley Gunn as he arrives, grasps his lapels and gives him a direct command: 'Ashley, I've had a drink so you're driving.'

There is no arguing with Debi in this mood. A few minutes later, Ashley Gunn's Jaguar, still with its new car smell in spite of having been briefly stolen, rolls to a halt opposite the Tollgate Bookshop. The three inside sit staring at the open door listening to the sound of a reassuring male voice over a PA system from within.

Debi Royce is first into the bookshop; Ivy Lewis and Ashley follow. The recorded voice comes to them from somewhere overhead.

"The Tollgate Bookshop welcomes all regular customers and wishes to apologise for the absence of staff today. Please feel free to browse as usual and if you wish to make a purchase, we trust you to leave the money in the box on the counter."

There follows a moment of *Vivaldi*, then the message is repeated. And so it continues while Debi and her entourage wander among the narrow corridors in bewildered silence. In the next few minutes, more customers arrive, stroll and browse the shelves in self-absorbed silence as on any normal day.

Ashley Gunn traces the voice to a shelf on the second floor and finds one of the speakers wedged in between *The Faber Book of Aphorisms* and a battered edition of *Brewer's Dictionary of Phrase & Fable*. Another is discovered behind a pile of *Asterix* books. By silent agreement, both are left undisturbed.

Debi says: 'I feel I should stay here. I've been responsible for this place for years. Why should today be any different?'

'You're not in charge any more, that's the difference.' Ivy Lewis steers her towards the door. 'What we ought to do now is tiptoe away and leave it to run by itself. Someone set this up and I don't think any of us is meant to interfere.'

Ashley Gunn backs her up and finally Debi is persuaded. They have grown used to the welcoming voice in the background, so a variation in the script as they leave goes unnoticed:

"...thank you for your visit. Please call again soon."

Twenty minutes later they're back in the White Lion broadcasting the news.

Perry Butt swivels on his barstool to confront Ivy Lewis. 'I suppose you're going to tell me this was orchestrated by your hero.'

'I'm saying nothing, but he dropped a strong hint that he doesn't believe in retirement.' Ivy looks into the old journalist's face. 'You believe in Robin Hood, don't you Perry?'

Butt chomps on loose dentures, peers at his pink gin and finally meets Ivy's stare.

'I'll believe in Robin Hood the day they scrap this hell-spawned railway.'

ANOTHER PEACEFUL DAY for Bob Sherman. He has no idea what the time is, and no interest in finding out. There have been visitors. Young Doctor Morley looked in earlier, brisk as ever, to give him the usual hurried examination. No reason has been given for this ritual but Bob accepts it stoically rather than encourage medical conversation of any kind. The doctor looked at his tongue, raised his eyelids with a thumb to peer in closely, seemed pleased with what he saw, flashed his quick, professional smile and left, leaving Bob to wonder if those unnaturally white teeth are real.

When the doctor left there was a quiet interlude, after which it seemed to Bob that a dense growth of bamboo had taken root in the far corner of the room and a party of Gurkhas emerged, complete with bush hats and kukris. They scouted around for a while and melted away as silently as they had come.

Some time later, Bob emerges from a doze and feels a presence. A man in a dark suit has been watching him from the doorway and now moves into the room, the floorboards creaking under his weight.

'Come in, please.' Bob allows himself a note of irony. 'I don't believe we've met.'

'Don't believe we have.' An effortless voice.

'Do you have business here?' Bob sits back and studies his visitor. 'Normally I expect people to introduce themselves. This time I'll give you the advantage – I'm Bob Sherman.'

'And you live here?'

'Man and boy, Mister...?'

'Taffin.'

'To what do I owe your visit, Mister Taffin?'

'Curiosity. Some of my people are working downstairs. You've met two of them.'

'People work here from time to time. I don't always know what they're doing.'

'They're fixing up some motors for you.'

'That's good of them.' Bob nods peacefully, his attention beginning to drift.

The next instant his eyes are wide open.

'I want you to concentrate, Mister Sherman.' Taffin leans

close to the old man. 'I need to know who those motors belong to.'

'They've been in my family for years. If they're still on my property, I suppose they belong to me. What is your interest in this, exactly?'

'They're worth a lot of money, Mister Sherman. If they're yours, someone's busy stealing them from you.'

'How bizarre. Who would do such a thing?'

'Has anyone asked you for documents, the kind of paperwork that goes with owning cars?'

'Documents, forms... not really my line of country – never have been. They're always asking me to sign things, flourishing sheaves of paper at me, asking if I know where this or that bloody document is. I tell them, I couldn't be less interested. You'll have a hard time finding my signature on anything. There's too much paperwork in the world.'

'Good thinking.' Taffin straightens up and wanders to the shuttered window. 'You get a lot of visitors?'

'People are in and out all the time.' Bob smiles to himself. 'Some are in my head, of course, but most of them are real enough. The doctor was here today. I don't know why he bothers – I never ask for him.'

'How well do you know this doctor?'

'I wouldn't claim to know him at all.' Bob considers for a moment. 'We had a family doctor for years, but he seems to have faded away. So has the family for that matter; there's only me left. This new fella's one of the more recent faces. Quite young – awfully white teeth.'

Taffin pauses in the act of opening the shutter, gazes out over twilight fields, watches rooks circling to roost in a scribble of trees.

'Good view of the barn from here,' he remarks. 'You ought to leave this open.'

'The doctor always shuts it. He says it lets in the draft.'

'You don't want to listen to doctors – especially ones you don't know. Is there anything I can do for you?'

'Kind of you to ask. I have everything I need.' Bob glances up at his visitor. 'If you'll forgive my presumption, you don't look like someone who would normally offer.'

'Nice talking to you, Mister Sherman.' Taffin wanders to the door, hands in pockets. 'I'll see you again.'

TWELVE

CHARLOTTE OPENS HER DOOR to find Mo and Shirley standing on the step. Shirley is clutching a copy of the Stoleworth Observer.

Mo asks, 'Any word from the boy yet?'

'I've heard from him.' Charlotte leads them to the kitchen. 'He's away doing a bit of business.'

'We were worried,' Shirley tells her. 'It's unusual for him to spend time away from home.'

'Yeah, I miss him like crazy – but don't tell him I said so.'

'He won't be too happy when he sees this.' Mo takes the newspaper from his wife, spreads it on the table and stabs at it with a finger like a Cumberland sausage. 'Them buggers have overstepped the mark this time.'

They all lean over to read:

NEW StarTrack ROUTE TO UNDERMINE LASHERHAM (writes Erica Lyle). StarTrack Ltd has revealed yet another alternative route for its proposed high speed rail loop. The Parliamentary Select Committee, chaired by The Rt. Hon. Gordon Glennan M.P. is considering a fourth option that includes a seven mile tunnel from the East Stoleworth turnoff to the western boundary of Lasherham. This latest development, fuelling uncertainty that continues to dog the StarTrack project, is likely to meet with strong local opposition. Tony Newton, Chair of Lasherham P.C., said: 'Everybody's sick of this. People's lives are being disrupted and you can't get any sense out of StarTrack.' No one from StarTrack was available for comment.

'You're right, he won't be happy.' Charlotte reaches for the kettle. 'No one around here's going to like this. It doesn't make sense.'

Shirley says, 'It's all about money and power with these politicians. They spend their time lining their own pockets and have the nerve to ask for our votes.'

'Don't get yourself worked up, Shirl,' Mo tells her.

'I don't know if they're all bent –' Charlotte plugs the kettle in and turns to face them, arms folded – 'but whoever's running StarTrack ain't that bright. All they do is dither and keep everybody confused.'

'Perhaps that's what they want to do –' Shirley makes a helpless gesture – 'so we're all impressed with how much power they've got.'

'Power to the People.' Charlotte punches the air without conviction.

'Yeah, why not?' Mo's voice. 'I don't even know who our MP is, but I'd like to know how often he turns up at the House of Commons. It don't matter what he calls himself, he don't represent me.'

'His sort don't even know we exist,' Shirley throws at him. 'It's all in-fighting, fiddling expenses and ignoring voters – until they want to get elected again.'

'We need to do something they can't ignore.' Charlotte is suddenly calm. 'How about we get people stirred up a bit?'

Three thoughtful faces stare at each other for a moment. Then, one by one, they start to nod.

'NOT GOOD ENOUGH.' Eric McDermott stands in the barn doorway, legs apart, hands on hips, the back of his head radiating disappointment as he stares at the five tarpaulins. 'There's eighteen cars here. I'm counting five and you haven't started the cosmetic work. You've hardly scratched the surface.'

'You're fucking joking.' Rick Bishop isn't having that. 'We've been working ten hour days, so I'll take a little respect from you.'

This time, Ed Pentecost shows no inclination to restrain his colleague and McDermott swivels to face them.

'You'll take whatever I think necessary – and spare me the attitude or I promise you life will get very uncomfortable. Clear?'

'Easy, Rick.' Ed sets a calming hand on Rick's shoulder. 'I've an idea the man wants you to take a pop at him. Not worth it.' He takes a pace in McDermott's direction. 'Now, Eric, if you're any judge of character you'll know none of us takes kindly to threats – so why are you trying to get my mate steamed up? I'll have an answer before we go any further.'

'The answer's staring you in the face.' McDermott's eyes narrow. 'We're talking money here – shed-fulls of money. Maybe you don't get the big picture but that's fine by me. All you have to do is work your arses off for as long as it takes and remind yourselves you're getting paid well over the odds for it. You don't ask questions, you don't get to give me lip. If you want respect, you'll earn it.'

He scans the faces in front of him. Ed's expression conveys nothing. Rick's jaw has slackened in a way that usually spells danger.

'One more thing –' McDermott turns to walk away – 'I'm the one keeping your paymasters sweet. Let's not give them an excuse to get difficult.'

'Did he just threaten to fire us?' Rick watches McDermott's retreating figure.

'He threatened not to pay us.' Ed wipes his hands on an oily rag.

'He was never going to pay us –' Rick watches McDermott climbing into the white Range Rover – 'but I ain't being fired by a twat like him.'

'BREAKFAST WITH A SMILE.' Mrs Dunphy brings a plate of bacon and eggs arranged as a face with a grilled tomato for the nose.

The Dunphys weren't sure about Taffin when he first arrived. The car caused a stir as it burbled in under the archway to the parking lot behind *The March Hare*. The red Ford Mustang is a larger car than the pub's limited space allows for and the man who got out made it look compact.

Paul Dunphy watched him approach with some apprehension. The slab of dark suit and slightly bow-legged walk suggested restrained menace, but the man was polite in a quiet way.

Later the same evening, both the Dunphys engaged Taffin in conversation over their bar and decided he was one who listened rather than talked. There was a disconcerting stillness about him but you could get used to that.

Since then, Taffin has come to appreciate *The March Hare*. Charlotte found the pub online, liked the look of it and booked him in. It's an ideal base for the matter in hand: fifteen minutes' drive from the farm where the motor collection is housed... and June Dunphy does a breakfast worth getting up for.

'Looks about right.' Taffin nods appreciation.

'That'll keep yer man from the door.' June's Irish voice is never less than comforting. 'Will you be wanting a look at the local paper?'

'No thanks, June.'

'You're happy with your own thoughts, then?'

Taffin thanks her without a word and she withdraws to the kitchen.

His own thoughts. Worth spending time on reflection at the moment.

His first concerns are in home territory. The Tollgate Bookshop plan is up and running, the day's work apparently hosted by a disembodied voice, courtesy of Tessa's brother Pierre. Charlotte does a drive-by every so often and reports that people are in and out browsing most of the time, much as when the shop was officially open. So far, there has been no attempt to interfere.

The end game is simple: show the owner, Gordon Glennan, that the community will have its way no matter what – and this applies even where his own property is concerned. As a strategy, it can't last; but it shows that anyone can be caught off balance with a bit of ingenuity; pressure can be brought to bear in surprising ways – and that's what a significant number of Lasherham locals require from Mark Twill Taffin.

The latest change of StarTrack route is more unsettling – a far bigger issue than the fate of a second-hand bookshop. Or is it? There is a common factor here that can't be ignored: in each case, Gordon Glennan is personally involved.

Reluctantly, Taffin acknowledges he will have to spend time in that man's company sooner or later, and he'd better come up with a result.

It's what's expected.

Like old times.

Taffin pours coffee from the pot June Dunphy has put in front of him, and adds warm milk. Paul and June know what breakfast is all about and take pride in every detail; even the toast is wrapped for warmth in linen napkins and there seem to be three kinds of marmalade. Bring Charlotte here when this business is sorted out.

Back to the present: Taffin takes out a notebook and a stub of pencil.

> *Further questions:*
> *Who does Silver (real name?) work for?*
> *Who does McDermott work for?*
> *Are Silver and McDermott connected?*
> *Is either of them Mister Adams?*
> *Who is Mr Adams?*

Taffin's pencil hovers over the page, then moves on with conviction:

> *Silver and McDermott work for same employer whose aims are: To restore classic motor collection (probably Bob Sherman's property).*
>
> *To put Muscle Motors out of business?*

Why? Personal grudge or fear of competition?
If personal grudge, WHO?

Bacon, eggs and coffee are the key to clear thinking and a decisive frame of mind.

'You enjoyed that, then?' June Dunphy comes to collect his clean plate.

'The best.'

'Oh, that's high praise indeed, Mister Taffin. I've an idea you don't give praise lightly.'

LASHERHAM is not easily roused. You could stand in the High Street all day holding a banner announcing The End Of The World and most people would step past you with a knowing smile.

You could shout and kick cans down the street and hardly attract a raised eyebrow. You could accost passers-by in the name of any number of worthy causes and come away with little more than loose change...

But mention StarTrack and people gather round.

Mo, Shirley and Charlotte have come to the White Lion for Saturday morning drinks. Ashley Gunn arrives while Meg is taking their first order. Debi Royce picks up on their conversation and sees a chance to light the fuse for a public demonstration of village feeling. It takes no time to raise spur-of-the-moment support. Ivy Lewis and Harry are all for it. Perry Butt and Mostyn were at the bar soon after opening time and could hardly avoid getting caught up in the spirit of insurrection – Butt by instinct, Mostyn out of duty. By noon, forty locals have gathered in the car park.

Someone produces groundsheets and spray paint. Groups set to work cutting and ripping up strips, with rhythmic accompaniment supplied by the *clacking* of shaken paint cans. The air is alive with shouted slogan suggestions.

Improvised banners rise up in the growing throng and someone suggests they all march down the High Street to the Bury Field.

The demo is on.

At Stoleworth Central, Sergeant Dave Walls takes a call from an anonymous Lasherham resident and before the march reaches the end of the High Street, Erica Lyle has left her desk at the *Stoleworth Observer* and is in her car heading for the scene.

The gathering has swelled by the time it reaches the Bury Field. Banners rock over the heads of the marchers with an assortment of hastily sprayed messages:

BACK OFF STARTRACK
AXE THE TRAX
TELL STARTRACK WHERE TO GO

There are others, too, rendered more or less illegible by over-excited use of spray cans.

A strident voice starts the chant – 'SCRAP STAR TRACK... SCRAP STAR TRACK...' and the crowd picks it up.

Once gathered in force, the assembly realizes it needs a focal point – someone to listen to – and there follows an exchange of questioning, challenging and competitive glances.

Tony Newton, Chair of the Parish Council, isn't used to spontaneous action and hesitates just long enough to discount himself.

Debi Royce believes decisions are taken by those willing to shoulder the burden – by those who show up, someone said – and is sporting enough to allow a moment's delay before stepping forward.

'Has anyone got a loudhailer?' she yells, but no one hears her.

Erica Lyle has parked across a private drive at the end of Church Street and arrives at Bury Field in time to see Debi Royce waving her arms.

That's where the story's going to be. Erica is at Debi's side in a heartbeat, urging people to gather round. Perry Butt, recognizing the instinct of a fellow newshound, grabs Erica roughly by the arm.

'Go for the throat,' he tells her. 'If you call yourself a journalist, forget the piffling political correctness that plagues your generation – write this so the bastards understand the contempt in which we hold them.'

Erica tries to shake off the gnarled hand that grips her, reads madness in the old fighting-cock's face and switches on her business smile.

'I'll write truthfully about whatever happens,' she assures him. 'Let me get on with my job.'

'It's not just the bloody railway.' Butt's plume of white hair stands proud from his blazing forehead. 'It's their gratuitous dismissal of the public – that's what rankles – their cynical indifference to the very people to whom they owe their positions – and these self-serving bloodsuckers should have their faces rubbed in it every time they dare to evade, prevaricate or condescend to us. Write it with bloody passion, no mercy, no prisoners, veins in your teeth – or don't write it at all.'

Erica tries to back away from the shower of spit that accompanies this outburst, then feels the force of it like an electrical charge hitting her nervous system at its core.

'You're fucking right I will,' she throws at him. 'You think I'd let Gordon Glennan off lightly after the damage he's done around here? Or his oh-so-charming wife, for that matter? No fucking way.'

'Good girl,' Perry Butt growls in her face; then he lurches off into the crowd leaving her to wonder what he must have been like in his youth.

Erica stations herself where she perceives the action to be – at Debi Royce's elbow. Debi has acquired a loudhailer and has begun to improvise with no clear idea of what to say to an impromptu gathering of chanting villagers.

'WHAT DO WE WANT?' she yells – then gropes for a follow-up line. The ongoing chant gives her the clue and she continues... 'WE WANT STARTRACK SCRAPPED... WE WANT IT CANCELLED... WE WANT TO KNOW WHY NONE OF US EVEN HEARD ABOUT IT UNTIL IT WAS A DONE DEAL... BUT MOST OF ALL... WHAT AFFECTS US MOST... IF IT'S COMING, WE WANT TO KNOW WHERE IT'S GOING.'

The throng rumbles approval: distant thunder.

Debi shifts up a gear. 'Where's it going? Take a wild guess – right through here if we're to believe the latest rumour. No one asked us how we felt about super-fast trains hurtling under our feet. No one mentioned StarTrack until the plans were well advanced – done and dusted – a *fait accompli.*'

The rumble swells...

'No one had the courtesy to mention we were going to have our lives uprooted. Why was that, do you think?'

... harder rumbling, with derisive undertones...

'Were they afraid we might object? Do they care? Could it be they don't give a stuff about any of us?'

The throng lets loose, thunder bellowing across the field...

'And who's in charge of this nightmare?' Debi Royce feels herself grow in stature as she surveys the faces before her. 'I'LL TELL YOU WHO – YOUR VERY OWN GORDON GLENNAN EM PEE, MINISTER WITHOUT BOLLOCKS – RESIDENT OF THIS PARISH. IT'S TIME FOR HIM TO TELL US WHAT HE'S GOING TO DO ABOUT IT... IT'S TIME FOR HIM TO EXPLAIN HIMSELF... HE CAN TELL US WHERE IT'S GOING OR WE'LL TELL HIM WHERE TO STICK IT. WHAT DO WE WANT?

Gale force, with no particular verbal content...

'...WHEN DO WE WANT IT?'

'NOW...' the crowd is ready to improvise.

'SCRAP STARTRACK...' she yells. 'TALK TO US, GLENNAN... TALK TO US, GLENNAN... TALK TO US...'

And that is the headline Erica Lyle was waiting for.

JANICE GLENNAN has a way of drooping her eyelids when she smiles. Her husband dreads that look; it goes with a gentle delivery that carries a razor-edge and can reach flashpoint without preamble in a second.

He knows she enjoys watching him on edge, wondering which way it's going to swing. If she lets fly, he will have to retaliate within reasonable bounds, and then she will revert to the sanctity of the Moral High Ground.

He is not, and never has been, a match for her. He relies on his status in government and such gravitas as he can muster to redress the balance, but public power and political influence count for nothing at home.

'The locals don't seem to trust you, Darling.' Janice sets the paper aside as if discarding a lightweight garment. 'They want you to explain yourself. I do hope you're not going to do that.'

'There's nothing to explain. StarTrack is in the national interest; I don't expect people who are directly affected to understand that.'

'They say you don't care, Darling. The consensus is you're chairing a bunch of indecisive has-beens, you're dithering over the route and you're indifferent to what ordinary people think – have you read this?' She holds the paper out to him.

'I've read it. What do you expect me to do?'

'They want a public debate. That could be interesting, don't you think?'

'They don't want a debate; they want license to question economic reality, deny any requirement for progress and hurl insults at a Minister of the Crown without fear of redress. I doubt if they're open to reason.'

'Are you really up to this, Gordon?' Janice sits back and studies him. 'You're a shadow of your former self. Too much creeping around corridors of power – not good for self-esteem, is it?'

'I haven't changed.'

'Something has. You're not your own boss, are you? You're somebody's mouthpiece – a man of influence, but still the instrument of another person's will. Whose? I wonder.'

'I work for the Prime Minister.'

'You have to say that, it goes with the job. But it's not the Prime Minister's drum you're marching to. You've managed to complicate things along the line, Gordon. Do you think I don't know that? You're not as inscrutable as you might like to think.'

The image of Frey-Morton's 'revolver that doesn't exist' appears to him in sharp clarity for a moment: the unexpected weight of it in his hand...

'You should have faith in me.' Glennan prowls the Persian carpet in their living room, hands behind his back in the style of a public figure. 'The world I have to occupy – the world that makes our living – is more complex than you could possibly know.'

'Which is why I ask the question again –' Janice lets her gaze stray round the room – 'Are you really up to this?'

'Why would you doubt it?'

'Look at yourself. Your ambition put you where you are but I wonder if you're comfortable with it. Power comes at a price.'

'Do you think I could stomach the distrust all politicians have to endure unless I thought some good would eventually come of it? You think I enjoy being pilloried, publicly attacked by people who haven't the guts or the gumption for public life? No, I don't – and I could do with just a bit of the support I used to get from you when I was a rising star in government. Right now I think you despise me.'

'Well –' Janice flutters the paper at him again – somebody does.'

TALK TO US, GLENNAN (writes Erica Lyle) WHERE'S STARTRACK GOING? Following the fourth change of route for the high-speed StarTrack rail project, locals are demanding to know when to ex-

pect a final decision. Saturday's march in Lasherham marks the latest show of Public frustration over mixed messages from StarTrack UK and Gordon Glennan MP, Chair of the select committee overseeing the project.

Campaigner Debi Royce said: 'This has gone on too long. No one knows where the track's going and the people supposed to be in charge don't talk to us. We've had enough and we want some answers. Talk to us, Mr Glennan.'

Tony Newton, Chair of Lasherham P.C., said: 'As a local representative, I must agree with the aims and objectives of this protest. The majority of people round here are dead against StarTrack and fed up with poor communication from the people running it.'

Another campaigner, Mrs Ivy Lewis, said: 'I'm willing to think the worst of most politicians but this takes the biscuit. I can't believe the likes of Gordon Glennan are the best we've got. If you want to get things done, there are people who can deliver – you'd better believe it. Don't ask me how I know, but I do. It's tragic there's no one like that in government.'

'What's that supposed to mean?' Glennan scans the article again, aware that he hadn't taken it all in the first time. 'Who the hell is Mrs Ivy Lewis anyway, and who are these people she thinks CAN DELIVER? Sounds like some kind of challenge, in which case she should name names and not feed empty threats like this to a hostile press.'

'The press will always be hostile, darling.' Janice watches her husband calmly. 'There was a film made about some thug who champions his village in time of need. A lot of people think that was based on someone who lives around here. Perhaps that's who she's thinking of.'

'Taffin,' Glennan muses.

'You even know the name, darling. I didn't think you had time for local gossip.'

THIRTEEN

'THIS PLACE STILL SPOOKS ME.' Julia watches through the caravan window as low clouds scud across the half moon. 'That big house kind of broods and I know there's stuff going on in it night after night. I feel sorry for the old boy who lives up at the top.'

Kath joins her. 'I know McDermott said they'd move us in there when it was done up but that was just more of his bullshit. I wouldn't spend a night in it now if you paid me.' She turns to Rick. 'How much longer are we going to be here? I'm getting fed up with takeaway.'

'Not long.' Rick is sitting on his bunk, feet up, reading an old motorcycle magazine. Kath peers at the cover.

'Nineteen fifty-four – not quite up to your speed, is it?'

'It's interesting. You wouldn't believe what they thought was modern in those days. Look at that bike.' He turns the page to show her.

'Promise you'll never turn up on anything like that. Where did you get this from, anyway? The paper's almost falling apart.'

'I found a box of them – old magazines and other stuff

when I was clearing out the Facel Vega. I was going to have a bonfire but this lot looked interesting.'

'Whatever turns you on, Lover. Anyway, how long do you reckon we're here for?'

'Like I say, not long. The Boss is around somewhere, I told you – Ed's seen him – so he must be figuring something out.'

'It can't happen soon enough for me.' Julia stands up and hugs herself. 'I wish Ed would finish up what he's doing, I'm getting cold.'

In the barn, Ed Pentecost is lying on his back under the Hudson with an inspection lamp, wondering what lunatic devised the front suspension. Rick was right – they're going to have to mill up some parts.

Footsteps mash the gritty concrete close to his ear. Doesn't sound like Rick's boots; certainly neither of the girls.

'Rick? That you creeping around?' Ed reaches to adjust the inspection lamp but sees only the bare expanse of concrete.

Somewhere in the distance a door closes.

BOB SHERMAN seldom ventures to the head of the stairs that lead to the depths of the house. He has everything he needs on the top floor and has no wish to subject his flimsy frame to the effort of clinging to bannisters and easing himself down, one step at a time, for no particular reason. He would only have to climb back up again; not appealing. But this has been a quiet day with no fanciful visitations; he is more than usually aware of activity on the lower floors and curiosity has brought him to his bedroom door.

Moving carefully, he switches on the landing light, hangs

his stick over the bannister and peers down into the stairwell, which grows darker with each descending flight. From what he can remember there are at least five rooms on each of the four floors below his, and that doesn't include the basement. Something is going on in one or other of those rooms every night; probably maintenance work of some kind; he has never been one to enquire about that sort of thing. Now and again, though, it would be nice to be brought up to date.

A movement two floors down catches his eye; a door opens and a figure steps into the corridor, glances up at the high light and sees Bob's face leaning over the top bannister.

'Mister Sherman –' a voice he knows – 'didn't expect to see you out at this time of night. You should be in bed.'

'I didn't expect to see you, Doctor Morley. I thought I was your only patient here.'

'And so you are. Off to bed now – I'll see you again soon.' The figure walks slowly into the shadows, down a flight of stairs and is lost to view.

After a while, Bob turns off the light, goes back to his room and shuts the door. He settles into his chair and reaches for something to read, wondering why young Doctor Morley would be in a room two floors below him without coming up to say hello.

Strange people, doctors. Surely those unnaturally white teeth can't be real.

THE STAIRWELL IS DARK AGAIN. The house is silent but for an occasional gust of wind battering the gables and moaning round the chimney stacks.

A torch beam cuts along the corridor two floors below Bob Sherman's rooms. The beam contracts and becomes a pool of light around a beefy hand scrawling an entry in a notebook with a stub of pencil.

Not easy finding your way around a strange house in the dark, especially when absolute silence is necessary. Patience is the secret; move as if in water, take your time and don't bump into anything.

Taffin allows himself a moment to reflect, slips the notebook into his pocket and sets off down the stairs. Some time later he is standing very still in the yard, breathing suspended, alert to the sounds of the night.

Earlier, on this very spot, he was aware of Ed stretched out under the Hudson with an inspection lamp, but was careful not to stray within earshot.

Someone else passed close and he heard Ed's voice demanding to know who was creeping around, and a few muttered remarks after that.

The hour that has passed since was well spent: old Bob Sherman's brief exchange with 'Doctor Morley' was useful. Taffin now has a clearer picture of who he's dealing with. The note in his book reads: *Tooth Fairy (Silver) is Doctor Morley.*

An owl hoots somewhere. The barn is closed up, so Ed is back in the caravan.

Taffin pictures Charlotte tucked up in bed in the Mitres Well Lane house, with Mo and Shirley on the other side of the wall if required; then he reminds himself she's not there: she's in Ashley Gunn's unfinished barn conversion and probably freezing.

He rubs his hands against the chill. Work to be done that won't wait. He watched from the shadows as The Tooth Fairy searched four rooms tonight. The man is going through the house meticulously, and will no doubt carry on until he finds what he's looking for.

Instinct says it's important to get there first.

'MAKING MONEY is one thing. Understanding what money means is something quite different.'

'I know what it means.'

'I wonder if you do.' Daniel Frey-Morton regards his visitor calmly. 'For most people, money is security, the illusion of freedom, purchasing power, a certain standing in society, the ticket to a life without worries. All trivial.'

'That may sound trivial to you but you're off any normal scale. You deal in billions – tens of billions, I believe.' Janice Glennan toys with the Champagne flute on the table at her elbow. 'Money is money. What is there to understand?'

'You make my point for me.' Frey-Morton lets his gaze wander around the characterless hotel suite. 'You, my dear, see it as a commodity – something to be amassed and enjoyed at leisure. It's because of people who think like you that money keeps circulating the way it does – finally accruing to a miniscule elite who know how to use it. With respect, you have no understanding of what real money can do.'

'Tutor me.' Janice Glennan ripples to a receptive posture, chin in hand, legs drawn up on the couch. 'I wouldn't want to miss the point.'

'I think the point is too subtle for you.'

'It hasn't been so far, Daniel.'

'Your values are childishly simple. They start and end with what you want for yourself. In your case the gold standard is your sexuality – on which you set a high premium by the way.'

'Now you're trying to offend me.' Janice pouts, avoiding his eye.

'If I tried, you would run for cover. You're not so fragile. You'll take a lot, but you won't take offense.'

'I hope you're not giving up on me, Daniel – you're not the type to give up on anything you start. I know you better than that.'

'Be very clear.' He holds out a hand and she moves to him. 'Things start when I say and end when I say. Don't kid yourself, Janice, you don't know me at all.'

'What I don't know, I can imagine.'

'You have no more imagination than that husband of yours.'

'Help me.' She looks into his face, passive, shoulders bare now.

'I'll tell you just once. There's only one kind of money worth the effort. It's called Fuck You Money and that's more than most people ever dream of. Your husband and people like him are hampered by limited imagination and low self-belief. Deep down, they know what they're worth and that's all they'll ever make.'

'Gordon's a wealthy man. Why knock yourself out making billions you can never hope to spend? What can you buy with all that money?

'You, my dear, heart and soul, and everyone like you. You and all the systems, the laws and law-makers you think are there to protect you. When you grasp that, the world is much cheaper than you think.'

Janice settles back, watching him. 'So money is power. That's obvious.'

'Your husband's a wealthy man – you just said it. So where's the power?'

'He has a certain amount of influence now. At some stage he will retire from public life on an enormous pension and be able to live very much as he wants – always assuming the pressures of office don't get him first. Those aren't bad prospects.'

'Pensions are poison.' Frey-Morton's gaze settles on some point in the middle distance. 'They encourage the illusion of security. Show me a man with a big pension and I'll show you a man who peaked too soon.'

'You're not a typical case. I can believe you've never thought about a pension.'

'But I have. My first employer, my mentor, had nothing but contempt for employees who expected him to supply lifelong security. When he was dying, he advised me to raid the corporate pension fund, which I did, to make my first billion.'

'Are you sure you trust me with that information?' Janice looks up at him, teasing.

'Quite sure.'

Janice smiles again. 'I don't think Gordon would approve. He claims some kind of moral code and still has some say in family matters.'

'As long as you allow it. You have the power, so you have the wealth. Take it and use it. Now –' Frey-Morton sits back and studies her – 'I need to see how slowly – with what infinite subtlety – you can shed that silk thing you're almost wearing. Go ahead, Janice – try to take offense – you won't convince either of us.'

FOURTEEN

AT AN HOUR he would normally describe as 'ungodly', Pierre is woken up by Charlotte tapping on the window of the van.

This is distressing for him on several levels. For some time now he has found that the first few seconds of consciousness come with a fleeting sense of futility that fades but leaves traces through the day. He is also aware of not looking his best first thing in the morning and is vain enough to care. More to the point, though, an agreeable dream lingers, taunting him with an atmosphere he would return to, given the chance.

'Stir yourself, you idle bugger.' Charlotte stares at his tight-knit face as he emerges from the sleeping bag. 'We've got to get you out of here one time quick.'

He leans over and opens the door. 'What's the problem?'

'The problem, my honey-voiced boy, is the bookshop is occupied by people you don't want to meet. Come on, move it.'

'The speakers are in there.'

'Leave them. Get your engine running and move out. I'll be right behind you.'

The Jeep is a few feet away, door open. Charlotte hurries back to it and fires up the engine with a deep V8 grumble.

Pierre casts around for his keys, fumbles them into the ignition and hangs on patiently until a clattering from behind tells him the camper is ready to move.

Charlotte waves him past and he heads for the gap in the hedge that leads out to the road.

A figure blocking his path. Pierre doesn't like to make rush judgments but can't help it this time: leather jacket sitting on square shoulders – this man isn't open to small talk.

Michael Wyatt watches the Camper van heading towards him and knows by instinct that the driver of this rattletrap will always come off second best at chicken.

Pierre pulls the Camper up with feet to spare, conscious of Charlotte's Jeep in his mirror. He can sense her frustration, knows she would have kept going and made the man jump clear, but that's not in his nature.

No time to think. The door is open and the man's face is inches from his own.

'Going somewhere?' Wyatt casts an eye over the interior and stares Pierre in the face.

'I was just leaving...'

'Oh, you were leaving? What've you got in there?'

'Nothing – just camping stuff.'

'Yeah, and my dick's a bloater. Get out.'

Pierre struggles for an answer but Wyatt's hand grips the front of his sweatshirt and pulls him half out of the cab.

'LET GO OF HIM YOU FUCKING APE.'

'You got something to say, Lady?' Wyatt turns to face Charlotte who has stepped out of the Jeep to confront him.

'You heard. Let go of him. We've got no business with you.'

Wyatt has released Pierre to give Charlotte his full attention and now stands squarely before her.

Charlotte looks past him to see Pierre floundering to sit upright in his driving seat. 'Get going, Kid. This clown ain't going to do anything.'

Pierre hesitates, torn between self-preservation and atavistic chivalry. Charlotte waves him away.

'YOU HEARD – GO. I'LL BE RIGHT BEHIND YOU.'

The camper lurches forward through the gap into the road and stops, Pierre looking behind, trying to measure the situation.

Charlotte turns back to the Jeep but Wyatt grabs her by the arm and spins her to face him.

'You ain't going nowhere, Lady.'

'Oh? Why's that then?'

'You're on private land. You've got some explaining to do.'

Charlotte is still watching the camper van and now waves it away with more urgency. She addresses Wyatt without looking at him.

'If this is private land, you're on it too.'

'You got a problem with that? What were you and that pimply kid doing – like them young, do you?'

'Get your hand off.' Charlotte forces patience into her voice.

'You haven't explained what you were doing here yet.'

'That's not going to happen. And you need to get your hand off me now.'

'Why would I do that?'

'Oh, look – he's escaping...' Charlotte watches the camper pulling away and in the same instant jerks her arm from Wyatt's grasp.

Wyatt lashes out by instinct catching her on the shoulder and hurling her face first against the door of the jeep. Charlotte, off balance, stumbles into the rear door and slips to the ground, struggling up, tasting blood on her lip, rounding on Wyatt with wildcat eyes, fist bunched.

'Whoa...' Wyatt holding up his hands, 'you need to be more careful – you'll do yourself a mischief.'

Charlotte staring him in the eye, wiping the blood from her mouth, turning to climb into the jeep.

Wyatt, feigning amusement, standing by the gap in the hedge. Charlotte rolls down her window.

'My friend is a nice guy – he stopped. I'm coming through now – you decide if you want to be in the way.'

She guns the engine. The Jeep clears the gap with inches to spare, Wyatt standing aside like a matador.

Greg Dupree comes out of the bookshop in time to see the Jeep go by. The sign hanging inside the door twists with the current of air: OPEN... CLOSED... OPEN... CLOSED...

There are no lights inside today, no browsing bookworms, no welcoming voice.

'IS YOUR BED NOT COMFORTABLE, DEAR?' June Dunphy sets a fresh pot of coffee in front of Taffin and looks at him with concern.

'Very comfortable.'

'Well how would you know? You haven't slept in it.'

'Working late.' Taffin lets his gaze rest on this hospitable woman.

'Strange work you do.' She pours coffee into his cup. 'You need your sleep, y'know.'

'I get plenty, love.'

'Well, I'm blowed if I know when. What kind of work is it you do?'

'Motor trade, mainly.'

'Which is why you have that lovely car. It looks like new but it can't be.'

'Nineteen sixty-six. It's a classic.'

'Your face almost went soft when you said that. I'll leave you to finish your breakfast.'

She takes his clean plate and withdraws to the kitchen leaving Taffin with toast, coffee and his notebook.

Progress: Tooth Fairy searching house for car documents?
Not found yet.
Sherman can't or won't say where they are.
If not in house, where?
Action: let Ed and Rick know what to look for.

Taffin puts the notebook away, finishes his coffee and is about to leave the table when his mobile rings.

'Mister Taffin?' An unfamiliar voice.

'Who's this?'

'It's Pierre. My sister is your masseuse. I've been doing a job for you – at the bookshop.'

'Going alright?'

'The job's over. Some men came and closed the shop. Your lady was there but she told me to get going so I had to leave her. I didn't want to because they were getting rough but she said I had to go. I thought I should tell you.'

'When?'

'Just now – maybe ten minutes ago.'

June Dunphy looks in to ask her guest if he needs anything more but sees only an empty table and a flash of red passing the window.

The Mustang's engine barks in the morning and fades into the distance.

ON THE HILLSIDE outside Ashley Gunn's barn conversion, the Mustang stands with the engine ticking as it cools.

Taffin takes off his dark glasses and stares into Charlotte's face. Bruised cheek and cut lip. She meets his eye with a challenge. 'You should see the other fella.'

'I will.' Taffin running a thumb gently over the bruise, looking into her eyes then closely at her lip. 'We need to get some Germolene on that.'

'Listen to you, Doctor Taffin. No bones broken, all my own teeth. I'll be alright.'

'This happened at the bookshop?'

'Young Pierre's a sweet lad but he worries too much. He shouldn't have got you back for this. Yeah, it was at the bookshop. No –' she catches his arm – 'you're staying here with me. I need comforting.'

'Who was it?'

'Never seen him before. You know the type – no space between hairline and eyebrows. I didn't get much of a look at the other one.' She leads him indoors and they settle down on an arrangement of tea chests and cushions.

Taffin continues to stare at her.

'You can stop smoldering,' she tells him. 'What did you expect? A developer's bound to have a few head-bangers on the payroll for when things don't go their way. I don't suppose Glennan hires people like that but they wind up working for him anyway.' She gets up and plugs the kettle in. 'We've got electricity here now, what d'you think of that?'

'Impressive.'

'Yeah –' she settles down beside him again – 'when are you going to learn?'

Taffin's gaze settles on her.

Charlotte watches him and continues quietly. 'You may not remember, but you promised me a long time ago there wouldn't be any more stuff like this. You were through with collecting and all the tricks that go with it. That's what you promised me.'

'I did.' Taffin nods.

'Not going too well, is it?' She cocks her head on one side and makes owl eyes at him.

'This problem came to us, I didn't go looking for it.'

'Someone's trying to torpedo our business – I know that – but you didn't really have to get involved with the bookshop.'

'True.'

'You did your bit to help. It was a nice idea and it worked for a while but it's time to let it go.'

'You reckon?'

'I do. Maybe this would also be a good time to call Ed and Rick back, get the business up and running again and stick two fingers up at any third-rate clowns who think they can stop us. You've beaten better odds before.'

'That's not the answer, girl.'

'Why not? This isn't exactly a polite business we're in, or hadn't you noticed?'

'I've noticed.' The hint of a smile.

'There you go then – business as usual. Why not just front it out?'

'I need to know who we're dealing with and why our business is a target.'

Charlotte gets up, drops tea bags into two cups, pours in boiling water and fills the silence by watching it brew.

'Why does it matter? When they see us back operating as normal, they'll realize whatever they was trying to pull didn't work and give up, won't they?'

'I'd like to believe that.' Taffin takes his mug of tea gratefully. 'I've got a feeling it ain't so simple.'

'MY HUSBAND ISN'T HERE.' Janice Glennan swings the front door closed but only succeeds in making the brass lion's head knocker judder on its mount.

The door swings open again. Janice takes stock: this man put his foot in the doorway without apparently moving a muscle. Dark glasses study her quietly.

'Move your foot.' Janice controls her voice in spite of warning sirens in her head. 'I won't tell you again. You're not coming in.'

'I don't want to come in, Mrs Glennan.' No attempt to project the voice. 'I want to speak to your husband.'

'We're not up yet. What do you mean by calling at this hour?'

'Tell your husband I'll be waiting right here.' Taffin moves effortlessly past her into the hall.

'I thought you didn't want to come in.'

'I changed my mind.'

'I'm going straight upstairs to call the police.'

'I'll chance it. Tell Mister Glennan to get up – we've got business to discuss.'

'Alright –' Janice Glennan moves to let the silk dressing gown hint at her contours – 'let's take another approach. What makes you think I can't speak for my husband? Discuss whatever it is with me.'

Taffin wanders across the hall and leans against the newel post. 'I'll be right here.'

Janice takes two shimmering steps to the stairs. 'You planted that stolen car here, didn't you?'

No response.

'What is it this time – the bookshop, or have you set your sights higher? StarTrack?'

'The sooner you get him down here, the sooner I'll be gone.'

'Oh, Mister Taffin –' the heavy-lidded eyes – 'it's such a pleasure to meet you at last. You may think your silent menace routine works on everyone, but you're well out of your league here, I promise you.' She sweeps past him up the stairs leaving a waft of Channel in her wake.

Ten Minutes later Gordon Glennan comes down to an empty hall. He glances left, right and left again. He is about to call upstairs to his wife but changes his mind: what's she supposed to do, anyway?

There's no one in the dining room, no one in the drawing room; the kitchen is empty. The study: his usual refuge. Strangely, it never occurred to him that anyone would come in here uninvited.

He has always thought of his desk as broad, imposing – a piece of power furniture befitting his position – but the man occupying the chair behind it makes the desk look insignificant.

'What do you think you're doing?' The words come thinly. 'That's my desk. Everything on it is private and confidential. You'd oblige me by getting out of my chair.'

'Sit down.'

'What? You don't give me orders in my own house.'

Gordon Glennan becomes acutely aware of a high-pitched singing in his ears and his visitor's unnatural stillness. He clears his throat and takes a seat facing the desk.

'Alright, state your business or I'm going to call the police.'

'I don't think you want to do that, Mister Glennan – not unless you want one of your employees charged with assault.'

'I don't know what you're talking about.'

'You have people working at the Tollgate Bookshop.'

'There's work being done there, yes – necessary work.'

'One of them used physical force on my partner this morning. I don't appreciate that, Mister Glennan.'

'I'm sure there was no malice involved.'

'We're talking serious assault.'

'No – you've got this all wrong. I don't hire people in that capacity.'

'Are you sure about that, Mister Glennan?'

'As sure as I can be – anyone working on my property is sub-contracted to do a job. I don't interview them all personally – my schedule wouldn't allow for it. I have to trust whoever hires them.'

'They work for you anyway.' Taffin rises slowly from the chair and ambles, hands behind his back, to the side of the desk. 'I hold you responsible.'

'I don't accept that, and who do you think you're

dictating to?' Glennan makes to rise from his seat but sinks back, obeying a downward hand gesture.

'Be calm, Mister Glennan. Don't get heated, it doesn't suit you.'

'I'm quite calm. I have no knowledge of the incident you're talking about, so what exactly do you expect me to do about it?'

'I expect you to stop all work on the bookshop until we find out which of your employees smacks women around.'

'Now wait a minute –' Glennan starts up again but pauses in response to the same gesture – 'If you think I can be intimidated by an unsubstantiated report, you can think again. Who is the woman who's supposed to have been smacked around, as you put it?'

'That would be my partner. When the time comes, she'll be able to identify the man who assaulted her.'

Silence settles. Glennan, seated in a guest chair in his own study, casts around for something to say and decides to try a change of tone.

'That being the case, I can understand why you're upset, Mister...'

'Taffin.'

'Yes, of course. Well, I can look into it, but that's the best I can do at the moment.'

'My partner won't be happy with that. She's a strong lady, not one to complain – but no one gives her a split lip and walks away from it. She and I think alike. You can understand that, Mister Glennan.'

'Let me be very clear – I'm not admitting liability for anything. I have business to attend to. You should leave now.'

'We're nearly done. You've got your finger in a lot of pies. We'll talk about StarTrack next time we meet.'

'Now look, Mister Taffin, I can sympathize with your coming to me with a private grievance, but StarTrack is work in progress and has no place in any conversation between you and me. I don't anticipate us meeting again.'

Taffin stops beside Glennan's chair, looking down, hands in pockets. 'We will, Mister Glennan. Believe it.'

'Is Mister Taffin giving you trouble, darling?' Janice Glennan stands in the doorway, dressed to impress. 'He's quite daunting when you first meet him but he's a pussycat really, aren't you, Mister Taffin?'

'He's just leaving.' Gordon Glennan seizes the moment to get up and appear to take charge.

'And he won't be back, will he?' Janice gives them both a glacial smile. 'Not if he knows what's good for him – and his good lady.'

'Nice room.' Taffin casts a critical glance around the study and ambles past her, pausing in the hall to address Gordon Glennan. 'You'll do what we discussed, Mister Glennan. And tell your wife that threats need to be handled with care. Get the balance wrong and they'll come back to bite you.'

FIFTEEN

'IT'S JUST A BOX OF OLD CRAP.' Rick Bishop hauls a soggy cardboard shape from under his bunk.

'Good crap, though.' Ed Pentecost takes a limp magazine from the depths. '"Motorcycle Mechanics", June 1955 – this is gold dust, Rick, you dozy git. What else have you got in there?'

'There's a few more motor mags. The rest looks like old worksheets, bills and stuff.'

Ed takes the box, sets it on the table and starts digging through the contents.

'You're a genius, Rick.'

'Yeah, but I'm too modest to admit it.'

'Look at this –' Ed holds up a clutch of thin card and wrinkled papers – 'logbooks, bills of sale, one for the Hudson with a letter to... Austin Oliver Sherman – that's got to be a relative of old Bob Sherman, so that one belongs to him for sure. This is magic.'

'Whatever turns you on.'

'Yeah...' Ed flips through the tattered papers in his hand. 'More logbooks, service records for an SS Jaguar, a load of stuff on a Chrysler Imperial... it's all here, Rick. This is what they call provenance.'

Rick is shuffling through another handful of papers. 'Here's an envelope of stuff on the Facel Vega – belonged to Mel Kinnear at one time. He's an old rock star – Kath knows all about him.'

The door opens and Kath and Julia climb into the caravan, bringing a waft of fresh air with them.

Julia peels off her jacket. 'It reeks in here. You don't really notice until you get outside. What have you got there?'

Ed goes to the window and looks out along the track.

'Is anyone around outside?'

'Not a soul. You can walk for miles here and not see anyone. You've been going through old magazines, I can smell them from here.'

'Not a word to McDermott.' Ed indicates the box on the table. 'I'm not sure what we've got yet, but we keep this out of sight and don't say a word about it to anyone.'

Rick picks the box up, weighing it in his hands.

'It ain't too much bulk. I can fit the lot in my rucksack.'

'Sounds like a plan.' Ed peers out of the window again. 'Time to talk to The Boss.'

NO ONE WOULD CALL Charlotte a worrier. For her, life with Taffin has always been a cocktail of risk and stability. The motor trade offers plenty of variety – and the risks, as she puts it, 'paint the colours a bit brighter'.

Until today she has never doubted her life partner's judgement, but watching him now – yes, she is worried.

'You haven't said much.' She prowls the freshly laid parquet floor of Ashley Gunn's barn conversion.

Taffin broods quietly, a dark shape against the window. Charlotte moves closer.

'You saw Glennan. What did he have to say?'

Taffin stirs. 'What can I tell you? He's a weak man. His wife's the one to watch. I'm still trying to work her out.'

'What did *she* say then?'

'Not a lot. She looks like a posh slapper but talks like a gangmaster. I'd say she's used to rougher company than her husband. She knows about what happened to you.'

'She said that?'

'Not in so many words. The geezer who took a pop at you works for her husband. Tell me again, what did he look like?'

'Your average gorilla. Dark, intimidating, gets off on it. You know the sort as well as anyone.'

To Charlotte's relief, the ghost of a smile touches Taffin's face for a moment. Then: 'You hear anything?'

They listen for a moment, picking up the sharp rip of a motorcycle engine rising to a bellow. Tyres scrunch outside and the engine cuts out.

Rick Bishop parks his hot Honda Fireblade, stretches aching limbs and is grateful to find the front door open.

Charlotte looks him over. 'What have you brought us, young Rick?'

'A raging thirst, for a start. I could murder a cuppa tea, unless you've got a beer handy.' He eases the rucksack off his shoulders and looks around the room. 'Nice place.'

He puts his rucksack on the trestle table, opens it up and pulls out the contents.

Taffin shuffles through the wad of documents, pauses to scrutinize the first few and nods appreciation.

'Give the man a beer.'

Charlotte rips the top off a bottle of Spitfire and hands it to Rick, who downs half of it in one go.

'I got here as quick as I could. Ed thought you'd want to see these.'

'He's not wrong. D'you know what it is?'

'Provenance, Ed said.'

'Ooh-er...' Charlotte clowns a learned look 'You swallowed a dictionary?'

'I swallowed a Spitfire – that's better. All I know about provenance is, if you haven't got it, all those motors we're working on ain't worth a light because there's nothing to say who they belong to.'

Taffin spreads the papers out on the table.

'You never did a better day's work, Rick. Tell Ed I said so.'

Rick tries a modest face, unable to handle a compliment. 'I'll tell him. I'd best be getting back before the Gestapo miss me.'

'Take your time, son. I've an idea your job's nearly done. You can tell Ed that, too.' Taffin is still going through the paperwork when Charlotte's mobile bleeps.

'Well, what have we got here?' She peers at the screen. 'That sneaky little sod.'

Taffin raises his head. 'What?'

'Little Pierre, the bookshop voice – what a smart little bugger. I saw him stop the van for a minute before I drove out of that field – never thought he'd have the brains or the bottle to get a picture. Here you are, that's the fella. Not a bad likeness, too.'

She shows Taffin the photo. Part of the jeep is clear. So is the figure of Michael Wyatt, standing back with a mocking matador pose, ushering it through.

Taffin studies the photo, shifts his gaze to some distant point, then turns to Charlotte.

'Tell Pierre he's done a good job.'

'He'll be so happy, poor little mite.'

Taffin shows Rick the mobile. 'See anyone you know?'

'He's got a fucking heavy boot. Yeah, I know him.'

'Easy with the language, son – ladies present.'

Charlotte strikes an imperious pose. 'Who are you calling a fucking lady?'

Taffin hands the mobile back to her, ambles to the window, looks out across the valley where *Muscle Motors* lies hidden beyond the trees and turns to Rick.

'It's all coming together, wouldn't you say?'

'WHERE THE FUCK HAVE YOU BEEN?' Eric McDermott leans against the caravan, watching as Rick dismounts and sets his helmet on the saddle. The Fireblade ticks softly as it cools.

'Taking a ride.'

'You don't take rides – not when there's work to be done.'

'So sack me.' Rick works his shoulders.

The caravan door swings open and Ed Pentecost steps out. Kath follows him and goes to Rick.

McDermott speaks quietly. 'I'll ask you again, where have you been?'

'And I told you.' Rick is in no mood for this. He has been riding hard all afternoon and the adrenalin charge has yet to give way to fatigue.

'Get this straight –' McDermott moves to face the three of them – 'you don't take time out unless I say you can, and that's not going to happen.' He strolls among them, hands in pockets. 'That's valuable machinery you're dealing with and – be very clear on this – if the smallest, most insignificant part goes missing I'll tear this place apart until its found. What's in the pack?

Instead of answering, Rick unslings his rucksack, gives it a shake and holds it upside down.

'That's it.' Julia appears in the caravan doorway and steps down behind McDermott. 'We've taken enough of your shit. I won't be called a thief by you and I reckon that goes for the rest of us. You think we're going to nick nuts and bolts from your precious collection? Or perhaps you think we're dealing in contraband windscreen-wipers and antique headlamps. Stuff you – piss off and learn some manners.'

McDermott's face sets hard. 'I warned you all about security from the start. You don't have to like it, you don't have to understand it – the money you're being paid says you'll do it without question. No one leaves here until the job's done, clear?'

'Very clear.' Ed moves in, puts an arm round McDermott's shoulders and addresses the group. 'You heard what the nice man said. No one goes anywhere without his permission. Eric –' he stares full into McDermott's face – 'you don't mind if I call you Eric? We'll do anything we like and go anywhere we want.'

'Don't put your hand on me, boy.'

'Just being friendly, Eric.' Ed makes a hands up gesture. 'I never trust people who don't like being touched – makes me wonder what they're hiding.'

McDermott turns to Rick. 'You always go riding with an empty backpack?'

'You got a problem with that?'

'I'll say it one more time. If anything goes missing, I won't answer for what happens. Your employers aren't all as understanding as me. I'm the nice guy – remember that. You wouldn't like some of my colleagues.'

McDermott makes eye contact with each of them in turn and walks away.

Stillness settles. Julia manages to radiate spent fury without a word. Kath, who has said nothing during the whole exchange, links arms with Rick.

Ed watches McDermott walk into the barn before breaking the silence. 'He's desperate.'

'I'd say so.' Julia controls her voice. 'He needs that paperwork but he can't risk letting us know there is any in case we start looking for it.'

Ed turns to her. 'That's about right. He's got half an idea we've found it, and no way of checking it out – his worst nightmare. He's desperate.'

Kath finds her voice. 'That was a threat – probably about seven on the Richter Scale. I don't think he was bluffing.'

'He's full of it.' Rick puts an arm round her.

'He sure is –' Ed speaks softly – 'but he ain't bluffing.'

Inside the caravan, by unspoken agreement, they start packing up their kit.

Ed glances out of the window from time to time, measuring the distance with his eye from the barn to McDermott's white Range Rover, from the caravan to the barn, from the bikes to the gate of the enclosure that leads onto the lane.

Instinct tells him they should be ready for sudden departure. McDermott has let the mask slip and shown teeth. Employers who started out as *a board of directors – a load of boring accountants,* have become *colleagues you wouldn't like.* And given McDermott's present dilemma, his unlovable colleagues could already be on their way.

Risk assessment. Ed can almost hear Taffin using the phrase, along with the word *balance*. If they decide to leave, it would make sense to take off during the night and be well clear of the place before they're missed. That won't be an option if McDermott's *colleagues* arrive in the meantime. No time for indecision if that happens. A fine balance of nerve and reactions...

'What do you reckon?' Rick is at his shoulder. 'The girls would be happier if we left now. So would I, but don't tell anyone I said so.'

Ed stares out at the bikes, parked ten paces away – his Triumph Sprint and Rick's Fireblade. In emergency, the four of them could mount up and be away, with all their kit, in less than a minute.

'We have to stick around. If we leave for no reason, that's as good as admitting we've got what Eric's looking for. We stay here unless someone turns up and if they do, that gives us a reason take off. It'll look like we just got scared and ran.'

'That's what I think.' Rick stares longingly at his Fireblade. 'I was hoping you'd talk me out of it.'

SIXTEEN

AS A CHILD IN THIS VERY HOUSE, Bob Sherman used to play with toy soldiers. He would set them out in orderly ranks on *papier mache* landscapes with their tin cannons and move them around, conduct their battles, send them off to skirmish, charge and retreat.

In those far off, comfortable days, any soldier would fit between his forefinger and thumb, much like the small figures moving around in the yard below right now.

Bob watches from his high window. There seems to be an unusual amount of activity down there. This is normally the quiet time, when the young people who work in the barn have gone back to the caravan to eat, drink and whatever they do.

Not tonight. Lights appeared in the lane a few minutes ago, then two large cars swung into the yard and the ground was alive with moving figures.

Hard to make out what's going on from up here, but some kind of discussion is taking place by the barn door and now a group of figures moves quickly towards the caravan.

Best open the window to hear what's going on.

Some kind of confrontation happening now. Voices raised. Shouts from the direction of the caravan. Two loud engines coming to life at almost the same moment.

Bellow of engines and two shapes burst through the milling figures and head for the gate, lights on, one behind the other as they swing out onto the lane.

Figures running back towards the cars, climbing in while they're moving, racing across the yard, sideways, straightening, demolishing a gatepost on the way out in pursuit of the motorcycles that can still be heard tearing away over the hills. A figure that was running slows down by the gate, stumbles and falls, lies still.

Was that real? Bob Sherman takes a deep breath of the night air, closes the window and the shutters and makes his way back to his chair.

Too much excitement for one evening.

JULIA SAW THE LIGHTS FIRST and immediately grabbed her backpack.

'We've got company.'

The caravan erupts as four pairs of boots make for the door.

Out in the night air, they pause as two cars swing into the enclosure and head for the barn where McDermott is clearly visible, framed in the glare.

'Walk slow.' Ed moves towards the bikes, mounts up and waits for Julia to settle in behind him. Rick and Kath follow suit silently.

By the barn, McDermott is faced with three men from the lead car. Snatches of the conversation just audible. Voices rising. McDermott pointing at the caravan. More figures joining from the second car, turning to follow McDermott's pointing finger, starting to run.

'That's our cue to leave.' Ed punches the starter button and the Triumph bursts into life. Rick's Fireblade starts up next to him. A handful of throttle, blast of air in the face, kick out for balance and the gates are rushing to meet them as they lean into the tight turn and burn off down the lane.

Eric McDermott breaks into a run in the direction of his Range Rover. He expected support from his backers but didn't imagine a word from him would get a trip-wire response like this.

This afternoon he told the man he knows as Doctor Morley that his employees might be nicking spare parts for rare automobiles; this seemed to touch a nerve. Doctor Morley flashed that chilling white smile and immediately made a call.

'They can steal all the cogs and trim and badges they want,' he remarked, through dazzling barred teeth. 'That's all replaceable. The paperwork isn't. You should pray it's still here somewhere – pray you're the one who finds it.'

Now McDermott is watching two motorcycles blaring off into the night, and it hits him with heart-stopping force that he has made a mistake for which he will be held responsible by people who don't forgive anything.

This thought has hardly formed when the swinging tail of an accelerating 4x4 pickup slams into his right side, gathers him up and hurls him away, staggering, a deep gong booming in his head until his knees melt from under him and all is quiet.

Nearly a mile away now, Rick Bishop's attention is divided between the Triumph's tail-light and his own rear view mirrors. He saw the headlamp beams swing out through the gate behind them, opened the Fireblade up to match Ed's pace and watched the pursuing lights dwindle in the distance.

Out on the main road, heading roughly south at 120 mph, he begins to relax and senses Kath, behind him, doing the same.

Ed in the lead throttling back, making a thumbs up gesture. No chance of being caught now.

A drift of cloud revealing a full moon. The song of the engines merging with the headwind rush.

This is what it's all about.

MO AND SHIRLEY are surprised to hear activity in the house next door, especially at 2.45 in the morning.

Shirley sits up in bed. 'Someone's moving about in your brother's place.'

The bed creaks like a galleon on a heavy swell and Mo rises to his feet to listen. At dead of night, Mitres Well Lane is usually the quietest spot on earth.

'You're right, Shirl', I'd best take a look – can't be too careful.'

Shirley, who everyone says would fit in one of Mo's pockets, helps him on with his coat and hands him a shotgun, which he instinctively carries open across his forearm.

Outside, he clicks the gun closed quietly and moves round to his brother's side of the house. Two motorcycles stand outside, still radiating heat.

Voices inside. Mo has always carried a key to his brother's house along with his own, and now lets himself in, light of foot.

Kath is in the kitchen, working her shoulders after a long, fast ride with a pack on her back, feeling secure for the first time in weeks.

The black figure **8** of a double-barreled shotgun facing her brings an inaudible scream from her throat and a whiplash contraction inside her.

'Jesus...' she sags, panting, holding onto the kitchen table. Focus. The figure **8** lowers and Mo's pumpkin face leans over her with concern.

'You alright?'

'I'm fine.' Kath straightens up. 'You nearly made me wet myself, Mo.'

The kitchen is suddenly full. Kath flops in a chair. Ed, Rick and Julia gather round. Kettle on. Mugs of tea circulate: order restored.

A window pane vibrates in response to a rumble – a V8 engine muttering outside. A moment later, Taffin and Charlotte are with them.

'You've done a fine job, all of you.' Taffin looks over the faces turned towards him. 'You've had your hands on some tasty machinery in the last few weeks. How does that feel?'

Ed snuffs a laugh. 'Made it worth living in a caravan.'

'I hope so.'

'And guess what –' Charlotte drops two fat brown envelopes on the table – 'now we know who all that tasty machinery belongs to. The name Sherman keeps appearing. One of the letters is to a Mister Robert Sherman, so it looks like he owns the lot.'

'The old gent in the attic.' Taffin puts a hand on each envelope. 'It's all his, whether he wants it or not. Mister Sherman don't seem interested in material things, but that's the way it is, and here's the paperwork to prove it. Good work, Rick, by the way.'

Julia says, 'Mister Sherman's a nice old geezer – real old fashioned manners. What makes me sick is they're robbing him.'

'Not if I can help it.'

'There never was a Cord.' Ed turns to the others for confirmation.

'Someone with a Mac created that.' Kath has recovered from the sight of Mo's gun. 'There must be a real one somewhere.'

'Changing the subject –' Ed gives Taffin a long look – 'I hope you don't ever feel like giving us the chop for real. You had us all believing we was out of a job for good.'

A hint of amusement touches Taffin's face. 'Your friend Eric had to buy it so I had to mean it. I suppose you want your jobs back.'

'Could be.'

'Well, that's handy – you're hired. How did you leave it with your friend Eric McDermott?

Julia's face hardens in recollection. 'He turned nasty when Rick got back, threatened us with his – what did he call them? – his *colleagues*, and he wasn't joking.'

Ed says, 'He reckoned we'd nicked something but he didn't know what, so he called for help. We rode out through a whole bunch of them.'

'We lost them.' Rick folds his arms, contented.

'Alright.' Taffin ambles among them. 'I still don't know who's targeting us or why. I aim to find out, which means we open up shop and let them come and find us. It's a risk and if any of you want to keep your distance, Charlotte and me won't think any the less of you.'

An eloquent silence follows. Ed and Julia confer without words. Rick and Kath do the same.

After a while, Julia meets Taffin's eye.

'No one talks to me the way that man did. He started getting snotty with us as soon as we got settled in. He tried bullying us, but he wasn't up to the job. He accused us all of stealing from him.'

'We did,' says Rick. 'I'd do it again.'

Ed looks across the table at Taffin. 'You don't have to ask – we're in.'

Taffin nods once. 'Good enough. We open up at nine tomorrow morning, clean up and have the workshop in action by midday. That alright with everyone?'

Charlotte says, 'I'll be on the phone to let the specialist press know. You should all get some sleep. Think of this as the end of a bad dream.'

SEVENTEEN

THE FIRST TIME DEAN ELTON heard the word *misanthrope* he thought it was a girl's name and wondered who she was.

When he found it featured in a psychiatric report on himself, he assumed it was a compliment and didn't bother to probe any deeper. Words don't matter much to Dean. He has found his way in life, working unconditionally for someone for whom he has genuine respect.

'Where to, Mister Morton?' – his first words at the start of any day, before the soundproof window goes up, isolating him from the occupants of the rear seats.

Today he has driven his employer to a remote stretch of high ground overlooking the vast panorama on the edge of the Chilterns escarpment. Daniel Frey-Morton is sitting alone behind him in the shadows.

A gunmetal grey Mercedes was waiting when they arrived and now the rear doors open and two men in suits step out. One waits by the Mercedes. The other smiles; a bright, white smile. Dean has seen this man often and each time his lip has curled unbidden. Cocky, slimy jerk, is Dean's assessment. Those teeth are asking to be knocked down the guy's fucking throat, and he prays that some day his employer will give him the order.

No sign of that happening any time soon. The teeth have privileged access to the back seat today, behind the soundproof window. Mister Morton has a use for this man and it's not for Dean Elton to question that.

In the back, Silver settles in beside Frey-Morton, avoiding eye-contact, ready for the question.

'What happened?'

'McDermott blew it.' Silver makes the statement without emphasis. 'The guys he hired were working fine, then he lost control. Something spooked them and they made a run for it.'

'You didn't find the paperwork.'

'I'll swear it's not in the main building. There's only the old man in there and he doesn't know what day it is.'

'Sounds like he's not the only one. Where's McDermott now?'

'Last seen in the yard. One of my drivers reckons he might have hit him with a pickup.'

'So what are you doing here?'

'You called for me, Mister Adams.'

The temperature seems to drop while Silver considers the wisdom of his remark.

'You don't ever come to me without answers.'

'My mistake, Mister Adams. I'll find out today.'

'That would be a good idea. Go.'

From the cocoon of his driving seat, Dean Elton watches Silver sprint towards the Mercedes, chalky teeth clenched.

Some day, he feels, he's going to get his wish. Some day soon.

FROM HIS LOFTY WINDOW, Bob Sherman gazes down at the yard. He has enjoyed a peaceful interlude; no activity all day until he heard a car arrive and decided to take a look.

People beetling around down there, two of them lifting a man from the ground, carrying him to a car that stands with all doors open. Doors slam. The car zig-zags, straightens, accelerates towards the gateway of the enclosure and hurtles into the distance along the lane.

Peace again. Bob Sherman makes his way back to his chair to immerse himself in the Arthurian legend that has fascinated him since childhood. *Arthur, The King in the West*: a book he hasn't looked at in a while. His world begins to make sense again.

MUSCLE MOTORS WOKE UP early this morning and is beginning to look businesslike. The office is clear of cobwebs, desk tidy, ledgers out, worksheets prioritized ready for the day ahead. Charlotte has spent the last hour on the phone renewing contact with her list of specialist publications, ticking them off one by one after each conversation.

The workshop door is open releasing a waft of oil, grease and hot metal. Ed Pentecost and Rick Bishop have wheeled the aging Dodge Charger inside for a complete refit and overhaul. There's a spirit of relief and optimism in the air.

Thirty miles to the north, the red Ford Mustang purrs a contented tune on a long, straight stretch of road. Taffin relaxes in the left hand driving seat, watching the long nose rise and rise again as he puts his foot down. No trace of the emotion he feels shows behind the dark glasses, but at his core he acknowledges this as perfection.

Private moments on such a day bring un-phrased

certainties into the foreground. His ideal picture doesn't require bright sun in a cloudless sky; the landscape he responds to is made up of muted greens moving in a warm grey wind with a pale road lancing to rolling hills on a cool horizon. A track by *Sounds Orchestral* called *Cast your Fate to the Winds* held that promise. Wistful, liberating piano: it reached him the first moment he heard it, years ago, and has never faded. He couldn't explain that to anyone: it would never occur to him to try.

The Mustang mutters through the village where *The March Hare* serves award-winning breakfasts – (bring Charlotte back here for sure) – and on towards the farm where old Bob Sherman will probably hear him arrive.

The gunmetal grey Mercedes fills his windscreen in a split second. Jerk the wheel left grazing the hedgerow on this narrow lane. Metallic jolt and scrape on the right rear wing. The Mustang rolling to a stop as Taffin twists in his seat to look back. The Mercedes past and gone without slowing.

Taffin walking slowly round his car, surveying the damage. Nothing Ed and Rick can't fix in a day or two, but it all costs.

Less at peace now, he climbs back in and fires up the engine. No mystery about that Mercedes. It stood for the best part of a day on the forecourt at *Muscle Motors*. Even with dark windows, there is no doubt in Taffin's mind that one of the occupants had teeth the colour of one of June Dunphy's white china cups.

BOB SHERMAN would like to believe Glastonbury Tor is Mount Badon, the site of Arthur's twelfth great battle against invading Saxon hoards, but he is not convinced.

A single archeological find – fabrics, bracelets, armour, any kind of weaponry of the early 6th Century – would seal it for him; but as far as he knows, nothing like that has ever turned up and the enigma remains to plague him.

No time for interruptions with that to contemplate. No visits, please: not just now.

A floorboard creaks. He closes the book and looks up. The visitor fills the doorway; dark glasses study him quietly. Bob returns the stare.

'Your face is familiar.'

'We've met, Mister Sherman.'

'And you told me your name, but I disremember it.'

'Taffin.'

'I remember your asking if there was anything you could do for me. Couldn't think of anything at the time.' Bob considers for a moment. 'I remember being agreeably surprised. You don't look the type who'd normally offer.'

'So you said.'

'Taffin –' Bob frowns, concentrating – 'suggests French ancestry. Probably Norman – *Norsemen*, you see – so the odds are you're a Viking. Do you know anything about your forebears?'

'Not a thing.' Taffin wanders into the room, pulls up a chair and sits down. 'I know something about yours. Interested?'

'I'm fairly well versed in my family history. Do sit down, by the way.'

Dark glasses dip slightly, acknowledging the irony.

'I don't think you'll be interested in what I have to say, Mister Sherman, but you should hear it anyway.'

'I shall, of course, hang on your every word.'

'There's a collection of motors downstairs, worth millions.'

'Yes, I gather people have been repairing them.'

'That's right.'

'I hope you don't want me to sign anything, Mister Taffin. I've devoted much of my life to avoiding documents, signatures, the paraphernalia that goes with all things legal, including that extraneous breed known as lawyers, with their outrageous bills and the distress and mayhem they bring to the lives of ordinary, peace-loving citizens. A murrain on all their flocks.'

'Glad to hear it.' Taffin produces a crumpled letter from an inside pocket. This is signed by a Mister Austin Sherman...'

'My uncle... Uncle Austin.'

'It says the whole collection passes to you on his death.' Taffin fishes in his pocket again. 'Here's his death certificate. You've been wealthy a long time, Mister Sherman.'

'There's Old Money in the family, and I suppose I'm all that's left of it.' Bob looks around the room, taking in the details. 'Any money there is, this old place swallows it up. Always something in need of repair.'

'Let's talk about the collection. It was an asset when your uncle died, but nothing special. Since then, values have gone through the roof. Like I say, millions.' Taffin leans towards the old man. 'Someone's trying to cheat you out of it and I aim to see they don't.'

'I appreciate your concern, Mister Taffin. If that's what you feel you must do, you must do it. I should make it clear that I have no interest in these motor cars but it's comforting to know they have a value. Who do you think is trying to steal them?'

'Your doctor, for one.'

'Young Doctor Morley, the fellow with china teeth? Seems a bit unlikely, doesn't it?'

'He ain't a doctor.'

'That's alright, I don't need one anyway.'

Taffin watches the old man, reaches out and puts a slab of hand on his shoulder. 'I don't believe you do. Have you got a phone here?'

'There's one in my bedroom. It never rings.'

Taffin gets up and walks into the next room. There is an old style phone on the bedside table. He lifts the receiver and listens. Nothing.

The old man is gazing into the middle distance when he gets back.

'Here's what I'm going to do for you, Mister Sherman...'

'Yes, yes indeed,' Bob turns to look at him. You asked if there was anything you could do for me... now sit down and I'll tell you.'

Taffin takes a seat, intrigued.

Sherman continues: 'There's a place called Mount Badon, the scene of a decisive battle in post-Roman Britain. Some people think it's Glastonbury Tor. I'd like to know if it really is. D'you think you could find out for me? You look like a capable sort of chap.'

Taffin sits back, blank features touched by a hint of amusement. 'I'll ask around.'

'I'd be grateful.' Bob Sherman shakes his head in wonder at the enormity of the task. 'Now, what was it you were going to suggest?'

'I'm going to bring a young lady here to fit you up with

a phone that works. She will make sure you can get in touch with me any time, day or night. How does that sound?'

'That's most generous.'

'It's most necessary, Mister Sherman, believe me.'

ERIC McDERMOTT lies in a bright corner of the Intensive Care wing of a small, private hospital. He has a broken right arm, a fractured pelvis and head injuries that appear to be minor. He has not yet regained consciousness.

The Resident Medical Officer who admitted him asked searching questions of the men who brought him in and is still not happy about the tone of that conversation. He wanted to know the patient's name, the name of his GP, details of the accident that brought him here and his relationship, if any, to the people with him. No answers were forthcoming.

The man who seemed to be in charge gave him a number to ring, which he did. The RMO was no wiser when the call was over, but he was clear on one thing: whoever he was talking to expected the situation to be dealt with, promptly, regardless of expense, and with a minimum of superfluous questions.

GORDON GLENNAN is not easy in his mind. In recent months he has felt increasingly unsure of the support he used to take for granted; the balance of his life seems to have been thrown out of true and each new development adds an unwelcome spin.

If he enjoyed any local goodwill, he has lost it now. Personal attacks from middle-aged women might be dismissed as spontaneous flare-ups but full-scale demonstrations and damning articles in the press and online are not so easy to shrug off.

As a politician, he should expect periods of unpopularity, but bastard fate has seen to it that this one coincides with a change in his wife's manner. She has always had the capacity to wound, but lately her eye for the exposed nerve is sharper. Something has changed radically and the suddenness of it has hurt him more than he would have expected.

Business, his usual refuge in times of stress, is no longer the catalogue of clear objectives it used to be. He has tamed his ego enough to accept the occasional summons to one of Frey-Morton's anonymous hotel suites, but the car park of one such hotel is a step beyond. He is not comfortable with the way the day is developing.

On arrival, he was met in the hotel lobby by a man he has never seen before – a broad man with a distant look in his eye and a battering-ram for a chin – who guided him, without conversation, to this stretch of bleak concrete where a midnight blue Rolls Royce Phantom is waiting.

'This is most unusual,' Glennan remarks, stepping into the back, trying to ignore his escort who now shuts him in with Frey-Norton and retires. 'I feel I'm being abducted.'

'You need to get a grip.' The flint eyes study him. 'How long do you expect to chair a select committee if you can't keep your home territory in order?'

Glennan frowns, surprised. 'There's nothing coming up I can't handle. People are suspicious of politicians – it goes with the badge.'

'You're getting bad press. Also, you're attracting the wrong kind of attention from local people. You had a visit, I hear.'

'People try to pressure me sometimes. It's just hot air.'

'Really? What exactly did Taffin want from you?'

'You heard about that?'

Frey-Morton makes a concessionary gesture.

'Well –' Glennan's brow darkens at the memory – 'he was carrying a torch for the bookshop. He enjoys some sort of celebrity status, if you can call it that. The bookshop is exactly the kind of local cause he would get involved in. He wanted to talk about StarTrack as well, but I didn't let him get that far. How did you hear about the visit?'

'How do you plan to react next time?'

'I'm hoping there won't be a next time but if there is, I shall ignore him, of course. How did you...?'

'And if he sues one of your employees for assault?'

'He's a cheap thug. He's not going to sue anyone.'

'You know something, Gordon,' the cold eyes settle on him for a moment, 'I'm beginning to have my doubts about you.'

Glennan takes a moment phrasing a reply, finds he has nothing to say and tries again. 'What's that supposed to mean?'

'It means, Gordon, that you need to listen when you're spoken to. I've made it clear you can afford to ignore any threat from Taffin or anyone associated with him.'

'I understand.' Glennan dismisses a disturbing image of *the gun that doesn't exist*.

Frey-Morton seems to be staring straight through him. 'A man like that has no authority to meddle in your business, and StarTrack is out of his league. Why haven't you taken that in?'

'I have – it's clear.'

'I don't want to hear he's been in your house. Next time, throw him out.'

'That's not so easy. He stayed for a while, then left without accomplishing anything.'

'He accomplished more than you're admitting. He shook your nerve.'

'He took me by surprise, that's all. There's nothing wrong with my nerves. I can deal with his sort.'

'You need to satisfy me of that.' Frey-Morton gazes out of the window.

Glennan takes a deep breath, feeling something inside him dissolve. 'You don't need to worry about me – everything's moving forward. I'm overcoming setbacks as I encounter them. What more can I do?'

'Show some commitment. Take control. Let the press into your life and calm them down. They want to hear from you about StarTrack, so give them something to chew on. I'm disappointed your instincts haven't led you there already.'

'I have to juggle with conflicting interests. It's not a game for beginners. I know what I'm doing and I have every intention of staying the course and drawing my pension at the end of it.'

'It's called politics – and by the way, pensions are poison, they encourage the illusion of security.'

'That's an extreme point-of-view, but...'

'Get that bookshop demolished, take control of the land my long-term plan requires and bring me a positive progress report within a week.'

The door opens as if by magic. Dean Elton picked up the signal from his boss and now ushers Glennan out of the car.

Walking away, pausing to look back, Glennan takes the

conversation apart in his mind, wonders why he didn't ask the key question and shakes his head as the truth strikes him. How could Frey-Morton possibly have detailed knowledge of his encounter with Taffin?

No point asking that; there is only one possible source.

From his driving seat, Dean Elton watches the politician walk away. The soundproof screen lowers and he half turns in his seat.

'Do you know that man, Dean?'

'I've seen his face, Mister Morton. He's on the news now and again.'

'You haven't seen him.'

'I haven't seen him. Where to, Mister Morton?'

'Drive. I'll let you know.'

The soundproof screen goes up.

KATH BREWER is only now beginning to realize what it is to work for Taffin – even by association. She was up at five this morning and now, late in the afternoon, she's ready for a break.

'Your first mistake was letting him know you could do computers and stuff,' Charlotte told her. 'You're on the unofficial staff for keeps now.'

Kath said, 'I don't even really know him.'

'You'll be fine with that, love.'

And so it turned out. Kath found herself in the passenger seat of the Mustang, heading north, with a man she had never seriously spoken to, and with no idea what to say. She knew what was required; all the equipment was in the back. What was there to talk about?

On the way, Taffin told her what he knew of Bob

Sherman and answered her questions when asked, but for the most part he seemed comfortable with silence, and that became the understanding between them.

Sherman was visibly intrigued by the iPhone Kath brought him, listened patiently while she explained it several times and eventually succeeded in calling the numbers she put in the *Contacts* list.

He didn't ask questions while she was installing a webcam facing his chair and the door, but worked out that the phone would need to be kept charged and asked her how to do it.

When Kath felt the old man knew enough to stay in touch, she looked at Taffin, who gave her a nod and they left without ceremony.

The next job was to transfer the equipment she installed in Ashley Gunn's barn conversion to the house in Mitres Well Lane. That's done now.

'There you go.' Charlotte produces tea in mugs and they sit at the kitchen table. 'You're done for the day. Rick can have you back and you've done something for us the Boss couldn't manage in a thousand years, for all his strange talents.'

'I wouldn't want to go back to that place again,' Kath tells her. 'The caravan was alright for a while but I felt threatened all the time we were there.'

'We can all put that time behind us, love. You're back home, the business is up and running. Think of this as a new beginning. It's like we never left.'

EIGHTEEN

ERICA LYLE is pleased with the way her nose is developing.

The re-launch of a classic motor dealership wouldn't normally attract her, but this one smells like a story. *The Stoleworth Observer* has a business section, which would certainly find room for it – and there's a motoring section as a fall-back position – but the enigmatic owner of *Muscle Motors* is ripe for an in-depth interview and that's where Erica's nose is leading her. He's a local celebrity with a dark past and she's never met him; that needs to be put right.

She arrives at the *Muscle Motors* office without prior warning and immediately walks into The Man Himself, on his way out.

'Just the man I came to see.' Erica's brightest smile reflects double in his dark glasses. 'Could you spare me some of your time?'

Charlotte looks up from her desk, ready to fend off a possible ambush. Taffin pauses in the doorway to study the woman in his path.

Erica plunges in, offers her hand, introduces herself rapidly and decides on the business angle as the most promising opener.

'I'd like to do a feature on the classic car market in general and Muscle Motors in particular. Is there somewhere we could talk?'

Taffin glances back at Charlotte with the hint of a shrug and leads Erica to the patch of forecourt recently vacated by the Dodge. The stump of a once massive oak presents itself and they sit down.

Erica produces her notebook, pretending indifference to the rough surface of the tree stump and the affect it's probably having on her white *Gerard Darel* skirt.

'So, where shall I start?' Her instinctive body language says *you can be open with me*. 'When people talk about you, it's always Taffin – no Mister, no first name or anything. Is it alright if I do that?'

A brief inclination of the dark glasses. Erica takes that as a *yes*.

'Thank you. Muscle Motors has been trading for some years now. Can you remember the exact date you opened?'

Taffin looks towards the office. 'Ask Charlotte. She keeps the records.'

'I will –' Erica makes a note – 'and you closed for a while recently. Why was that?'

'Improvements.'

'Does that mean you're upgrading the service – aiming higher?'

'Something like that.'

'Tell me about the company. What were your ambitions for it when you started out?'

'Make a living.'

'But I suspect there's more to it than that.' Erica searches his face. 'Looking around, these are not just any old cars. Every one I can see from here is a show-stopper.'

'We always have tasty wheels here.'

'Would you say your core market is classic car enthusiasts – collectors?'

'Certainly.'

'Especially Americana?'

'That's the way it's worked out.'

'So, would these beefy American beasts be your personal preference?'

'That's my preference.' Taffin indicates the red Mustang.

'Looks like you've had a ding on the rear wing.'

'No problem. The lads can fix that.'

Erica pauses. Time for a change of pace.

'You don't strike me as someone who talks about himself a lot. I'd like a little background on the man behind *Muscle Motors*. Is that alright?'

The suggestion of a shrug. Erica continues.

'You have quite a reputation locally. You know what I'm going to ask next, don't you?'

Dark glasses turn to her. The double reflection again.

'That film –' she returns the stare – 'fact or fantasy? Is it about you and if so, is it a true story?'

'Some people think so.'

'But what do you think? – you're in a unique position to comment and, after all, you're the one all the controversy's about.'

'I don't think about it.'

'I doubt that.' Erica makes a note, flips to a new page and pushes her hair back for thinking time. 'Let's turn the clock back a bit. What did Taffin do in his youth, before

Muscle Motors? Where you always in the classic motor business?'

'Not always.'

'What were you doing before?'

'Freelancing.'

'Well, that covers a lot of possibilities. What was your speciality?'

'Keeping the balance.'

'That sounds suspiciously like book-keeping – and you don't look the type at all. Were you a loss adjuster?'

'Not exactly.'

'You'll have to help me – I don't know what the balance means in this context.'

'Balancing what's owed with what's paid.'

'That's a phrase I haven't heard before. What exactly does it involve?'

'I'll make it simple for you.' Taffin studies her for a moment. 'There's always someone looking for more than they want to pay for. That's alright, it's part of the game. The motor trade's a good example – it's full of chancers so you expect it.'

'You mean everybody wants a deal.'

'Sure. But you get the odd one who don't want to pay at all, even after they've got the goods. That's when the balance needs restoring.'

'That sounds like debt collecting to me. Who did you work for?'

'Strictly freelance.'

'Putting the balance right?'

'That's it.'

'I understand.' Erica applies herself to her notebook,

dismissing a mild wave of insecurity. 'I can see how people wouldn't argue with you.'

The dark glasses incline slightly. Erica meets the gaze again.

'Everything about your operation suggests size and strength. Do you enjoy power?'

'I don't like what it does to people.'

'That's not quite what I asked. I mean, do you like the idea of wielding power?'

'Same answer.'

Taffin sits very still and Erica notes that he never moves unnecessarily, creating an impression of unassailable calm. Even so, there must be thresholds that shouldn't be crossed. She decides to push it.

'Would you take on StarTrack?'

'Why would I want to do that?'

'It's what some people expect of you.' Erica flips back through old notes. 'I covered the demo in Lasherham. Feelings were running high that day and there were hints that Gordon Glennan might be up against stiffer opposition than he knows. Have you met our Mister Glennan?'

'Certainly.'

'Is he someone you could do business with?'

'Not out of choice.'

'Let me quote you what a Mrs Ivy Lewis said...'

'I know what she said.'

'You read my article?'

'I heard a first hand account.'

'She think there's someone around here who'd make a better job of looking after public interests. Who would that be, d'you think?'

She tries to meet the gaze of two dark lenses.

There is a lot of silence in a whole minute, then:

'Do you read at all?'

'Yes, of course.' Erica holds his eye-line.

'Read Russell Chambers Gates – anything you can get hold of. He writes about human behaviour – says most of our energy is wasted worrying about things we can't influence.'

'I get it.' Erica opens a clean page, makes a note and looks up again. 'StarTrack is a step too far. You're a victim of your own reputation. What else does Russell Chambers Gates talk about?'

'Balance.'

'So do you. What's he got to say about it?'

'If at all possible, make sure nobody's dead because you're alive.'

'That's an interesting thought.' Another note goes in the book. 'I can believe many things about you, Taffin, but I don't see you as a pacifist.'

Erica waits for a response, aware of an expressionless face turned towards her. After a while Taffin gets up and strolls away towards the workshop, leaving her wondering where to start.

NIGHT. All switches are off in the workshop. Ed Pentecost turns the main lights out in the stores and closes the steel door.

The lights are out in the office, too. Charlotte closed up and left an hour ago. Rick has been gone for a while.

Silence settles.

In Mitres Well Lane, Taffin sits with his feet up, watching Charlotte's fingers stray across her laptop and wondering when she found time to get comfortable with computers. He can see the screen over her shoulder as she manoeuvres a view of the office at Muscle Motors, switches to the workshop interior, then the forecourt.

She turns to him. 'Magic, wouldn't you say, young man?'

'Impressive.'

'Yeah, but not very entertaining. I come home from work, turn on the laptop and have a lovely time watching the place I work at, except I'm not in it. You reckon we'll ever get a visit?'

'Quite likely.'

'You wish, don't you? You want to see that bloke who tried to shove me around.'

No response. Charlotte glances at him.

'How did your interview go?'

'She asked questions. I answered them.'

'Not all of them, I bet.' Charlotte switches views again and they both gaze at the workshop interior for a while. 'Do you remember in *The Godfather*, when the families go to the mattresses? It feels like that's how we're living at the moment.'

'Except we ain't gangsters.' The blank countenance fights back a smile.

'Yeah, well not everybody would agree with that, Mark Twill Taffin. Look at you – you're never going to pass for a romantic poet.'

'I don't look like a book-keeper either – so the lady reporter said.'

'Strange, that.' Charlotte leans over and pats his midriff. 'You need to get rid of that beer gut.'

She switches through views of the office interior and the forecourt. All seems quiet.

'How long d'you reckon we need to do this?'

'We've got something they want. They ain't going to stop unless they find it somewhere else, and that ain't going to happen because we've got it.'

Charlotte shakes her head. 'It's a lot of fuss over a shed full of old bangers.'

'We make our living out of old bangers, girl – and some of the ones in that barn are worth serious money.'

'The ones in that barn don't belong to us, young man.'

'No, they belong to a nice old geezer who lives in an attic. I'll introduce you one of these days.'

The phone rings, breaking in on their musings.

Taffin gets up to answer it and at the same moment a shadow shifts on the screen.

Charlotte leans forward to stare at it and shouts: 'We've got company. Someone's in the office.'

Taffin turns to look, phone in hand, as Julia's voice comes down the line with a single question:

'Is Ed there?'

IT WAS THE OBVIOUS PLACE TO LOOK. Taffin's flashlight plays along the coarse grass flanking the track to *Muscle Motors* and picks up Ed's recumbent form.

A heartbeat later Taffin is on his knees checking for signs of life. A pulse; shallow breathing. Instinct says don't try to move him. Taffin rising to his feet, searching a pocket for his phone.

No thought for anything else in this moment.

Unaware of two figures emerging from the trees behind him.

The attack is swift, silent and efficient.

Taffin half turning as locked hands club the side of his head and two punches take him in the midriff, doubling him up.

Pain and fury taking over. Taffin bellowing rage, staggering sideways, hurling a shoulder punch into the dark, spinning into a right hook, never seeing the punch that takes him on the temple, hardly feeling impact with the ground.

Some time later Rick Bishop's bike swings into the lane, the headlight beam slashing across the Mustang telling him Taffin is here, somewhere.

A moment more and Rick finds them, fumbles for his phone, makes the emergency call, then three more calls to Charlotte, Julia and Kath in quick succession as he waits twenty minutes, or an eternity, for the ambulance to turn up.

Two paramedics manhandle two heavy men onto stretchers and into the ambulance; the clash of doors and they're gone into the night in a swirl of blue lights heading for Stoleworth General.

The roar of Rick's bike mingling with the sirens as he swings round to follow.

CHARLOTTE AND JULIA join Rick in the soulless glare of a hospital corridor. Doctor Murphy approaches. He looks as if he hasn't slept or changed his white coat in a week.

He wants to know about their relationships with the patients and fails to disguise his unease about people who arrive in this condition: these are not accidental injuries.

Both men are in a stable condition, he tells them, and

will be kept under observation overnight. Neither is fit to be discharged; scans are being arranged. No more information at this stage. He advises them to come back in the morning.

Charlotte and Julia insist on staying. Rick is disinclined to leave them but they insist he should go home and look after Kath. He is more relieved than he cares to admit. Hospitals give him the creeps.

NINETEEN

MAURICE TAFFIN is not given to depression. He is Mo – relentlessly peaceful, good-natured and disinclined to speak ill of anyone.

It's been a long time since Shirley has seen him in his present mood. He left the house this morning to roam the hills around Lasherham and she hasn't heard from him since.

At this moment he is on the hillside by the Church with the whole village spread out beneath him. Across the valley to his left, Mill Lane winds up to join Mitres Well Lane, out of view on the far side of the hill. A mile to his right he can see the acreage belonging to the bookshop. According to the most recent change of route, StarTrack will come out there if those in charge of it get their way.

He dismisses the thought. StarTrack is not on his mind today. Matters closer to home are more pressing and he is doing as he always does, letting nature put him at ease. His pipe is burning evenly, matt-black and peaceful. Wisps of smoke snatch away on a gentle wind. He is in a calm place. In spite of which he cannot dismiss alien stirrings of outrage directed at anyone who means harm to his family.

Mo began to sense all was not as it should be when his brother's business went quiet and Charlotte couldn't conceal her anxiety.

To a countryman, tuned to the music of every day, a wrong note crept in at that point and a clanging discord left echoes of a time he thought was firmly buried in the past.

He knows his brother has often stood on this very spot, reflecting on whatever it is he turns over in that impenetrable mind of his. Now he, Mo, is doing the same, but with no hard facts to chew on.

No point brooding. He feels the need for company and sets off down the hill towards the High Street, the White Lion and sanity.

Ashley Gunn is leaning on the bar when he gets there and Mo joins him without a word. Meg pours him a pint and waves away his offered payment.

'You don't look yourself, love,' she remarks. 'That's on the house.'

Ashley Gunn nods approval and Mo is suddenly aware that here, at least, problems can be shared.

Ashley says, 'I hear your brother discharged himself from A and E. Have you seen him?'

Mo shakes his head. 'Charlotte says he don't want to talk to anyone. You know how he gets.'

'He's a quiet one,' Meg moves closer, mopping imaginary beer from the bar.

Ashley watches Mo solemnly. 'Is he going to be alright, d'you think?'

Mo shrugs. 'They patched him up in the hospital and wanted to keep him in overnight at least, but he didn't fancy staying there and I don't blame him. He walked out as soon as he could. Charlotte's looking after him now.'

Meg keeps mopping, more slowly. 'What about Ed Pentecost? How's he doing?'

'They don't tell you anything, do they? Charlotte reckons they think he might have a skull fracture.'

'That doesn't sound good.'

'Someone really laid into the pair of them.'

'Any idea who it was yet?'

'You tell me.' Mo dips to his beer. 'It's been a long time since we had anything like this. Something ain't right.'

'You can say that again.' Ashley Gunn speaks without looking at either of them.

'What do you reckon?' Mo glances at him. 'You know my brother as well as anyone. Someone don't want him around and I'd give a lot to know who it is.'

Ashley shakes his head. 'I can't say.'

'You could if you had a mind to, though.' Mo finishes his pint and signals Meg for two more. 'You know I keep well clear of my brother's business, Ashley, always have. I ain't got the kind of mind for what he does, anyone'll tell you that – but I've said it before and I'll say it again – I know when there's something people ain't telling me.'

RICK BISHOP takes a handful of throttle and hunches up against the blast of cold air, his view of the rising sun sloping left, right and left again as he launches the Fireblade into the bends towards Stoleworth.

Fury and guilt are driving today. Fury at himself for not being there when the attack took place; guilt, for the same reason.

Kath managed to calm him down last night, arguing that he had no way of knowing what was about to happen and probably wouldn't have come out of it any better than the other two. They're no walk-overs, she pointed out; someone must have got to them before they knew what was happening.

The ride absorbs some of this morning's adrenalin but Rick is still highly charged as he walks into Stoleworth General.

Doctor Murphy is still on duty.

'Mister Taffin discharged himself last night, against my advice.' The doctor refers to a clipboard without looking at Rick, whose presence he finds at least as unsettling as the two who were brought in at the start of his shift.

'Is Mister Pentecost here?'

'He is –' more reference to the clipboard – 'are you a relative?'

Rick is about to say no, but says 'Yes.'

The Doctor doesn't believe him but hesitates. Saying no to this hard-breathing leather-clad person is likely to spark off a scene he doesn't need. He directs Rick to the ward and leaves it to the nursing staff.

Julia is at Ed's bedside and gets up as Rick approaches.

'He's sleeping now,' she tells him. 'They thought it was a skull fracture but it turns out not to be, thank God. He's got a couple of cracked ribs and bruising everywhere and they say he'll have a hell of a headache when he wakes up.'

'I should've been there.' Rick still has a wild look in his eye.

Julia looks him over. 'No one saw this coming – not like this, anyway. Don't beat yourself up.'

'I hear The Boss discharged himself.'

'He wasn't in great shape, either, but no one felt like giving him an argument and Charlotte took him home.'

Rick takes a close look at his long-time friend and colleague in the bed and turns to Julia.

'You reckon he'll be alright?'

'He'll do. I'll let you know if there's any change. Off you go, Rick – you don't look happy in places like this.'

Rick puts a hand on her shoulder – an attempt at the reassuring gesture he's seen Taffin use many times – and marches out.

The Fireblade gives him comfort again and a while later he pulls up outside the house in Mitres Well Lane.

Charlotte opens the door and leads him into the kitchen. 'I'm glad you're here. He wants to see you. Kath said you'd gone back to A and E. How's Ed?'

'He's pretty beat up but they reckon he hasn't got a fractured skull. Julia's with him.'

'That's a load off, anyway. Himself's in the shed. Go and say hello.'

Rick goes round to the back of the house, taps on the door of the shed and eases it open. Taffin is sitting on the table by the window, a broad silhouette against the light. Dark glasses slip into place.

'Sit down, Rick.'

Rick finds a chair and sits down, searching Taffin's face against the glare for signs of damage.

'You alright?'

'I took a beating, son. Never saw it coming. I must be slipping.'

'Nah – not you.'

A hint of amusement touches the highlit profile.

'Not just me, Rick. We all have to watch our backs at the moment.'

'We know who we're looking out for now, at least.'

'We know some of them. I doubt if we've met the whole crew. Someone's pulling the strings and I still don't know who or why.'

'What do we do now?'

'You and Kath should keep your heads down until I can see things clearer. That's not up for discussion, Rick –' Taffin moves a hand against the objection – 'I'm thinking of Kath, and so should you.'

'What about the business?'

'The business keeps running. I'll be there, so will Charlotte. Everything normal on the face of it, except you'll be keeping an eye on us with Kath's magic cameras.'

'What about Ed and Julia?'

'Ed ain't fit for much right now. When he recovers, the same goes for them.'

'I don't like it.'

'That's how it's going to be anyway.'

'You mean, you're just going to sit there at Muscle Motors waiting for someone to turn up and take another pop at you – and maybe Charlotte this time?'

'I won't be sitting around, son – nor will Charlotte. Someone's playing games and I need to stay ahead of them. That means working out how they think and what they want.'

'They want us out of business.'

'No one would argue with that. So they start by hijacking you and Ed, leaving me short of skilled men. It don't work because you guys won't play ball and they was never going to pay anyway – you know that, don't you?'

'We worked it out. They didn't own the cars we worked on, so they were gambling on the paperwork turning up.'

'Which you obligingly found for us.'

'And I was going to have a bonfire with it if Ed hadn't worked out what it was.'

'Team work. Balance of skills – you get it?'

'Sure. I still don't like leaving you to run the place without us there.'

'Don't worry about it. They won't catch us on the hop a second time. I'm working on adjusting the balance in our favour.'

GORDON GLENNAN stands at his study window gazing out over his garden. It looks good in the failing light and he finds himself wishing he had time for it. Life is too full of other things. His wife hired a gardener years ago and Glennan tries to remember the man's name. Bill, he thinks, but he probably wouldn't recognise him in the street.

Janice is off somewhere again; he has no idea where she is this evening and it occurs to him that there is no real contact between them any more. A married man with all the trimmings, but no marriage.

This would be as good a time as any to commune with nature, smell the freshness of mown grass and stroll along the herbaceous borders wondering what the various plants are called.

The lawn feels good underfoot and he ambles along clean-cut borders, breathing deeply, making a conscious effort to clear his mind of everything but the present. Rooks settle in the treetops, making harsh remarks to each other. Or are they crows? Some sort of language among them, he feels. Nothing makes that much noise without a reason. Except, possibly, The House of Commons.

At the foot of a dense hedge he finds a wrought iron bench and sits down, wishing he had thought to bring a cigar.

The phone ringing in the house. A distant jangle, easily ignored. If he were in his study he would monitor it and call back later if necessary. Right now he has no inclination to stir himself. Let it ring.

When it stops, he relaxes, surprised to find how easy it was to resist the intrusion.

It rings again. This time he lets his gaze wander over the twilit garden.

'You have reached Gordon Glennan's private line. Please leave a message.'

Glennan smiles at the imagined sound of his own, calm voice, keeping callers at bay.

A moment to register that the voice was not in his head, but real. How could that be possible?

'You really don't want to talk, do you?'

A new voice, soft grit, inches from his ear.

A snatch of breath as Glennan's scalp seems to freeze and contract. A certain numbness.

A beefy hand holds a phone where he can see it.

'D'you want to leave yourself a message?'

Glennan struggling for words, half turning. A dark form moves behind him and the bench shifts under the weight of a man who takes up more than his share of the space available.

'Settle down, Mister Glennan. You have nothing to fear from me.' Taffin makes himself comfortable, watching the pencil-black pattern of trees against pale evening light.

Glennan feels weakness in every limb. 'What do you want?'

'I promised we'd talk again.'

'We have nothing to talk about. You scared me, I admit, but I can't react to threats – my hands are tied.'

'I understand that, Mister Glennan. I'm not the person you need to worry about. You won't believe this but I'm here to help.'

'You're right, I don't believe it. How can you possibly help me?'

'Maybe we can help each other.'

'Mister Taffin, I'm a Minister of the Crown with responsibilities and pressures you can't even imagine.'

'You'd be surprised what I can imagine.'

'I'm also human, with all the frailty that implies. You can intimidate me – you're doing a fine job of that – but I can't react in any way that would make sense to you.'

'Well –' Taffin rests a heavy arm along the back of the bench – 'let's think about that for a moment. Where's your pressure coming from?'

'Where do you think? I serve the government.'

'You should be used to that. Where else?'

'That's enough, isn't it?'

Taffin lets the silence settle. Glennan would like to get up and head for the house but lacks the resolve and is sure the effort would be wasted. Better to try steering this bizarre conversation himself.

'Alright, Taffin – I'm sure you keep up to date on current

affairs locally. I've upset a few people around here and I regret that. I'm aware that your lady friend was hurt by someone you think was working for me. If that is indeed the case I am very sorry – I hope she's feeling better now – but my influence extends only so far. Being held to account is the price one pays for being in politics.'

'You know what bothers me?' Taffin muses at the distant trees. 'You've got some people working for you who definitely aren't civil servants. I wonder where they're coming from.'

'You're probably talking about manual help for various projects I deal with. As I told you last time we spoke, I don't know who hires everybody. It's not what I'm here for and, frankly, not my concern.'

'You don't know who's working for you.'

'That's the way of it.'

'Or who hires them.'

'I can't honestly say I know who hires them.'

'You see, that's not what people want to hear from a man in a responsible position. You don't know who works for you or who hires them.'

'I'm afraid not.'

'Your wife does.'

Glennan draws breath to respond and checks himself. Finally: 'My wife has no place in any conversation between you and me. I'd be grateful if you'd leave her out of it.'

'You're not kidding either of us, Mister Glennan. Where is she tonight?'

'I don't ask her where she is every minute of the day.'

'She wouldn't tell you anyway. Let's be frank, you play by her rules. I can see her thumb print on the top of your head from here.'

'You can think what you like.' Glennan feels the bile rising in his throat: the truth, thrown in his face by a cheap thug.

Taffin watches a pair of rooks making for the treetops. 'Let me tell you what I'm thinking. If you could see where your wife is tonight, you wouldn't have to ask where the pressure's coming from.'

'That's a very offensive suggestion. My wife has commitments...'

'Your wife's taking you for all you've got – and I don't just mean money. Your career, social status, contacts in high places – it's all hers to play with.'

'You don't know her at all.'

'I know heavyweight backing when I smell it, Mister Glennan. She felt safe enough to threaten me. That don't happen a lot.'

Glennan huffs a bitter laugh. 'I can understand why.'

Taffin lets his gaze stray over their surroundings.

'You have substantial property – a lot more than we're looking at here. Your wife's a fortunate lady, with or without you.'

'What are you implying?'

'I'll bet you're well insured on top of everything else.'

'I'm not discussing my private life with you.'

'You should discuss it with someone, Mister Glennan. You're not safe, the way things are – too exposed.'

'This is ridiculous. You seem to be saying I need some kind of bodyguard.'

'You should think about it.'

'I don't move in those circles.'

'You're right in the middle of them.'

A cacophony of rooks in the treetops, high overhead.

Taffin watches the big birds flapping, subsiding, flapping again.

'Let's be straight with one another. We're enjoying a pleasant evening. We're not strangers any more, so no need to be formal. I'll call you Gordon.'

'I'm not comfortable with first name terms.'

'Humour me.'

'Alright, if that's what you want. I'd like to go in now. I think we've said all there is to say.'

'You're in too much of a hurry. Let's talk about StarTrack.'

'I can't comment on that, as you very well know...'

'Why does the route keep changing?'

'For very good reasons which I've explained many times. We're exploring possibilities to make sure the final route is the best option.'

Taffin's attention drifts upwards as more rooks circle to land.

'Have you ever seen the three card trick, Gordon – Find the Lady?'

'I'm familiar with it, yes. It's a well-known con.'

'That's what it is, Gordon. It don't matter how many times you watch it, or how carefully you watch, you're never going to get it right because someone wants you to keep guessing.'

'What point are you making?'

'What happens every time the route changes?'

'There's an outcry in the affected area – that's bound to happen...'

'What else happens?'

'Each new proposal sets off a cycle of activity. The

Select Committee researches the new route, weighs up the implications, hears objections, takes advice...'

'What else?'

'Then I have to keep everyone concerned apprised of the situation...'

'Prices drop.'

Taffin studies the afterglow on the mackerel sky while Glennan searches for a reaction.

'Oh, there are many factors that influence property prices, Mister Taffin.'

'But nothing like not knowing if your house is going to stay standing.'

'There are generous compensation schemes for anyone who's likely to be affected. You should read up on the proposals and stop scaremongering – because that's all this kind of talk amounts to.'

'Meanwhile you keep people guessing. Property prices don't recover because everyone's waiting for a decision, and each time there's a new route, the area of uncertainty gets bigger. How am I doing, Gordon?'

'Where are you getting this from?'

'I watch, listen, put pieces together.' Taffin turns his head to study Glennan's profile. 'And I ain't heard you say I'm wrong.'

Glennan huffs his half laugh again. 'You think it's all a big plot to undermine the property market?'

'That's what it does.' Taffin lets the rooks take over for a while, then: 'Do you read, Gordon?'

'When I get the time.'

'You should read Warren Palmer.'

'What does he write – thrillers?'

'Economics. He reckons all economic theory is guesswork. You have to look at who's pulling the strings to make sense of it.'

'That sounds – rather cynical and strangely academic.' Glennan struggles to connect what he's just heard with the man who said it. 'What else?'

'He's got this idea he calls *Economic Truth*, but says it can't work because banks, bombs and billionaires manipulate the economy.'

'You're surprising me, Taffin. Why do you read this stuff?'

'Why not? All you can do is improve your mind.'

'Who are you quoting now?'

'Russell Chambers Gates. He writes about how people behave. Reckons we stay primitive because half of us waste time trying to get rich and the other half waste time trying to stop them. He calls it *Miseconomics – a study of social cramp*. You'd enjoy it.'

'I've never heard of either of those people.'

'Hard to come by. I get old copies through the Tollgate Bookshop. I believe you know it.'

Glennan is working on a reply to this when headlights slash across the hedgerows; tyres chew the gravel on the drive and a Volvo pulls up.

Janice Glennan gets out and heads for the front door.

Taffin sets a hand on Glennan's arm. 'I believe your wife is home. Why don't you call her over?'

Glennan is torn between getting up, pretending he was out strolling the grounds, which he never does, and staying where he is in the shadows. He holds his breath, willing his wife to let herself in before she senses his eyes upon her.

'Good evening Mrs Glennan.' The soft voice carries, without effort.

Janice Glennan pauses in the act of letting herself into the house.

'Who's that?'

'Come and join us. It's a pleasant evening, we're having a chat.'

Janice takes two steps towards the lawn and sees the two seated silhouettes. 'Who is WE?'

'Me and your husband. We've been getting along famously.'

Janice pauses. 'Is that Mister Taffin? I'm surprised to see you here, I must say.'

'That doesn't surprise me, Mrs Glennan.'

'I heard you had an accident.'

'News travels fast.'

'I hope you're fully recovered.'

'I'll do. My colleague isn't so good.'

'Shouldn't you be looking after him, then?' Janice has come to the edge of the gravel drive and now stops rather than trust her heels to the soft grass.

'I'll be on my way presently.' Taffin shows no sign of stirring. 'Don't you want to know what we've been discussing?'

'Nothing you have to say could interest me, or my husband.'

Taffin rises to his feet, hands in pockets, and looks down at Glennan. 'Why don't you tell her what we've talked about, Gordon?'

'Oh – Gordon, is it?' Janice stares at her husband as he emerges from the shadows.

Taffin ambles towards her. 'Me and your husband have some shared interests. You don't mind that, do you? Tell us about your evening – what's Mrs Glennan been up to?'

'That's it – this conversation is over.' Janice looks past him to her husband. 'It's time to come in, Gordon. Say goodnight to your new friend.'

Taffin is close to her now and turns to gaze at the darkening horizon.

'I don't believe you like me, Mrs Glennan. I think you've been talking about me behind my back. Shall I send my colleague your best wishes when he recovers?'

'You can do what you like. Gordon, I'm tired and we've got things to talk about. Good night, Mister Taffin. I don't expect to see you here again.'

Glennan moves to guide his wife to the door, glancing over his shoulder as he goes.

'You should leave us alone, Taffin. There's nothing here to interest you.'

'Think about what I told you, Gordon.'

TAFFIN SITS FOR A WHILE in the Mustang contemplating the gibbous moon before twitching the key, bringing the V8 to life and burbling away into the night.

The lights are on in Glennan's study now. Janice closes the curtains and turns to her husband.

'Sit down, Gordon. It's time we had a serious talk.'

'I think we should.'

'You don't need to look so solemn, I'm not about to leave you. Maybe that's what you'd like but it's not going to happen.'

'It wouldn't be my choice, Janice. All I ever wanted was

a wife, a career and a healthy pension at the end of it. What do you want to talk about?'

'You're too accessible here. You should base yourself in the London flat. Knightsbridge is a more fitting place for a Minister anyway.'

'I notice you didn't say *we*.'

'We don't see much of each other these days, or hadn't you noticed? And by the way, pensions are poison – they create the illusion of a secure future.'

'Poison, you think. Well, that's a point of view.' Glennan pauses. 'I've noticed you come and go as you please with no regard for me. I haven't asked questions. Maybe I should.'

'We're grown-ups, Gordon. Grown-ups in a prominent position. You don't want the tabloids snooping into your private life any more than they have already, do you?'

'My private Life? What about *our* private life – yours and mine – I wonder what they'd make of that. The press loves to humiliate a minister and I'm sure there would be at least three players involved. I'd be interested to read about that.'

Her hand is faster that his reactions and his head explodes with the force of it.

Glennan staggers, stares at her, composes himself.

She speaks softly, triumph and venom in her voice.

'Be very careful, Gordon.'

Glennan nurses his cheek, turns and watches her in the mirror as he speaks. 'I don't know where you go or what you do. The press latches onto anything, however trivial. We saw it with the ludicrous stolen car prank –' he snorts dismissively – 'childish practical jokes.'

'But things like that attract attention, and you don't want that, do you?'

'Are you suggesting I've got something to hide?'

'Oh, not *suggesting*, Darling. You're up to your neck and people sense it – especially in a place like this. You need to be out of the way in London.'

'You mean I should be where people like Taffin can't drop in on me.'

'What were you thinking of, spending time with him?'

'He surprised me.'

'That's what he's good at. You shouldn't have let him in.'

'No, I mean I found him surprising.'

'He's a crude thug – a vulgar *garagiste* with an ego the size of one of those awful cars he peddles, inflated, no doubt, by the movie everyone says is about him.'

'He's no fool. I'd say he's a shrewd judge of a situation. And by the way, a *garagiste* is a maker of wines – from Bordeaux, I think.'

'So what is it he wants you to think about?'

'He made some assumptions about the StarTrack project. Guesswork, I suppose, but alarmingly accurate.'

Janice watches her husband and he meets her gaze, chilled for a moment by those drooping eyelids. She moves towards the door. 'You need to tread carefully, Gordon – very carefully.'

'How did you know he'd had an accident?'

She pauses. 'I overheard some of your conversation.'

'He didn't mention it to me.'

'A lucky guess, then. His sort is always in and out of trouble, usually of a physical nature.'

'You said, news travels fast. You must have heard it from someone.'

'That's something for you to wonder about, Darling.' Janice stares him down. 'Or you can ask your new friend what he thinks.'

TWENTY

ED PENTECOST is aware of people around him. There have been voices for some time but he hasn't been able to raise any interest until now. He feels inclined to comment and is astonished at the excitement this causes.

'What did I say?' He feels this is a reasonable question and is surprised by the enthusiastic noises that follow.

A woman's face looking into his, looking away to talk to someone else and back to him. A man asking how he feels. Ed doesn't know either of these people and says so.

Footsteps coming and going and after a while Julia is there, holding his hand and asking if he can hear her, which of course he can.

'He can hear me,' Julia tells someone.

'Of course I can fucking hear you,' he remarks.

Julia's explosive laugh. 'You'll have to watch your language in here, Ed. The nurses aren't used to it.'

Sounds of general amusement suggest the nurses are most definitely used to it.

Ed tries to sit up but hands restrain him. He moves his head and everything is suddenly clearer.

'You look better.' Julia is scrutinizing his face. 'That

bruising looked horrific when they first brought you in but it's settling down now. You're definitely the best-looking beetroot in the ward.'

'Good to know.' He looks up at her with appreciation.

'You've got to take it easy for a bit. You took a kicking and your ribs are going to be sore.

'Everything's sore.'

More faces he doesn't recognize; someone telling him it's a good sign he feels the soreness. It means his body is repairing itself.

'Where do they get all this crap they tell you?' He asks Julia the question and she squeezes his hand and nods to the unknown people.

'He'll do.'

AT ABOUT THE SAME TIME, in a private hospital a hundred miles away, Eric McDermott is causing concern. He is still comatose. The medical staff monitoring his condition still have no idea who he is. Doctor Clemens, the Resident Medical Officer who admitted him, was told the patient's name on arrival but has been unable to extract any further information.

McDermott's visitors have been terse and obviously impartial, their only apparent connection being business of an unspecified nature. There seems to be no personal interest in this patient at all.

Paradoxically, his condition is clearly important to someone. The costs are considerable but the funds are there, with the proviso that no attempt should be made to pry into his background.

No one tending him is comfortable with this but the

hospital administration is in no position to argue. Intensive Care has to be paid for.

'It can't last indefinitely, of course.'

'I'm not sure I understand, Doctor Morley.' Clemens looks up from his notes. 'Our instructions were that we should look after Mister McDermott for as long as necessary.'

'There has to be a limit. He is not an employee of ours. We are only doing what common decency dictates.'

'I gather he is not your patient, Doctor Morley.'

'I am not a medical doctor.' A flash of white teeth.

'I misunderstood.' Clemens refers to his notes again. 'Mister McDermott's condition is critical. We know nothing of his personal circumstances but some provision will have to be made for his continued stay with us.'

'Regrettably I can't guarantee that. My employers are only bystanders in this sad situation, you understand. We are happy to pay Mister McDermott's expenses up to a reasonable limit, but eventually we must step aside.'

When Doctor Morley has left, it occurs to Clemens that he has no contact details for the people who brought McDermott in, and no contingency for continuing his treatment when the funds dry up.

In the meantime he has a patient who is on his own and shows no sign of recovering.

A SKIP FULL OF OLD BOOKS hangs suspended on four chains before being swung onto the truck.

Michael Wyatt watches the load settle and thumbs his mobile. 'I've got a ton and a half of heavy reading here. What do you want done with it?'

Silver's voice answers: 'The driver knows where to take it. You'll recognize the place – you've been there before.'

'Good enough.' Wyatt puts his phone away and shrugs at Greg Dupree. 'It's not our problem.'

He slaps the cab door twice and the truck pulls away.

Wyatt and Dupree make a final tour of inspection inside the bookshop. The floorboards creak, as ever. Their torch beams flicker along row after row of empty shelves and finally they let themselves out, lock up and leave a lifeless building behind them.

'WHO SAW THIS HAPPEN?' Perry Butt swivels on his bar stool to face the lunchtime gathering in the White Lion.

'No one, apparently.' Ivy Lewis flings her arms in a helpless gesture, almost knocking Butt's glass out of his hand. 'The front window is empty and you can see some of the ground floor shelves through it. They've all been cleared and if that's anything to go by there isn't a book left in the place.'

'Theft – vandalism.' Butt's plume of white hair rises in outrage. 'Someone has to answer for this.'

'Guess who –' Ivy's voice takes on its public address tone – 'I'll tell you – everyone's favourite Member of Parliament, Gordon *StarTrack* Glennan, local benefactor, creep *extraordinaire* and owner of the Tollgate Bookshop.'

'Never mind that,' Harry Hawkins interrupts. 'Where are all those books now, that's what I want to know.'

'That would appear to be the key question.' Mostyn studies his half of bitter. 'There were thousands of books. Hiding a hoard like that would be no easy matter.'

'We're in the hands of philistines,' Butt booms. 'You

don't imagine an invaluable cache of reading matter means anything to people like that. The whole lot is probably blazing away at this very moment – that, or they're being tipped into a landfill site somewhere.'

Ashley Gunn has walked in through the door marked *Gents* and catches the end of the conversation.

'There was a skip outside the bookshop yesterday,' he remarks. 'If the stock's been cleared out, it could be traced through the skip hire company.'

'Maybe.' Harry Hawkins is skeptical. 'They deal with demolition all the time. It ain't like the Antiques Roadshow when they get involved.' The assembly nods with him as he turns to Ivy. 'This is when we need your hero.'

'He's in bad shape at the moment.' Meg pauses in the act of running her ever-present cloth along the bar. 'Discharged himself from hospital. His mate Ed's still in there. I thought you all knew.'

They all knew; the nodding becomes more profound.

Perry Butt surfaces again. 'I understood Robin Hood was retired.'

Ivy Lewis shakes her head. 'I don't think so. That was him who got the bookshop to open when it was meant to be shut. I'll swear he was behind that.'

Butt is about to comment but Mostyn risks interrupting him. 'If Mister Taffin is still inclined to help in some way, perhaps this is an occasion when an approach would be justified.'

To his embarrassment, Mostyn has struck a chord. All eyes turn to him and the nodding becomes more animated.

'I didn't mean me,' he explains.

'Good God man, this is your chance to shine.' Perry

Butt swivels to face him. '*In peace there's nothing so becomes a man as modest stillness and humility* – as you yourself can testify, Mostyn – *but when the BLAST OF WAR blows in our ears, then IMITATE THE ACTIONS OF A TIGER – stiffen the sinews, summon up the blood, disguise fair nature with HARD-FAVOURED RAGE, lend the eye A TERRIBLE ASPECT.* Go on, Mostyn – LEAD US INTO THE BREACH.'

'I'd rather not.' Mostyn covers his glass against the shower of spittle.

Ivy Lewis puts an arm round him. 'Don't worry, love – Harry and I'll go and see him. We've been before so he knows us.'

TAFFIN stands outside the office at *Muscle Motors*, hands behind his back, staring at the skip that now occupies the space where the Dodge Charger was until a couple of days ago.

The skip was there when he arrived at ten to seven this morning. He has wandered around it, ascertained that it contains an enormous number of books of all sizes, and is now weighing up his options.

He has no doubt who arranged this delivery. The Tooth Fairy – what did he call himself? Silver – had a couple of gorillas with him; Charlotte identified one of them from Pierre's photo. No doubt they were tasked with clearing the bookshop and dumping the contents here; The question is, was it Silver's decision to bring it here – if not, who is pulling his strings? – and what kind of response does he expect?

Silver must know he, Taffin, is not likely to make this a police matter. For one thing, it wouldn't be hard to establish ownership of the consignment. This is the contents of a building owned by Gordon Glennan, removed, presumably, on his instructions or at least with his consent.

No victim, no crime.

Taffin wanders along the track towards the road and back again. One option would be to make contact with Glennan, ask him what he wants done with his skip load of books and watch his reaction. But would Glennan himself have ordered the contents of his shop to be planted at *Muscle Motors*? It would be a vindictive act, calculated to do damage, and Taffin seriously doubts that Glennan has that in his nature.

Dark glasses slip into place. Another turn around the forecourt to reflect, pausing every so often to stare at the skip, as if to divine its reason for being there.

It seems to be saying: *'Your move.'*

That, he is sure, is what he's meant to think.

Which means the smart move is to do nothing.

If this is a game of Who Blinks First, Taffin's dull stare can handle it.

TWENTY-ONE

IVY LEWIS has a vivid memory of her last visit to Muscle Motors with Harry Hawkins. Now they're back, as hesitant and uncertain as before.

They walk straight past the skip without registering what they've seen and tap nervously on the office door. The door swings open. Ivy and Harry see themselves reflected doubly in the dark glasses, and in that moment Ivy realizes they've just seen what she was going to ask Taffin to find. No words come so she makes a mute gesture in the direction of the skip.

Taffin lets his gaze settle on the pair.

Ivy suffers brain-fade a moment longer before snapping into action. 'We had something to ask you but it looks like we don't need to.'

'Let me guess –' Taffin stares past them – 'you found what you came looking for.'

'That looks like it, over there.' Ivy follows Taffin's eye line. 'We came to ask a favour but you seem to have beaten us to it. You must think we're always on your doorstep asking for something.'

'Not at all.'

Harry finds his voice. 'The bookshop's been cleared out. We were all wondering where the stock went but it looks like it's sitting over there, so we shouldn't waste any more of your time. Come on Ivy, no point us hanging around.'

'Wait a minute –' Ivy wants to know more – 'what's the idea of bringing the books here?'

'Good question.'

'But you don't want to answer it.' Ivy's eyes sparkle as she wags a knowing finger. 'Just one more question, then you can tell me to shut up. What happens to the books now?'

'I'll tell you.' Taffin takes a long look round and stoops to meet Ivy's eye. 'We'll put a cover over them so they don't get wet, then we'll wait and see who turns up to claim them.'

Ivy frowns. 'No one's going to claim them. Strictly speaking they're Gordon Glennan's property and he obviously doesn't want anything to do with them.'

'Someone'll turn up.' A hint of amusement touches the broad features for a moment. 'They won't be able to resist it.'

'There you are –' Ivy turns to Harry Hawkins, triumphant finger raised – 'he's baited a trap. What did I tell you? I said he'd do the right thing by us if humanly possible.'

Harry takes Ivy's arm to lead her away, remarking over his shoulder, 'Ivy's always had a lot of faith in you. We'll leave you in peace.'

Taffin nods quietly, and at the same moment his gaze freezes on the track beyond them as a gunmetal Mercedes slides among the shadows and stops.

Ivy has seen it too. 'More visitors, Taffin. You're popular today.'

Taffin leaves the office doorway and ambles after them, hands in pockets.

Silver leaves the Mercedes and approaches, smiling politely at Ivy and Harry in passing, stopping in Taffin's path. 'I came to see how you're getting on.'

A movement in the shade of the trees by the Mercedes. Taffin assumes Silver is not alone.

'Same as usual.'

'Same as usual...' Silver turns the response over, reflecting. 'You haven't forgotten about my client, I hope.'

'Mister Adams? I never give him a thought.'

'You should. He thinks about you. Have you found him a car yet?'

'No.'

'I'm sorry to hear that. You should try harder.'

Taffin nods slowly and turns to look at the Mercedes. 'Tell your mates there's nothing to interest them in my office.'

'You're a surprising fellow, Taffin. Why would you say a thing like that?'

'We got them on camera.'

'No chance. You should check your equipment.'

'My colleague got a headache the same night. Those gentlemen need to answer for that.'

'I can see how you'd feel like that.'

'Unreliable men.' Taffin shakes his head heavily. 'They had a go at me, too.'

'Someone assaulted you, Taffin? That sounds unlikely.'

'Funny old world, ain't it?' Taffin has ambled round Silver, causing him to turn.

'You must have upset someone, Taffin. I hear it can get rough in the motor trade. Which reminds me,' Silver's bright smile hardens, 'your colleague's former employer had an accident – he's in intensive care – witnesses say your colleague was there when it happened.'

Taffin takes a leisurely pace forward and Silver's face freezes to an agonized rictus.

'Listen to me very carefully –' the voice is whispered gravel – 'I know two of your names and I ain't convinced by either of them. You've made a mistake planting the books here. Your boss won't be happy.'

While Taffin is saying this, Silver is slowly cockling over the nerve-shattering pain in his navicular bone.

After another moment, Taffin shifts his weight, releasing Silver's foot from the underside of his heel. Silver risks a cautious step, gasping with the pain. A glare of teeth reflected double in dark lenses.

Looking back, Ivy Lewis mistakes Silver's posture for laughter.

'Look Harry – Taffin must've told that man a joke. There's a sight I never thought I'd see.'

As the two of them walk on towards Harry's car, Silver takes two hobbling steps, staring venom at Taffin, then composes himself.

'You really don't want to mess with me, Taffin. You're a long way out of your depths and there's no way back.'

Two doors open on the Mercedes. Wyatt and Dupree have noticed Silver's change of posture and are happy to intervene.

Taffin leans close to Silver's ear. 'Your associates are joining us. What are you going to tell them?'

'They know how to deal with the likes of you, Taffin. They don't need telling.'

'Last time we met, they helped my colleague unload a

car from the low-loader. They'll take instructions from me again.'

Taffin watches Wyatt and Dupree approach, strolls to meet them, hands behind his back.

'I was telling Mister Silver he ain't fit be in charge of you lads. He's got no judgment, and what's worse, no manners.'

Wyatt moves in close; Dupree moves round to Taffin's other flank.

Dupree's face glows with triumph. 'He's a mouthy fucker, isn't he?'

Taffin turns to him. 'You're the one I want to talk to. I've got a job for you.'

'You've got a job for me?' Dupree swells with anticipation of payback, spreading his arms. 'Here I am.'

Taffin stares him in the face, aware of Wyatt on his right.

'The gentleman beside me hit a lady. Your job is to pick him up.'

On the last word Taffin adjusts his balance, right arm, fist bunched, slamming sideways taking Wyatt on the point of the jaw.

Dupree's eyes wide as Wyatt falls backwards full weight.

Silver moving in, seen in peripheral vision, right hand coming from his jacket.

Taffin's right hand clamping on Silver's wrist. The gun glimpsed in an instant.

Taffin's left arm locking on Silver's forearm. Right hand jerking down against the elbow angle. Pistol and bone cracking in unison as Silver cries out. Taffin's left leg booting him away to sprawl on the rough ground.

Taffin stooping to retrieve the revolver.

Dupree staring down the barrel as Silver squirms at his feet. Wyatt stirring, making no effort to rise.

A moment to reflect. Taffin examines the snub-nosed 38 in his hand. 'Sneaky,' he remarks. 'Either of you clowns carrying?'

Dupree cautiously opening his jacket to show no weapons.

'The other gentleman?'

'How would I know?'

'Check him out.'

Dupree takes a step towards Wyatt, stoops and opens his jacket.

'Look for yourself.'

'You do the looking.'

Dupree glares at him and makes a thorough search of Wyatt's clothing.

'Nothing.'

'Pick him up.'

Dupree braces himself and hauls Wyatt to his feet. Wyatt's head lolls as he brings Taffin into focus.

Silver has worked himself to a kneeling position using his left arm to support his limp right. 'You're dead, Taffin.'

'Tell your Mister Adams I know who you're working for. Explain to him you tipped me off yourself. The skip was your mistake.'

At the same moment, Ivy Lewis and Harry Hawkins are strapping themselves into Harry's car. Harry glances back at the scene, just visible through the trees.

'I'll tell you what –' Harry nudges Ivy's elbow – 'whatever Taffin said to those fellows must've been crippling. They're still rolling about on the ground.'

'I DON'T LIKE THAT THING.' Charlotte peers at the 38 revolver as Taffin thumbs the release to drop the cylinder sideways.

'I don't care for it myself.' Taffin ejects the rounds into his hand, one spent. 'The Tooth Fairy was trigger-happy.'

'Was he shooting at you?' Charlotte's round eyes.

'I had hold of him. He didn't hit anything.'

'What are you going to do with the gun?'

'Put it in the safe.'

Charlotte shakes her head. 'I don't like it. Who are we dealing with? I thought they were just run-of-the-mill idiots but it looks like they fancy themselves.'

'They're just window-dressing for some fat cat.'

'So who's the fat cat – that geezer who came shopping for Ed and Rick?'

'McDermott – nah. The Tooth Fairy says he's in intensive care somewhere.'

'What happened to him?'

'Accident.'

'Too many accidents just lately.' Charlotte takes the revolver from him and opens the safe. 'Look at me, Babe – you wouldn't use this thing, would you?'

'Not my style. Never has been.'

'It doesn't belong here.'

'Better here than with them.'

Charlotte searches his face. 'So what happened after you finished smacking them about?'

'Kath was watching on her laptop and told Rick. He turned up in time to help out. We checked their car to see if they had any more surprises like that –' he gestures at the revolver – 'then we packed them off.'

'That ain't the end of it. They'll be back, for sure.'

'Not till they've got their instructions, girl. The Tooth Fairy won't blow his nose without word from higher up, and his boss won't be happy with him.'

'That's the question, isn't it – who is his boss?'

'Mister Adams.'

'Great –' Charlotte clowns her joy – 'Mister Adams. Who is Mister Adams?'

'I don't know his real name but he's the geezer who wants a 1937 Cord.'

'You reckon?' Charlotte looks into Taffin's face, absently picks something from his lapel. 'That's just bait. He don't want a Cord, young man – he wants you.'

'He wants me out of business.'

'It's personal. Mister Adams has got it in for you big-time.'

'It's business, girl. You know how the trade works: half goodwill, half bluff.'

'This ain't bluff. There's plenty of ways to put us out of business if that's all he wants. A bit of wrecking and vandalism – he's got the guys to do it and obviously money ain't his problem. Instead, he pushes – a little bit at a time – like he's teasing you.'

Taffin stands very still while she picks more flecks off his lapel. Finally he moves to the window.

'I didn't want to hear that.'

'You've thought it, though – I've seen you. You don't get to hide from me, Mark Twill Taffin.'

'Personal...' Taffin turns the word over as if examining a rarity.

'That's what I said. So... what do we do?'

'First thing, get you safe. I know a place.'

'You're not hiding me away, young man. Who's going to look after you?'

'We'll take a short holiday. Just the two of us. You need a break and I need time to think.'

TWENTY-TWO

DEAN ELTON doesn't care for hospitals much; he's seen too many of them, mostly half-gutted structures with soiled walls, corridors full of dust, debris, confusion and the shrill babble of humanity in torment.

This one is nothing like that: the floors gleam under strip lighting and there is no sound above the whisper of a closing door. His reflected image marches with him along a glass wall, prominent jaw and black cheese-cutter cap giving his profile the appearance of an adjustable wrench.

He has seen Doctor Clemens, who wanted to know his relationship with the patient and was clearly not happy with the reply.

Clemens is getting used to apparently unattached men arriving for treatment: first the one called McDermott – still comatose – and now the person who brought McDermott in, the one who calls himself Doctor Morley. There is a pattern developing. Who and what these people are is not Clemens' business but all his antennae are telling him to be vigilant.

Elton is indifferent to quietly spoken people in white coats. He has business with Doctor Morley and that's what counts at the moment. He finds Morley in an immaculate cubicle, sitting on an inspection bed with his arm in a sling.

'Hello Silver.'

'Who the fuck are you?' Silver's teeth flash malice.

'Don't look so worried, I'm not a doctor – but then, neither are you, Doctor Morley. All you need to know is, I'm a visitor come to see how you're getting on. Don't you like visitors?'

'What do you want?'

'A bit of respect, for a start.' Elton sits on the bed beside Silver, taking satisfaction in the resulting flinch. 'That looks painful –' he prods the sling with a finger – 'hurts, does it?'

'Yes, it hurts.' Silver recoils, glaring at him.

'Broken?'

'Dislocated elbow, since you ask. They're going to pump pain-killers into me so I don't hit the roof when they put it straight. Do me a favour and keep still.'

'Delicate things, elbows.' Elton prods the sling where the arm bends, raising a sharp cry from the patient.

'What's your fucking game?'

'No need to be hostile. Like I said, I'm just looking in to see how you're keeping. Mister Adams is worried about you.'

'Is that right?' Silver turns cautiously to look him over, noting pale eyes that convey nothing. 'How come I haven't seen you before?'

'I'm the invisible man.' Elton almost smiles. 'Mister Adams wanted me to give you a message.'

'I'm listening.'

'Good news and bad news. Which do you want first?'

'Give me the good news.'

'Nah, let's go with the bad news first. Mister Adams feels

you've lost your touch – you're behind the curve – not up to the job in hand.'

'It's work in progress. We've had setbacks...'

'So I hear. One of your colleagues is in a bad way.'

'McDermott – he's in a coma.'

'He's not expected to survive.'

'How do you know that?'

Elton shrugs. 'Just the way it is. You're through.'

'What do you mean, I'm through?'

'You're done – finished – off the job. Want the good news?'

'Sure,' Silver sneers at him, 'I'd love to hear the good news.'

'Mister Adams has another job for you. Don't mind a bit of travel, do you?'

Silver stares at a point in the corner, struggling to take in what he's heard. 'No, I've got nothing against travel. Where?'

'There's some business in the Caribbean he feels you could oversee. British Virgin Isles. Hot climate, fancy hotels, nice girls.'

'What kind of business?'

'Financial. I didn't ask the details. How long will that take to mend?' Elton gives the sling a nudge, raising another gasp of pain.

'About three weeks. Less if they do a good job.'

'Less would be better. You could travel as a wounded hero – private yacht, all the trimmings. You wouldn't mind that, would you?'

Silver draws breath. 'I could live with that.'

'You'll have to earn it.'

'Sure,' Silver shrugs, 'how?'

'You discharge yourself from this place as soon as they fix you up. No discussion, no paperwork, you disappear.'

'That doesn't sound like a problem.'

'There you go – think positive. Finally, there's your colleague to consider.'

'What about him?'

'He's not expected to survive.'

Silver takes a few moments to absorb this, during which time Elton stares at nothing in particular. After a few moments he rises to his feet and leaves.

ED PENTECOST is not used to being driven. Julia watches him trying to straddle his Triumph, then takes his arm and guides him to the Jeep she borrowed from the *Muscle Motors* pool.

'I was just getting the feel of it,' he tells her. 'Give me another minute and I'll have it fired up.'

'How do you expect to control a bike when you can't take two steps without clutching your ribs and using foul language?' she demands, helping him into the passenger seat and stowing his stick beside him.

'I feel like an old geezer,' he mutters.

'You're my old geezer, so do as you're told.'

They arrive at Muscle Motors as Rick Bishop and Kath are dismounting from the Fireblade, taking off their helmets.

Ed glares at them. 'That's what we should be doing.'

'Stop moaning. The Boss wants to see all of us and I said I'd get you here. You don't see him screaming around on two wheels, do you?'

Taffin is waiting for them in the doorway and stands aside to let them in.

'Glad to see you on your feet, Ed.'

'I'll be glad to get rid of this.' Ed brandishes the stick, stumbles without its support and let's Charlotte sit him in a chair.

'Is he giving you a hard time, love?' Charlotte gives Julia her mock-sympathy look.

'He's a miserable git. I have to put his socks on for him because he can't bend over without turning the air blue.'

'You behave.' Charlotte waves a cautionary finger at Ed. 'We won't have any of your fucks and buggers in here. This is a family business.'

Taffin stands at the window with his back to the room as the group settles down. Finally he turns to them, hands in pockets.

'We've attracted the attention of some rude people lately,' he remarks. 'You're all aware of the problem and I don't mind saying I'm proud of the way you've been handling it. This business don't amount to anything without you.'

Appreciative nods all round: compliments from Taffin are a rarity and this almost sounded like a show of emotion.

Charlotte casts her eyes skywards. 'Get on with it, you're embarrassing the staff.'

'We've got two choices.' Taffin ambles amongst them. 'We can shut down and hide, or stay open and risk another visit. We know what these people are, so it has to be your decision. I'll go with whatever you decide.'

A brief exchange of glances. Ed says, 'Stay open.'

'Wait till you've got all the facts.' Taffin raises his hand, a rumble of steel on wood and all eyes fix on the revolver sliding to a halt on the table.

'Where did that come from?' Rick peers at the gun.

'The Tooth Fairy pulled it on me. I had to take it off him.'

'It was loaded –' Charlotte glances at Taffin – 'and he didn't mention it's been fired – the geezer tried to shoot him. This raises the stakes more than somewhat, wouldn't you say?'

Rick looks round the table. 'I agree with Ed – stay open.'

Taffin says nothing, aware of a stir in the room. After a while Kath says: 'This is a real threat, isn't it?' She turns the revolver round with a finger. 'This thing isn't a toy.'

Taffin nods quietly. 'You get the point.'

Julia says: 'The point is you could get killed messing with these people.'

'Nothing's worth that.' Charlotte folds her arms and looks at each of them in turn.

'So what are we going to do?'

'We could go to the police,' Kath offers, without conviction.

'And tell them what?' Charlotte shrugs and stares at Taffin. 'You can bet that gun ain't registered, it's been fired, and guess whose prints are all over it.'

Taffin strolls to the window and stares out. A murmured remark behind him.

'What was that, Ed?'

'I said, "Which way would your brother tell me to go?"'

Taffin turns to him. 'He'd tell you to run and hide.'

'Would he?'

'This time, he would. Your necks are already stuck out a mile because you're with me. It's personal and I can't let that put you guys at risk.'

'You said it was our decision. What happened to that?'

The room falls silent.

Finally, Julia says: 'This business belongs to all of us because we work here. Look at Ed and Rick: they've built it as much as you have. Me and Kath are involved in our own way, especially recently. This is what we do, and anyway, where would we hide?'

Sounds of agreement work their way round the table. Charlotte leans back and looks at Taffin, head on one side.

'I told you they're all barmy.'

'That's why they work here.' Taffin produces dark glasses and slips them on. 'So you've decided we stay open.'

'That's about the size of it.' Rick picks up the revolver and examines it. 'Oh, look – it's got my prints on it too.'

Taffin reaches out and Rick reluctantly hands the gun over.

'Good enough –' Taffin pockets the weapon – 'so it's business as usual.'

A general exhalation while this sinks in. Taffin continues: 'I said I'd respect your decision. Now here's mine. We could all do with a break, so it's time for our annual holiday. We take three weeks off. The four of you get to go anywhere you want, within reason. Let Charlotte know where, she'll book flights and hotels on the company so no one'll be out of pocket. Try to behave when you're in a foreign country.'

A profound silence settles in the room. After a while, Julia says: 'You sneaky bugger.'

'Watch your language, girl.' Charlotte attempts a parody of Taffin's voice. 'This is a family business.'

IT IS A REMARKABLY LARGE endowment for a small cottage hospital, but the management isn't about to quibble: it's at least enough to provide another Intensive Care Unit, or any other facility the administration might choose to specify.

The benefactor insists on anonymity but that's not unusual: philanthropy comes in various guises. In this case, some preferential treatment and a high degree of discretion are implicit. The wellbeing of a valuable medical facility trumps everything.

Doctor Clements knows he should be celebrating but finds it hard to dismiss the sense of something dark behind this windfall. It is not the first donation from the same source, he is sure of that. He is equally sure of its connection with two recent patients about whom he knows nothing, both of whom he has now lost.

The one named as McDermott never regained consciousness: he died three nights ago. There is a question mark over an alteration to the IC staff rotor that evening that resulted in the patient being left unattended for a brief but crucial period. There will, of course, be an enquiry, but Clemens has little faith in such procedures: the patient is dead; the hospital administration will make a show of tightening up the system; legal advisors will be briefed and in a few days the tragedy will have been eclipsed by more pressing matters.

The patient Clements knows as Doctor Morley – not a medical doctor, by his own admission – discharged himself yesterday, less than a day after an operation to reset his right arm at the elbow. He was full of pain-killers and hopefully will have access to more when the need arises, as it certainly will. Nursing staff reported he complained of claustrophobia, insisted on going for a walk in the hospital grounds and never came back. He left no personal effects behind and there are no contact details on record for Doctor Morley.

The fact that he and McDermott knew each other, or at least worked for the same organization, ought to be cause for concern; but no one seems inclined to initiate any kind of investigation or ask questions. Detective work holds no appeal for Clemens; the day-to-day deserves his undivided attention.

TWENTY-THREE

IN THREE WEEKS, THE WORLD HAS TURNED. Lasherham's collective consciousness has undergone a seismic shift from suspicion of all things political to a swell of unrestrained triumph over the forces of uncaring officialdom.

Erica Lyle writes:

STARTRACK DERAILED and goes on to relish the details:

Gordon Glennan MP, Chair of the Select Committee overseeing the StarTrack project, last night announced the 'indefinite suspension' of work on the High Speed Rail loop designed to connect the Capital with commercial centers in the West Country. In a statement to the press, Glennan said, 'This should not be seen as a decision to scrap the project for good, but the latest studies have cast doubts on its long-term viability and value for money. Cost projections are a factor and returns on such a major public investment have been called into question. In the light of these findings, the committee feels it would be irresponsible to proceed with the existing plan at this time without a lot more research at our disposal.

'HE DID IT,' crows Ivy Lewis. 'I told you he'd pull something out of the bag and here's the proof.' She brandishes the paper like a battleaxe.

Perry Butt swivels on his bar stool, eyebrows cocked. 'We've all read it, Ivy. It's gratifying to see common sense prevailing, but by what possible measure can you chalk this up to your Robin Hood?'

'You think Gordon Glennan just woke up one morning and said to himself: "Hmmm, what were we thinking – StarTrack's got to go"? Of course he didn't – someone persuaded him – no prizes for guessing who.'

'Ivy, my darling, this is mindless hero worship. By all means wallow in it if it makes you happy.'

'You miserable old killjoy,' Ivy nudges him, slopping his pink gin, 'they'll probably make another film about this, then you'll see.'

Mostyn frowns over his half of bitter. 'I must say, Ivy, given the enormity of any such task, I find the likelihood of Taffin's involvement in this outcome – joyful as it is – most unlikely.'

'You're all a bunch of old dead-beats,' Ivy tells them. 'Here's the best news any of us have heard in ages and all you can do is put a damper on everybody's enthusiasm. Let's have some credit where it's due.'

'What could that gentleman possibly have done to achieve this result?' Mostyn offers the question to those gathered round the bar.

'I'll tell you what I think he'd say to that –' Ivy's face sparkles – 'don't ask.'

'WHAT DO YOU LOOK LIKE?' Charlotte stares in disbelief at Rick Bishop as he follows Kath into the front office at *Muscle Motors*.

'Hasn't he got spindly legs?' Kath turns to present Rick for her examination. 'Wouldn't have guessed it, would you? Most people think he's all bike leathers from the waist down.'

Rick seems at ease in baggy shorts and a purple Hawaiian shirt with multi-coloured parrots on it.

'What's wrong with my legs?' he demands.

'They weren't that colour when you went away.' Charlotte walks round him with a critical eye. 'The sun must suit you.'

'*Obrigado*,' says Rick.

'That's his word of Portuguese, Kath remarks. 'He uses it all the time.'

Rick isn't going to let that stand. 'Tell her your bit of Portuguese then.'

'*Quanto e este?*' she announces. 'How much is this?'

'You found time for some shopping, then?'

'Not a lot. Rick discovered sunbathing and after that all we did was eat, drink and sleep. All I had to do was drag him out of bed to go to the beach.'

'*Obrigado*,' says Rick.

The door opens and Ed Pentecost walks in, still limping but without a stick.

'*Bom dia*,' he announces, with an expansive gesture.

'Can we make English the official language now?' Charlotte waves them all to chairs as Julia joins them, carrying Ed's walking stick. 'Has he been behaving, Jule?'

'Definitely not.'

'The four of you are revoltingly tanned.' Charlotte examines them each in turn. 'I'm dead jealous.'

'Where did you and Himself get to?' Kath asks.

'Not far. He found a great pub in this quaint little village and we spent a few days pigging out, wandering around, admiring the view and ignoring everybody. Quiet stuff. We got some help unloading the skip before we left. One end of the machine shop is wall to wall books.'

Ed looks up. 'You didn't have any unwanted visitors while we were gone?'

'Nothing. I can set your minds at rest on that score.'

'*Obrigado*,' says Rick.

Ed starts struggling to his feet. 'I haven't seen the Boss. Is he here?'

'Not right now.' Charlotte puts a restraining hand on his shoulder. 'He went off first thing this morning to meet someone. I didn't ask who.'

AT THIS PRECISE MOMENT the red Mustang is pulling into a parking space on the roof of a multi-story car park.

Taffin relaxes in the driving seat listening to his engine cooling, watching the approach of a figure in a charcoal suit, complete with crisp collar and tie.

Gordon Glennan lets himself into the car in response to Taffin's signal and closes the door.

'I could wish you hadn't come in quite such a conspicuous vehicle,' he begins. 'With any luck, nobody's looking, but you can never be sure. People know my face.'

'What am I here for, Gordon? Or do you want me to call you Minister, since we're on your patch?'

'My patch...' Glennan looks out across the spread of West London below them. 'You think I have any credibility left here – or anywhere, come to that?'

'I don't know, Gordon. Why ask me?' The ghost of a smile brushes the blank features. 'I'm a cheap thug.'

'You're the only person in this sorry affaire who's told me anything approaching the truth. You once said, maybe we could help each other. Now's the time.'

Taffin studies the profile of this man of politics, reading the tension.

Glennan continues: 'You've read the papers. StarTrack's dead. What do you suppose that means?'

'A lot of people are very happy, where I come from.'

'Sure. The unfeeling politician didn't get his way. People Power wins out. I'm guessing some of the locals will even credit you with a famous victory. Am I right?'

Taffin shrugs. 'That don't make any sense.'

'No it don't – doesn't – but that's how the world works sometimes.'

Taffin lets his hands wander over the Mustang's steering wheel. 'What am I here for, Gordon?'

'Well, that's the question, isn't it. I'm going to break Parliamentary protocol and tell you the truth. You don't mind that, do you?'

'I'm listening.'

'StarTrack was a myth from the beginning. It was never going to happen. The Select Committee was a charade.' Glennan glances sideways for a reaction; the broad features tell him nothing. He continues: 'You got it right. Property values dropped along all the proposed routes. They'll start recovering in due course but the damage is done.'

'Tell me about the damage.'

'A lot of prime development land has changed hands – and I'm partly responsible, God help me.'

'You work for the government, Gordon.'

'I wish...' Glennan waves a helpless hand. 'That's usually the excuse for any stroke a minister pulls. Policy – staying on message. I wish I could pin this on a government directive, but not this time.' He pauses, shaking his head. 'The government, from Number 10 downwards, wanted StarTrack from the beginning. My job was to make it work.'

'What went wrong?'

Glennan shifts uneasily in his seat. 'I must be insane, talking like this to you.'

Taffin gazes out across London. 'This meeting was your idea, Gordon. You can get up and leave any time.'

'I think you guessed it. I got suckered into another job as well. Not my idea, but irresistible once it was on the table. Very lucrative – beyond your wildest dreams. It meant abuse of privilege on an unthinkable scale but hell – I was tempted, I did the sums and caved in.' Glennan slaps both hands down on his knees, rocking forwards. 'If I could turn the clock back three years...'

Taffin lets him settle.

'They say no man can serve two masters.' Glennan fishes out a handkerchief, twists it in his fingers. 'I thought I understood the business world, but it's got levels I never imagined – like another planet. It was easy to get drawn in, but the pressure kept on building, and one day I had a moment of clarity and realised there was no way back.'

'Two masters –' the voice is a whisper with tone – 'who's the other one?'

'Just your average member of the Super-Rich with billions to play with. You meet these people when you move in government circles. This one's not high-profile so you probably wouldn't know his name.'

'Try me.'

'Frey-Morton. I doubt if it's the name he was born with. He made his money building shopping centers. Don't ask me where the original finance came from.'

'How did you meet him?'

'At a reception after some function – I don't remember what for. Someone introduced us. My wife was there, I remember. We talked for a while. Later he got in touch and things started picking up pace from then on.'

'Your wife.' A pair of eyebrows lifts above the dark glasses.

'My wife, Janice. You've met her.'

Taffin caresses the steering wheel again. 'Your wife doesn't like me, Gordon.'

'You seem to have touched a nerve.'

'It's my rustic charm.'

'She thinks you give me ideas. She's not wrong. These days, when I look at her I feel – I don't know what to call it – self-loathing, revulsion, jealousy...'

They both sit quietly for a while.

Taffin inclines his head. 'You know what's going on, don't you?'

Glennan puffs a bitter laugh. 'She let slip a casual remark in an unguarded moment. I said something about my pension. She told me pensions are poison because they create the illusion of a secure future. That didn't come from her. I heard it first from Frey-Morton, in exactly those words.'

Taffin becomes absorbed in the scenery for a moment,

then: 'Your billionaire friend used her to get to you. What's yours is hers – what's hers is his.'

'So it seems. I had my suspicions but I didn't see that coming. Her signature carries as much weight as mine and there isn't a damn thing I can do about it – not unless I want to be exposed as the prime mover in the fraud of the Century – and she'd do it.' Glennan wraps and unwraps the handkerchief round his hand. 'Now I feel personally threatened.'

'That's the only way, son. If it ain't personal, you ain't threatened.'

'I mean I have the sense of being in real danger – and I'm not talking about anything abstract like career and reputation – I mean physical danger. Can you understand that?'

'That's why I'm here, isn't it, Gordon?'

Glennan sighs, reaches for the door handle, lets it go again. 'I need some weight in my corner – someone who doesn't think along conventional lines. I'm a politician, not a...'

Taffin lets the silence draw out while Glennan fumbles for the word.

'Frey-Morton produced a gun at one of our meetings, like a grotesque conjuring trick. One minute it was there being tossed around like a toy, then it was gone. How am I supposed to deal with a maniac like that?

Taffin peers at a spot of dirt on the windscreen.

We've got more in common than you think.'

'You know the type, then?'

'Could be.'

'Could be...' Glennan echoes the phrase and falls silent for a moment. 'Frey-Morton knows your name.'

Glennan feels dark glasses turn on him. 'Go on.'

'He says you ruined his old boss – his business mentor – a man called Sprawley. Does that mean anything to you?'

'I remember the name. I never met the man.'

Glennan nods, distracted, and turns his attention to twisting the handkerchief again. 'You know the position I'm in. There's no one I can ask this so I'm asking you: what would you do?'

Taffin watches him passively.

'Seems to me you've got two choices.'

'I'm not going to like either of them, am I?'

'You got yourself into this, Gordon. Don't expect sympathy from me.'

'I accept that. What are my two choices?'

'You can behave like nothing's happened – bluff it out, cry foul when they point the finger, call it a smear campaign. You're a politician – act like one.'

'I might wind up with some remnant of a career, I suppose. What's the other choice?'

'Put your hands up to messing with the committee and take the bad guys down with you.'

Glennan bows his head. 'I'm not sure I would survive that. I think you'd soon be reading about a tragic accident. These are not people who play by normal rules.'

'Maybe the bad guys have got a weakness.' Taffin reaches for the ignition and the V8 rumbles into life. 'Be patient, maybe they'll show it.'

Gordon Glennan climbs out and pauses.

'I may have to call on you.'

Dark glasses incline slightly in acknowledgement.

Glennan closes the door and watches the Mustang

drift along the ranks of parked cars, listens to the engine muttering away down the spiral exit lane and feels, against all reason, that a weight has been lifted.

'I THOUGHT Mister Adams might want to see me before I go.' Silver stands by, cradling his plastered left arm while Dean Elton stows his cases in the back of the Porsche Cayenne Turbo S.

'He's a busy man.' Elton gives him a parody of a pleasant smile.

'Where are my instructions?'

'You worry too much. In a couple of hours you'll be in your private cabin on a luxury yacht, and then it's cruising all the way to the Caribbean.'

'I'd like to know what I'll be doing when I get there.'

'Destination, the British Virgin Isles – that ought to tell you something. A bit of business to sort out – child's play to a man of your abilities.'

'That doesn't tell me a lot. When I take on a job I expect to be prepared.'

'Very commendable.'

'So how about giving me a clue?'

'No point asking me, I'm just your driver today. You'll get your instructions on the voyage. The crew knows who you are.'

'I don't know them.'

'Don't worry about it, they're the soul of discretion.' Elton slams the tailgate shut and opens a back door for his passenger with heavy-handed ceremony.

Silver climbs in awkwardly and fumbles with the seat belt. 'I can't strap myself in.'

Elton leans across him to click the belt into place.

Silver winces. A glare of white teeth.

'You're a gentleman. I'll send you a postcard.'

'Mister Adams doesn't like postcards.'

'Fine, no postcard, let's just get moving.'

'Relax, you're going to a dream location in the height of luxury. The crew will spoil you to death.'

THE RED MUSTANG pulls up outside the front office at Muscle Motors. Taffin climbs out, stretches his limbs and wanders inside.

Charlotte looks up from her computer.

'You've got that look on your face, young man.'

'What look's that, girl?'

'The one that says you've worked something out.'

Taffin sits down, causing distress to a flimsy office chair. 'The troubles we've been having go back a long way.'

'Are you any closer to who it is?'

Taffin makes a wavering hand in reply.

Charlotte nods. 'Someone with a grudge from way back.'

'Looks like it.'

'That narrows the field down a bit.'

The same wavering hand, then: 'I had a job offer today.'

Charlotte swivels to face him. 'I hope you told them to stick it.'

'This was more of a request – flattering, in a way. It came from a Member of Parliament.'

'Gordon Glennan Emm Pee?'

'You've got it.'

'What does Mister Glennan want from my boy? Does

he know we've got his books? That could be a nice second career for you – librarian.'

The immobile features twitch imperceptibly. 'Mister Glennan don't feel safe.'

'I'm not surprised. Maybe he shouldn't put so many noses out of joint. So he wants you to babysit – don't the government supply bodyguards for the likes of him?'

'Not any more. He's been misbehaving. Fell in with the wrong crowd.'

'I see.' Charlotte swivels left and right, rhythmically. 'D'you mind if I ask you a personal question?'

'Ask away.'

'Are you still up to that kind of thing? I mean, don't get me wrong, but you don't like to move any faster than you have to.'

Taffin lifts a languid hand. 'I didn't promise anything. He just needs someone to call on when he can't sleep.'

Charlotte scrutinizes him. 'He's a politician, love – I'm surprised you're giving him the time of day.'

'I've met his wife. Anyone stuck with her deserves all the help they can get.'

TWENTY-FOUR

TO ANYONE in a contemplative frame of mind, the warm wind rippling the treetops along the valley could sound like a sigh of satisfaction. Lasherham is at ease. The spectre of trains shooting at bullet speed from a tunnel close to the village boundary has been set to rest. The rumour of a housing development on ten acres of land behind the old bookshop sounds civilized by comparison.

'It's all gone quiet,' Julia remarks.

The assembled company of *Muscle Motors* stands back to admire the freshly renovated Dodge Charger, now an immaculate example of its marque in deep bottle green with a broad central strip from nose to tail.

'I'll tell you why,' Ed Pentecost whacks his hands together in triumph, 'that's because this baby stands us in at ten grand and it's worth eighty to the right buyer – maybe more.'

'Think big.' Charlotte makes an upward gesture. 'You'll go a long way to find another one like this.'

'That's not what I meant.' Julia levels her camera and kneels for a low shot of the car. The shutter *clacks* several times as she moves round it. 'I mean everything's gone quiet.

I'm surprised McDermott hasn't been back looking for us. I'm not sorry – don't get me wrong – but we didn't part on good terms and he never struck me as the forgiving type. And what's happened to that scumbag with the teeth?'

'He won't be back.' Rick Bishop plants both thumbs in the belt of his jeans. 'Him and his gorillas got a good kicking last time they was here.'

Charlotte looks up, privately amused, and looks down again. 'Don't write them off. Like Jule says, they're not the forgiving type – none of them are.'

'Maybe they've given up.' Julia moves round the car with her long lens, looking for angles. 'What are the odds?'

'Fifty-fifty.' Taffin detaches himself from the office doorway where he was leaning and ambles over to stand by the Charger.

'You reckon?' Julia straightens up and turns to look at him.

'They should have come back the next day.' Taffin weighs an invisible balance in his hands. 'It's been weeks. Something ain't working out for them.'

Julia steps back to line up a long shot. 'I keep thinking they might turn up any time.'

'We've got better things to think about today.' Taffin stoops to examine the car's interior. 'This baby's got four hundred and forty cubic inches to play with. Right now we should be finding out if it goes as good as it looks. What do you reckon, Ed?'

Ed Pentecost runs a clean rag over the Charger's wing, takes a deep breath and climbs in. The engine turns, turns, barks and hammers the stillness flat.

'THE CHURCH, THE PUB, THE LIBRARY AND THE POST OFFICE –' Perry Butt executes a practiced 180 degree turn on his bar stool – 'take any one of those out of the equation and the village stops functioning.'

'And now they're talking about closing the Post Office.' Meg wipes the bar with unusual savagery, addressing the back of the old journalist's head. 'Don't you love the way THEY feel free to dispose of things WE can't do without?'

The old Post Office occupies the ground floor of a looming Victorian building on the corner of the High Street and Station Hill. The sorting office, on a separate lease, extends behind it. The main building is privately owned and the owner wants to sell.

'I wonder who THEY are this time.' Ivy Lewis has caught the scent of a new cause and is already winding herself up to marching pitch.

'No mystery there –' Ashley Gunn pulls up a bar stool and flicks an eyebrow at Meg, who pours his pint without a thought – 'the building belongs to Alice Becker. Her old man died, remember? You must know her, Ivy – she's Debi Royce's sister.'

'I hadn't put it together.' Ivy shakes her head at her own denseness. 'No wonder Debi's kept quiet about it; her own sister depriving us of the Post Office – that must be embarrassing.'

'I can't understand why she'd want to sell.' Meg attacks a particularly offensive beer stain. 'She's a nice lady – comes in here now and again.'

Ashley is ready with the answer: 'She's broke. John Becker was into the horses in a big way, but didn't bother to study form. He left her a pile of debt and the Post Office building.'

'I'm sorry about that,' Ivy makes a tragic face, 'but there's no way something we all value should depend on any one person. It's not right.'

'Aha!' Perry Butt raises a clenched fist high above his plume of hair. 'Your Marxist soul is showing through at last, Ivy – or do you lean towards Trotsky?'

'I don't know what you mean but there's nothing new about that. There ought to be some show of public support for the Post Office.'

'And there we have a predicament.' Perry Butt gazes critically at his pink gin. 'You can hardly engage your Robin Hood to use his persuasive skills on a friend's sister. I'm not suggesting Mister Taffin isn't up to the job, but it would hardly be... cricket.'

In the corner by the fireplace, a large, silent man in a black cheese-cutter cap sits over his beer.

So far, Dean Elton has hardly bothered to tune into the conversation at the bar – what he did pick up put him in mind of *The Archers* – but the name he has just heard would bring a cold smile to his face if he were inclined to let it show.

AT THREE O'CLOCK IN THE MORNING Alice Becker sits bolt upright in bed trying to make sense of the crash and gush of glass that brought her to the surface of sleep.

The silence sings, the echo playing in her mind as she tries to locate it. In the house or outside? No husband to reach for anymore: no John to protect her. Light on. Stay in the room; watch the door. First instinct, reach for family. She fumbles for her mobile, finds Debi's number and waits, breath held, picturing her sister groping for a bedside phone, wondering who this could be ringing in the small hours...

'Debi?'

'Alice? Do you know what time it is?'

'I've just heard a crash. It sounded like a bomb going off – I don't know...'

'A bomb? Have you called the police?'

'No, I'm calling you. I can't go downstairs Debs – there might be somebody there. I've always hated going downstairs by myself at night.'

Alice hears her sister conferring with her husband and feels the pang of isolation. Debs still has Rodney. Rodney, bald and jolly, someone to turn to in the night.

Debi's voice again: '*I'll* call them. Give me a moment to put some clothes on and we'll be right over.'

By three forty-five the house is a blaze of light. Alice, frail and trembling, has collapsed on the settee in the living room, Debi perched on the arm next to her. Rodney lets in two uniformed officers, one of whom wants to know exactly what Alice heard while the other takes a look around with a flashlight, inside and out.

'It wasn't a bomb.' PC James comes back inside, bringing with him a waft of cold night air. 'It's a good job you've got these internal wooden shutters, or you'd have had a lot more damage. What you heard was this –' he holds up a block of concrete – 'dirty great chunk of stuff hitting the window. It must have made a hell of a boom.'

Alice struggles to comprehend. 'Why would anybody do that?'

'That's what we're trying to find out.' PC Bailey, more sympathetic, squats down in front of Alice. 'Can you think of anybody who might want to scare you? Any neighbour disputes, for example?'

'No, the neighbours are fine. We're all on friendly terms.'

'Anyone further afield who might wish you harm?'

'I can't think...' Alice turns to her sister for comfort.

'Alright,' Bailey straightens up. 'Me and my colleague are going to have another look around outside, see if there's anything that might help trace a suspect. We'll get a statement from you when you're feeling up to it, and make a crime report.' He turns to Rodney. 'Can you and your wife keep this lady company for a while?'

'We're up now,' Rodney tells him. 'I hope you find something helpful. In the meantime I'll see where she keeps the kettle.'

At four o'clock, PC James is at the door again, speaking to Rodney.

'Can you check with the lady if that's her silver Peugeot 206 outside?'

Rodney confirms that the car belongs to Alice. James continues: 'You might not want to tell her this just yet, but someone's aerosoled BITCH across the nose and windscreen.'

'Bloody hell –' Rodney glances over his shoulder at the two women on the settee.

'My feelings exactly. That tells me this is more than a random act of vandalism. This is intimidation.' James turns off his flashlight. 'There's nothing more we can do for the moment. It's just the two of us covering the whole area tonight. It would be helpful if any of you could think who might have done this.

'THANKS DAVE, I OWE YOU ONE.' Erica Lyle has regular chats with her brother-in-law, Dave Walls at Stoleworth Central, ostensibly about family business. This morning it's been time well spent; she wrote her headline while he was still on the line.

WIDOW'S NIGHTMARE TERROR ORDEAL.

Several phone calls and a brief drive later, Erica has enough to flesh out the story:

> *Lasherham resident Mrs Alice Becker became the victim of a 'Terror' attack on her home in the small hours of this morning. 'It sounded like a bomb going off,' she told her sister, Mrs Debi Royce, who alerted local police. The explosion that woke Mrs Becker proved to be the sound of a block of concrete hitting a downstairs window, amplified by the vibration of internal wooden shutters. Further inspection revealed offensive language sprayed on the bodywork of her car at the same time, leading police to believe the attack was personally motivated. The investigation continues.*

'PC BAILEY TO SEE YOU.' Charlotte opens the living room door with Bailey looming behind her.

Taffin looks up and flicks the TV to mute, turning a re-run of *Top Gear* into a frantic mime. Bailey steps in and stands in front of him. He knows Taffin by reputation but has not met him before and there is a grain of curiosity in the back of his mind. Instinct says keep this firm and formal.

'We're making routine inquiries about an incident that took place last night, not far from here. Local knowledge is often the key to identifying a suspect, or suspects – so that's what I'm here for.'

'Sit down.' Taffin indicates a chair and the officer settles himself, being sure not to look comfortable.

Charlotte standing in the doorway, arms folded.

Taffin, at ease in his chair, turning a blank gaze on Bailey. 'Who have you spoken to?'

'This is my first call. Your name came up as someone who might be able to help.'

'Why us?' Charlotte's neutral voice.

'You're known as a man with roots in the area –' Bailey is careful to look Taffin in the eye – 'and your name comes up in connection with – how can I put it? – you have history in the debt collecting business.'

Taffin says nothing. Charlotte moves in to stand at the officer's shoulder. 'D'you hear that, young man? Your name's come up in connection with an *incident*?' Then, to Bailey, 'What sort of *incident* would that be?'

Bailey, not sure who he is talking to, switches between them. 'There was an attack last night on the home of a lady who lives by herself – a widow – and we can safely say it was personal.'

'You won't have heard.' Charlotte turns to Taffin. 'Debi Royce's sister had a rock through her window and someone wrote BITCH on her car in aerosol.'

Taffin nods, considering. 'That sounds personal.'

Bailey keeps his eyes on Taffin. 'Do you know of anyone locally who might have a grudge against the lady?'

'Say what you mean, son.'

Bailey, not used to being addressed as a kid by a member of the public, lets go of caution. 'I suppose you've reached the age when policemen look young.'

An easing of atmosphere in the room; Bailey is aware of

quiet amusement on both faces.

'Ask your question.' Taffin's eye strays back to the screen where an SUV is sliding backwards down a mountain track.

'I thought maybe you could help me with some names – the odd local misfit who wouldn't mind putting the wind up a widow, for a consideration.'

'My partner asked why you came to us.'

'Alright –' Bailey sits forward – 'I wanted to get an opinion from – to put it crudely – local muscle, which is the way people see you. You've got a reputation – they even made a movie about you.'

'Did they?'

'You know what I mean. A lot of people think it's based on you. Is it?'

'Have you seen it?'

'I haven't. I don't get to the movies a lot. I'm more interested in facts and I set great store by local knowledge. In this case, the victim owns the Lasherham Post Office and she's upset a lot of people by putting it up for sale. Her sister feels someone might be trying to frighten her out of selling it.'

'Unlikely.'

'You're known to be a public spirited man with a talent for making people see your point of view.'

Charlotte examines her fingernails.

'I'll tell you what,' Taffin turns an expressionless stare on the policeman, 'I'll ask the question for you. Did I aerosol a widow's car and chuck a rock through her window?'

'That's about it.' Bailey returns the gaze.

'That's more like it, son. I can't give you names but there's a pair of geezers been hanging around lately and a job like that wouldn't be beneath them. Definitely not gentlemen. Not local. If they did it, someone hired them.'

'That's a start.' Bailey stirs uneasily. 'So the question is, who around here might do the hiring. Any thoughts on that?'

'I'll give you a thought.' Charlotte taps Bailey on the shoulder. 'The geezers my ol' man's talking about have been giving us a hard time for a while. If they're the ones who did Alice's place, it's because someone reckoned your lot would think of us first.'

'Interesting.' Bailey considers for a moment. 'You're suggesting this might not have been about the Post Office at all.'

'Probably not.' Taffin's eye strays to the screen again.

'You're going further than that, though; you're implying the attack was staged to implicate you, personally, in something dirty.'

'Look at it this way,' Taffin gives Bailey his full attention, 'people who care about their Post Office ain't the type to hire some clown to put the frighteners on a respectable lady. People like that sign petitions and write to the paper. They don't pay for muscle and they know better than to come to me. Does that answer your question?'

DEBI ROYCE SPENT LAST NIGHT with her sister and stayed on this morning calming her down. They were on the second pot of tea when Ashley Gunn turned up uninvited to clear the shattered glass from the window frame, repair the woodwork, replace the pane and sand and repaint the damaged internal shutter.

'No problem,' he assured them, when Alice offered to

pay him. 'No reason why some idiot with a rock should cost you money.'

Alice has started thinking clearly enough to rifle through her husband's desk drawers in search of insurance documents, but Ashley's colourfully expressed views on the insurance industry have left her staring blankly at the wall.

'Strong language, Ashley.' Debi gives her sister the tenth hug of the day. 'Alice had a sheltered upbringing, in fact we both did.'

'True though, isn't it? Who needs the paperwork?'

Ashley clears up while the sisters inspect his handiwork and thank him profusely, brimming over with self-reproach for being shocked by his outburst. They've both heard language like that before, just not used with such graphic precision.

They watch Ashley stash his tools in his Jaguar and drive away, then turn to each other with the same question in mind. Alice gives it voice: 'How did he know exactly what needed doing?'

Debi shrugs. 'News travels fast.'

They turn to go into the house and pause at the sound of a large engine growling at the gate. Alice clings to her sister as a red Mustang noses into the drive and a lumbering figure in a dark suit climbs out.

'It's alright Alice, I know him.' Debi disentangles herself from her sister. 'Mister Taffin, isn't it?'

Taffin nods. 'Would this lady be Mrs Becker?'

'I'm Alice Becker.' Alice eyes him warily.

'I heard what happened. Has Mister Gunn been yet?'

'He's just left.'

'He's a fine craftsman. You couldn't do better.' Taffin

strolls to the Peugeot parked by the garage and runs a critical hand over the crude aerosol lettering. 'This needs attention.'

'I don't know how to get it off.'

'My lads do. They'll take it away for a couple of days and bring you a replacement car in the meantime.'

'That's very kind. Won't it be expensive?'

'They charge the same as Mister Gunn.'

'I don't know what to say.' Alice looks from Debi to Taffin and back again. 'Shouldn't I let the insurance know? My husband believed in insuring everything up to the hilt, but I don't know if we're covered for vandalism like this.'

'Maybe.' Taffin makes a dismissive hand gesture. 'It don't matter.'

'It's not just the damage...'

'You're wondering who did it.' the hint of a smile on the blank face.

'Of course I am, who wouldn't? I know people are upset about the Post Office and I've been worried sick about having to sell it but I haven't any choice. This is all horrible – and that crash in the middle of the night...'

She shrinks away as Taffin approaches but the huge hand on her arm is unexpectedly light. 'You can forget about who did it – those scumbags are my problem now.'

Debi Royce looks into her sister's face. 'That's what you wanted to hear, isn't it?'

Alice nods. 'I'm very grateful, Mister Taffin, but why should people I don't know help me?'

'You didn't ask for this.' Taffin glances at the Peugeot, hands in pockets. 'It needs sorting. Ashley Gunn's your man for fixing up buildings. My lads fix cars.'

Alice watches as he strolls to the Mustang.

'I've heard your name before, Mister Taffin. My sister thinks you might have had something to do with getting StarTrack stopped.'

Taffin slips dark glasses on and considers for a moment. 'Nothing to do with me.'

Debi Royce huffs a half laugh. 'The consensus says it had a lot to do with you.'

Alice feels her confidence returning. 'It sounds as if you're being too modest. What is your line of business?'

Taffin becomes absorbed in the scenery, hands behind his back. 'I maintain the balance.'

'You'll have to explain that for me.'

He turns to face her. 'In general, people want to be left in peace. It don't always work out.' He indicates the flowing scrawl of BITCH across the Peugeot.

Alice nods. 'Someone wanted to frighten me. The police were sympathetic but I don't suppose this is high on their list of priorities.'

'So the balance is wrong.' Taffin climbs into the mustang and rolls down the window. 'The law depends on respect. Take that away and it don't work.'

'That's very profound.' Alice raises an eyebrow in her sister's direction.

'Read Russell Chambers Gates, *"On Balance"*.' Taffin raises a slab of hand in salute, the Mustang gargles thoughtfully and is gone.

TWENTY-FIVE

FROM HIS LOFTY WINDOW Bob Sherman looks down at the yard and across to the open country beyond its gates.

Things have been quiet lately. There was an interlude of daily activity when some young people were staying in the caravan and the smell of bacon and coffee wafted up at first light. Then came a night of uproar and racing engines with dark figures darting here and there in the shadows. That was over quickly and the memory has receded; he couldn't say how long ago it was.

Young Doctor Morley doesn't come anymore and Bob is not sorry. He was what Uncle Austin used to call a *Wrong'un*. There was a large, monosyllabic man in a dark suit who came a couple of times, once with a girl; they did something to his telephone and fitted small cameras to the walls that gave him a vague sense of wellbeing. He remembers those visits with some pleasure. He remembers enjoying that man's company and would like to see him again. *Taffin* – memory serves up the name without effort – French sounding, probably Norman. The man was going to find something out for him: Mount Badon – Glastonbury Tor – that was it. Got his number somewhere on this strange phone they left with him. It's still plugged into a wall socket. Leave it there, they said, to keep it charged up.

Bob picks up the iPhone and peers at it, trying to make sense of its blankness. No buttons or switches on things anymore. He squeezes it with his thumb and the screen comes to life for no apparent reason. Colourful symbols: one actually says *Phone*. Memory coming back. The girl was patient with her tuition. Get adventurous and try it out...

Activity in the yard below diverts his attention. A huge articulated truck pulls in through the gates and stops under his window. Two, three men get out and open the back, which drops as a ramp.

He watches as they manhandle a sleek white car down to the ground and wheel it with difficulty towards the barn, out of his line of sight.

What was he doing? The phone. Let's see if it works.

AT THE SAME MOMENT a hundred miles away, Gordon Glennan is staring from his fourth floor apartment at the traffic snaking along Brompton Road.

Here is London, laid out before him, a sight he would have considered idyllic at one time; now a *tableau vivant* of infinite loneliness.

...That is the land of lost content,
I see it shining plain;
the happy highways where I went
and cannot come again.

When did he consign that to memory? Long ago, in more innocent times. He wanders through the empty rooms, stopping at another window, gazing out. Strange how easy it seemed to rise through the ranks and float on the surface, buoyed up by wealth, influence and plenty of time to enjoy it.

Now he daren't show his face outside for fear of – what? The press? Not yet: the StarTrack story is still easy enough to explain away, and will be until the truth comes out, as he is sure it must.

What then? The fear is real, a lead weight inside him. He has dipped his toe in a world of criminality that's going to drag him down while Frey-Morton walks away, tramples more lives, makes other fortunes.

Legal or lethal? You have to be involved to know the difference.

His own wife will bury him with a smile, with hardly a flicker behind those drooping eyelids. But is she any safer than he is? Glennan closes his eyes. Janice lives on cold confidence – and by Frey-Morton's code, loose talk kills.

And there's the root of it. Forget the press; never mind the disgrace; a deadly threat stalks him now and there's no safety in this apartment or out on the street.

Sounds in the hallway. Something happening in the next apartment or someone at his door? The walls seem to be closing in and there's no time for caution. He grabs his coat and marches out, not looking to right or left.

The mirror in the lift shows the face of a hunted man, collar turned up.

Through the foyer: did two seated figures rise to their feet as he passed by?

Out to the seething street with a backward glance – not sure if he was followed. A taxi; where's a taxi when you need one? Where to anyway? Not thinking straight. A member of HM Government not thinking straight. Arm raised by tribal instinct and a taxi pulls up, disgorging an elderly couple who fumble for change while he stands close and leaps in as soon as they move from the door, leaving them wondering if that heavy-breathing pushy bastard was What's-his-name, the Minister of... whatever.

The driver leaning an ear for instructions. Name a place, anywhere.

'Lancaster Hotel.'

A man's face stooping to look in at him as the taxi pulls away. Was that face in the foyer as he went through?

'Lancaster Hotel it is...' The driver has recognized him and wants to talk. 'So you're not going to waste billions on that StarTrack, then? Thought better of it?'

Glennan makes vague acknowledgement and pulls out his mobile in self-defense. And it comes to him, like the slap of a distant shock-front, that there is no one who would want to hear from him.

'WAVE TO THE CAMERA, MISTER SHERMAN, we can see you.' Kath watches her screen as the old man turns on unsteady legs until he is looking right at her.

'You can really see me?' Bob Sherman waves the iPhone at her and advances with a benign smile. 'This gadgetry is truly extraordinary.'

'What can we do for you, Mister Sherman? Is everything alright?'

'Yes, yes, never better. I thought it might be worth telling you about what's happening here. There hasn't been much going on for a while, in fact that's something of an understatement, it's been wonderfully peaceful.'

'I'm happy to hear it.' Kath glances at Charlotte, who

has moved up to look over her shoulder. 'What's happening now?'

'Some people have turned up in a large lorry that contained a white motor car. I couldn't really describe it but I suppose it's another of those rare and valuable machines you and your friends were working on. They've just wheeled it into the barn.'

'Are the people still there? Could you describe any of them?'

'Three chaps in overalls. I can't see their faces because I'm looking down on them. I think they're leaving now – do you want me to check?' He turns and shuffles to the window. 'Yes, the lorry is driving away. One of the fellows has just closed the gate, and they're off. It's all peace and quiet again.'

Charlotte takes over from Kath. 'Thank you for letting us know, Mister Sherman. Are you sure they've all gone?'

'I can't see anybody. I must say, I'm quite proud of myself for getting this phone to work – and you can really see what I'm doing, can you?' Bob makes an attempt at a dance step, turning slowly.'

'We're following every step. That was very elegant.'

'Thank you. I used to be rather good.'

'You haven't lost it. Is there anything else we can do for you?'

'I'll be happy to see any of you when you're passing this way.'

'We will be very soon, Mister Sherman.'

'Bob – call me Bob.'

'Thank you Bob. One or other of us will be with you before you know it.' Charlotte turns to Kath. 'Where's Himself gone – he'll definitely want to know about this.'

Kath looks out of the window. 'The Mustang's still here so he must be around somewhere.'

'No – he's off again.' Charlotte has caught a glimpse of the Jeep heading away along the lane. 'Why can't the bugger ever tell me where he's going?'

TAFFIN WALKS INTO THE LOW-LIT BAR at the Lancaster Hotel and pauses. The place is practically empty but for a bow-tied barman and a scattering of transitory guests; no regulars in a bar like this.

Gordon Glennan, hiding in a corner behind a copy of the *FT*, cockles a page to check out the new arrival's silhouette: a slab of dark suit and that characteristic slightly bow-legged walk. A sigh of relief.

A moment later Taffin is sitting beside him without apparently having covered the distance.

Glennan peers round his paper. 'You move fast for a heavyweight.'

'You called me. You sounded desperate.'

'I didn't know who else to contact.'

'I'll ask the same question as last time we met –' Taffin speaks without looking at him – 'what am I here for?'

'I'm being followed.'

'What d'you want me to do about it?'

'I don't know. I'm being watched. I can feel it.'

'Recognise anyone in here?'

'I don't think so. I came in a cab and I didn't see anyone follow me in.'

'So whoever it is, you've lost them.'

'It looks like it, for the moment – but I can't stay here all day. I'm expected to show my face in various places, but

I don't feel secure enough to do that.' He peers gloomily around the room. 'I thought you might be able to come up with an idea.'

'Time we was going.' Taffin hands him a bunch of keys. 'Get down to the car park. Look for a grey Jeep – the number's with the keys – get in and wait for me. Take your time. Move slowly.'

'What are you going to do?'

'Just do as I say, Minister.'

Taffin watches while Glennan rises to his feet, folds his paper and walks too quickly to the door, stumbling on the shallow stairs on his way out.

When he is out of sight, Taffin orders a beer at the bar and allows himself time to enjoy it. When he is sure no one followed Glennan out, he pays and leaves.

The Jeep is two levels down and he takes his time reaching it. Glennan is sitting in the back, shielded by his paper, and starts visibly as Taffin gets in.

'Was I followed?'

'Only by me.'

'You probably think I'm paranoid.' Glennan now feels secure enough to let irritability show. 'There was definitely someone around all the time I was at the apartment. No doubt about that – I could practically hear them breathing through the door at one stage, you know what I mean? Nothing you could put a finger on but you can sense when someone's paying close attention. I felt unsettled all the time I was there.'

'You're used to having the press underfoot. No one's interested now and you can't get used to it.'

'Alright, you've had a wasted journey. I apologise.'

Glennan folds the paper and shoots Taffin a bleak look. 'Just take me back to Knightsbridge and I'll lie up in the apartment in the hope that eventually I'll feel safe enough to show my face in public.'

Taffin turns to face him, one arm along the back of the passenger seat. 'I don't know if you're paranoid, Gordon, but you're not safe. You need to disappear for a while.'

'How can I disappear? I've got nowhere to go.'

'That's why you called me. Sit back, read your paper and don't ask questions.'

THREE MEN STAND AT THE RAIL watching the yacht's wake cut a milky trail on the lead-grey swell of the Atlantic.

'Looks like we're turning.' Silver has got used to shouting over the rush and hiss of the ocean; he steadies himself against the steady rise and fall, still inclined to hang on to anything solid in spite of his painful right arm.

'It's necessary.' The crew member to his left speaks English with an accent Silver can't identify. The man at his right shoulder hardly speaks at all.

The wake, usually straight as an iron track, has described half a circle. The darkening eastern sky that should be behind them is now to their right.

'I don't pretend to be a navigator –' Silver sets his glistening teeth against the wind as the ocean sucks and heaves – 'but we seem to be heading back the way we came. Have we got a problem?'

'We make full circle. It's necessary.'

'Why?'

'Don't worry about it.'

'I'll tell you what worries me –' Silver is serious now –

'we'll be in the Virgin Isles any day now I and I still haven't been briefed on what I'll be doing when we get there.'

'Plenty of time.'

'For you, maybe. I still don't know what I'm expected to do and I need to think about it, so chop chop – let's get on with it.' Silver glances at the wake again. 'And you still haven't explained why we're going in a circle.'

'It's routine – safety practice.'

'I don't get it.' Silver holds tight to the rail. 'What's going round in circles got to do with safety?'

'When there's a man overboard we make a circle to look for him and maybe rescue him if he's lucky. It's correct safety procedure. Regular practice is important.'

'I don't see that going round in circles takes any practice – give me the wheel and I could do it. This is a fucking waste of time – there's no man overboard and if there was, they wouldn't stand a cat in hell's chance in the dark – so straighten this thing out and get me to where we're going.'

'Be patient one minute more.'

'Don't tell me to be patient, pal. I'm the VIP on this trip, and I'd be obliged if you'd remember it.'

'This is true.' The man to Silver's left nods briefly to the man on his right.

Silver aware of a silent exchange.

A hard hand under each armpit heaving him up – feet clear of the deck.

A moment's realization – teeth barred, eyes wide, a half gasp snatched in the air, hands spread to claw the wind, body turning over one last time, impact on water like a sheet of steel. All sense frozen.

THE MAP, printed on carpet tiles, takes up most of the floor space in this otherwise featureless hotel room.

Daniel Frey-Morton paces along two sides of it and walks to the middle.

'Ten by ten. Do you know what you're looking at?'

'I've never seen a map you can walk on. That's Stoleworth behind you, isn't it? And you're standing on Lasherham.' Janice Glennan steps carefully across the detailed landscape. 'I'm standing... in a field five or six miles away.'

'Rather more, in a Westerly direction. Mostly open country at the moment. A new metropolis by the time we've finished.'

'But Daniel, this is huge. It's unthinkable.'

'To some people.'

'How do you expect to develop an area this size?'

'A step at a time –' Frey-Morton paces the floor again – 'with patience, purpose and clear thinking. Now perhaps you begin to realise what real money is for.'

'This carpeting can't have been cheap.'

Frey-Morton turns a cold stare on her. 'Understand, we're talking about money as a simple tool. In the right hands it becomes limitless. It redefines ownership, thus reserving control for visionaries. Not one person in ten million has any grasp of that.'

'You want your own town.'

'Towns become cities – and I've no intention of living in it.'

'A soulless new town, then.'

'I imagine it will appeal to a high-energy market – entrepreneurial people, apartment-dwellers who prefer to base themselves in a town that never sleeps with every amenity close at hand – shopping malls, fitness centers, gaming and gambling facilities, hotel and conference complex –' Frey-Morton is pacing now, head down – 'and a prime attraction to put the scheme on the map – the most complete classic motor museum in the country. Planning will require a concession to what they call *affordable housing*, but that will add an interesting dynamic.'

'Well, what can I say?' Janice looks for somewhere to sit; the furniture has all been pushed against the walls. 'Most people would call this insanity.'

'Your husband would, I'm sure. He reached his limits long ago. What about you?'

'Am I part of this?'

'You will be instrumental. Think of yourself as venture capital. Beyond that, it depends how you handle yourself.'

'I've already handled my husband. I hope you're suitably impressed.'

'You enjoyed it. He's a broken man now. That's life – he's served his purpose.'

'He has the Knightsbridge apartment at his disposal. He'll be alright.'

'If he survives. Men in public life are a fragile species. As for you, you're overdressed; and I need the touch of silk. You must choose which bit of the county you want to fuck over.'

'WHERE TO, MISTER MORTON?' Dean Elton takes his seat behind the wheel and inclines an ear for instructions.

'Portsmouth. I shall be at sea for a while. In the meantime I need you to do some tidying up.'

'Just say the word, Mister Morton.'

'I understand Gordon Glennan has gone missing.

You know him by sight. Find him, as a matter of urgency, whatever it takes.'

'Right, Mister Morton.'

'I have no use for amateurs. The men who were watching him clearly didn't take their work seriously enough. You'll liaise with them, use them as you see fit.'

'Understood.'

'Gordon Glennan is a weak man with the capacity to do a lot of damage. His political career is finished and he lacks the moral fiber to cope with his inevitable public disgrace. I do not expect him to survive.'

'Elton nods slowly. 'I understand.'

'His wife may be useful in locating him but if she can't help, feel free to think of her as collateral damage.'

'Understood.'

'Now we come to Mister Taffin. I don't believe you've met him yet.'

'That's correct.'

'It's time he was out of the way.'

'Whatever it takes, Mister Morton?'

'An elegant outcome would be preferable. Right now he's looking for a rare car – a Cord. He will soon know where to find it and when he does he'll want to drive it himself. I don't expect him to get far. Look in the glove-box beside you – what do you see?'

Elton leans to flip open the glove-box, takes out a mobile phone and holds it up. 'A white smart phone.'

'A white smart phone.' Frey-Morton looks away. 'It has the Cord's number. Text 812 and the driver will get the surprise of his life.'

'Understood.' Elton takes a moment to prioritize.

'What will you expect of me after that?'

'I will expect you to take early retirement.'

Elton says nothing for a moment, then risks a look over his shoulder at his boss. 'I'll need to work, Mister Morton. I'm not a wealthy man.'

'You will be. A package has been put in place so you will never have to work again.'

A taut silence while Elton casts around for words, then: 'I don't know what to say, Mister Morton. That's more than I could ever have asked for.'

'You didn't ask. You will earn it. There are conditions.'

'Of course, Mister Morton. May I say, it's a privilege...'

'If I should require your services in the future I'll expect you to respond immediately. Be assured I will always know where to find you. That aside, your time will be your own to enjoy – with unlimited resources. I take it you accept.'

'Of course, Mister Morton.'

'Drive on.'

TWENTY-SIX

THE CORD 812 was built in 1937 and was by far the most eye-catching car of the year. That, at least, was the opinion of the New York dealer who bought this particular one for himself: a sedan, finished in cream. The 1936 Cord 810 had caused enough stir, but this new one was sleek, mean and supercharged, with a pair of chrome external exhaust pipes on each side to show where that extra grunt was coming from.

Highly desirable, this cream Cord sedan: a personal statement about the man who drove it. But, being in the automotive business, the first owner soon traded it in for something newer and less troublesome.

The second owner was a Major in the US Army who pulled strings and took his Cord to war with him. In 1945 it was stolen while parked for the night in a small Bavarian town, and the Major was repatriated before he had time to look for it.

In 1956 the cream Cord, now sadly discoloured, was noticed in a side street in Innsbruck in the Austrian Tyrol. Locals said it had been there for some time and no one remembered how it got there, so an enterprising enthusiast called Kurt Stark took it on and restored it to running order. The car looked and sounded rough but it ran well enough, even though no one quite knew what to call it.

Eventually bureaucracy caught up with Kurt and required him to register the car that had long since become his property by default, and was therefore his responsibility. There was no original paperwork with it and the system wasn't equipped to recognize a rare make, so the cream Cord 812, now dull grey, was registered as a Volkswagen.

Its fortunes then took a new turn. Kurt had his car shipped to London, where he had been advised the market for exotic vehicles was picking up and he might be able to get a good price for it. The Cord arrived at the London Docks with a consignment of new Volkswagens, where a young man, also new to the country, had a job washing the cars as they came off the boat.

When Kurt turned up to collect his car, this young man was there to meet him and, by chance, was able to recommend a place for him to stay while he was trying to turn his asset into cash.

Kurt had been ill advised: the Cord didn't sell and eventually he was forced to hand it over as part payment for back rent to a London entrepreneur and property owner named Arch Sprawley.

Time went by. The Cord was put up on blocks and was still listed among Sprawley's effects when he died. It was bequeathed in his will to the young man who had first recognized it as something special while he was washing it at the docks.

The young man was Sprawley's protégée, 'the son he never had', a natural speculator with all the flare and dynamism you could wish for in a successor.

His name was Daniel Frey-Morton.

BOB SHERMAN is deep in the Dark Ages, reading and rereading the reference to the Arthurian legend in Churchill's *History of the English Speaking Peoples*.

For the second time in as many days he is disturbed by the sound of an engine under his window.

Yesterday he saw some men in overalls delivering a long, curvaceous car to the barn. This was of no interest to him. A rare Cord 812 was just another shape on wheels and he had forgotten about it before the delivery truck was out of sight.

Even so, visits are not an everyday occurrence. He lays Churchill aside, eases himself out of his chair and takes his time walking to the window.

A dark grey Jeep is parked in the yard. Bob opens his window and leans out. No sign of activity. It occurs to him that perhaps young Doctor Morley has come back to plague him, but dismisses the thought and returns to the sanctity of his chair, his book, and a world that doesn't keep demanding his physical attention.

Down in the yard, Gordon Glennan strains his neck to look up from the Jeep. 'Are you going to tell me what the fuck we're doing here? There was someone looking out of that top window a moment ago.'

'Don't worry about it.' Taffin opens the rear door to let him out. 'You wanted somewhere to disappear. We've arrived.'

'This feels uncomfortably like abduction.' Glennan stretches his legs and looks around. 'I'm putting my trust in you, Taffin. I hope you're not going to abandon me in the middle of nowhere. I've got nothing but the clothes I'm standing up in and no toothbrush.'

'We'll get you some stuff. In the meantime, I'll make you comfortable, show you the security measures and introduce you to the occupant. You'll be fine.'

Taffin shows him to a flaking, ill-fitting wooden door, lets him in with a key and leads him up several flights of creaking stairs.

'This doesn't look secure to me.' Glennan peers grimly to right and left on each corridor as they climb. 'Look at the state of these walls. The place ought to be condemned.'

'Plenty of life in it yet.' They reach the top floor and Taffin uses a keypad to open the attic apartment.

Bob Sherman looks up from his book, takes a moment to focus and recognizes the broad figure in the dark suit.

'Well, blow me down – Mister... Taffin. What a pleasure to see you. I spoke to your good lady just the other day. She promised me one of you would be dropping by, but I didn't expect you to appear so promptly.'

'Good to see you, Mister Sherman.' Taffin stoops to offer the old man his hand.

'I haven't met your companion.' Bob leans to look at Glennan, who is standing in the doorway. 'Is he another of your telephone people? Does he play chess?'

'He's Gordon.' Taffin steps aside to let the two shake hands. 'He needs somewhere to stay for a few days.'

'I haven't much to offer.' Bob indicates the confined space with a limp hand. 'There are plenty of rooms downstairs; I recommend the one that opens out onto a flat roof. At one time I thought of turning it into a kind of roof garden, but never got round to it. He's welcome to that.'

'It'll do.'

'While I think of it, there was something you were going to look into for me – Glastonbury, or Mount Badon, as I prefer to think of it – the scene of Arthur's last great battle against the invading hoards.'

Taffin resists a smile. 'I'll see to it now.' He thumbs his phone, waits a moment and Kath's face appears. 'A job for you, Kath.'

'Where are you?' Kath stares at him from the screen. 'Charlotte says you took off like a bat out of hell and didn't tell her where you were going.'

'Tell her she worries too much. Ever been to Glastonbury?'

'The rock festival? I went one year.'

'Describe it.' Taffin holds the phone where Bob Sherman can see the screen.

'Pandemonium,' Kath tells him. 'Heavy metal, mud, writhing bodies everywhere.'

'Good enough. I'll be back tonight.' Taffin turns the phone off and looks down at the old man. 'Sounds like a great battle to me.'

Bob stares at him, open mouthed. 'I say, that girl is remarkable. Where does she get her information?'

'She works hard.'

'D'you know,' Bob rises unsteadily to his feet, 'I believe I can accept that as confirmation. Glastonbury and Mount Badon are one and the same place. I'm very much in your debt.'

'My pleasure.' Taffin turns to Glennan who has been standing by without a word. 'Your turn, Gordon. Time to take a look at where you're staying. It ain't the Ritz but It'll do for a few days.'

'Very kind,' Glennan nods. 'And yes, I play chess.'

THE ROOM BELOW BOB'S ATTIC is a step beyond shabby and one wall shows signs of damp, but there's a fat mattress on the iron bedstead, a table and chair in the corner and a single ceiling light.

A French door opens onto a flat roof, which is at least twice the area of the room. Glennan steps out, grateful for the extra space; somewhere to spend time, breathe fresh air and appreciate the landscape.

This building is hard to date. Around 1800, he guesses, or maybe earlier, but extensions have been added over the years and the roof terrace he is standing on is clearly one of them.

Taffin said this place was secure and Glennan is inclined to believe him. Creature comforts must take second place for now; at least he won't spook here the way he did in the Knightsbridge apartment – unless his nerves are totally shot to pieces. In which case no amount of protection will do any good.

Down in the yard, Taffin's Jeep describes a U-turn and heads out through the gate. Glennan watches until it is out of sight, then goes inside, wondering if Bob Sherman knows or cares that a Minister of the Crown is staying under his roof. Perhaps the old man can at least lend him something to read. Or offer him a game of chess.

MICHAEL WYATT wasn't planning to work today and had no intention of getting up to answer the door until a splintering crash told him someone had kicked it in.

A moment for his head to clear. Loud noises are commonplace in this run-down apartment block. First thought, Silver has come back with new instructions. That would make sense; Silver rented this apartment as a base and deserves a bollocking for keeping them hanging around with back pay owing.

Silence, then someone whistling patiently outside.

Wyatt swinging his legs off the bed, blundering out to the hallway with all the fury of a man disturbed, face ghastly with rage. 'Who the fuck are you?'

'Get dressed.' The man in the black cheese-cutter cap seems unconcerned. Dean Elton has dealt with the likes of Wyatt many times and is more than happy to show him how if need be.

Wyatt takes a moment to size up the odds. Heavy frame, evenly distributed, arms folded. He decides to move slowly. 'Who do you think you're talking to, pal? I'm under contract – not available... get it?'

Greg Dupree, roused by the disturbance, appears from another room. 'Who's making all the fucking row?'

'You too –' Elton shifts his gaze to Dupree – 'get dressed and step on it.'

'Go fuck yourself, you snotty shite.' Dupree takes a step forward. 'We don't work for you.'

'Yes, you do.'

'I don't think so.' Dupree's beefy face glows with the prospect of taking this man apart.

'You work for Mister Adams.'

A pause hangs in the air.

Wyatt speaks. 'You know Mister Adams?'

'I work for him – you work for me.'

'We've got a contract with Silver.'

'He's retired.' Elton studies their faces: typical failed military. 'Don't look at each other, look at me.'

'Who the fuck *are* you?' Dupree again, moving closer.

'I told you to get dressed. Prove to me you're not the slow-witted moron you look and jump to it.'

Dupree is quick. Hammer blow to the body with locked fists, left and right elbows to the jaw and knee to the groin.

None of it connects.

Elton stands back to look at him, one hand flashes and Dupree slams back against the wall, senseless before he hits the ground.

Elton turns to Wyatt.

'Mister Adams isn't happy with you.'

Wyatt stands very still. 'We don't know Mister Adams – never met the man.'

'You know who Mister Gordon Glennan is, don't you.'

'Sure – we've got him under observation.' Wyatt shifts his weight, warily.

'You lost him.'

'No problem. We know where he lives.'

'Really?' Elton takes a leisurely step forward. 'So why aren't you on his doorstep?'

'Taking a break.' Wyatt squares up, ready to react. 'Glennan's got a place in Knightsbridge. We can find him any time.'

'So where is he now?'

'Right now? I couldn't tell you.'

'That's disappointing. Mister Glennan is missing. No sign of him anywhere. That's not good; Mister Adams likes to know where he is at all times.'

'We're on it.' Wyatt glances at the silent form on the floor.

'You're on it.' Elton stoops, places a hand on Dupree's neck for a moment. 'This one's through. Put him in his room and shut the door.

This time Wyatt doesn't hesitate. It takes him a few moments to haul Dupree's inert weight down the corridor and deposit it on the bed.

The final effort of lifting it causes an unnatural exhalation of breath and the truth hits Wyatt like an electric shock: this man will soon be cold.

'You got a problem with that?' Elton watches him from the door.

Wyatt shrugs, trying to find somewhere to look.

'Close, were you?' Elton's cold eye.

'I hardly knew him.'

'No memories then – that's a healthy attitude. We can't use amateurs.'

Wyatt straightens up. 'What now?'

'You understand what just happened?'

'Yes.'

'And you know what that means as far as you're concerned.'

'I didn't see a thing.'

'I think you did.'

'Trust me – I don't know what happened.'

'I'll tell you what happened. This fellow had a fatal accident and you were there. It doesn't look good.'

'I didn't touch him.'

'That's not the way I remember it. But then, no one's ever going to ask me. I'm not here.'

Wyatt staring wide-eyed at nothing, finally focusing on the man in the black cap.

'Relax.' Elton folds his arms. 'We're going to discuss damage limitation.'

'What does that mean?'

'It means you doing everything it takes to find the missing Minister, Gordon Glennan.'

'I can do that.'

'Possibly, but we won't leave the planning to you. Tactical sense is called for and I think your talents are more basic.'

'What do you want me to do?'

'Exactly what I say without question. You and your late colleague lost track of Mister Glennan's movements.'

'He's got to be in his apartment...'

'Forget it. It's empty.'

'So where do we start?'

'He could be anywhere, so we won't waste energy looking for him. Instead, we get smart. We flush him out.'

'How?'

'By you doing what I tell you. I'll say it one more time: get dressed.'

TWENTY-SEVEN

ALICE BECKER'S PEUGEOT was in her drive when she woke up this morning and she immediately called her sister over to look.

'That's an amazing job.' Debi Royce peers at the paintwork. 'It looks like it did when you first had it.'

'You know what bothers me?' Alice is still shaky from the night she was vandalized. 'I didn't hear them deliver it.'

'They obviously didn't want to disturb you.' Debi steers her into the house. 'Reasons to be thankful – you're not a BITCH anymore. I got a paper on the way over. That's my contribution – you can make us breakfast.'

When tea and toast are on the table, Debi glances at the paper, pauses and looks again.

AT THE SAME TIME, a couple of miles away, Taffin lowers himself face first on to Tessa's massage table, dismisses Gordon Glennan from his mind for the moment and resigns himself to the magic hands. First contact; always sensational.

'Haven't seen you for a while,' Tessa addresses his shoulders. 'Been busy?'

A non-committal grunt from the buried face, which she takes as affirmative.

'My brother enjoyed the bit of work he did for you. I've never seen him so animated.' Tessa digs in with some force. 'Knotted muscles. What have you been doing?'

Taffin says, 'Keeping out of trouble', but the sound comes out as a muffled blur. This is fine with Tessa, who has learnt from years of experience to decipher the unique language of the massage table.

A sound from the adjoining room. Pierre has arrived to read the paper and make himself a bacon sandwich from her fridge. She hears him pause, hears the rustle of newspaper, hears him mutter 'Bloody hell', and makes a conscious decision not to let him interrupt her.

ASHLEY GUNN has made an early start this morning. A few grace notes need to be added to his barn conversion before he puts it on the market. Taffin and Charlotte left it in fair condition after spending time there, but a restored property needs to look and feel fresh.

On the drive up to the site he stops at the village shop for an egg sandwich and picks up a paper as an afterthought.

Once in the barn, he appreciates the smell of cedar on some subconscious level, but what he wants is coffee.

While the kettle is boiling he picks up the paper and turns instinctively to the property section, ignoring the front page. No tempting properties catch his eye and he tosses the paper aside, glances at the front page, pauses to look again and slowly takes a seat to read, coffee forgotten.

IN THE WHITE LION, Meg makes preparations for opening time. When the papers arrive she places them on the usual table and carries on putting the place in order.

The regulars don't normally start turning up until eleven. Dan the chef arrives and goes to work in the kitchen. She hears him singing to himself as the pans begin to clatter.

Meg straightens the pile of papers, glances at the front page and looks again. Her daily routine is set, solid, automatic and is seldom, if ever, interrupted. Today she hesitates, takes a copy over to the bar and begins wiping the surface with a cloth as she reads. Her hand moves slower as the news sinks in. She purses her lips and looks round the empty bar, wishing there was somebody to share this with.

It won't be long now. People are going to want to discuss today's main story. The usual faces will be in early and there can only be one topic of conversation.

RICK BISHOP parks his Fireblade outside *Muscle Motors*. Ed dismounts from the pillion and the two of them go into the office. The TV is on in the background. Charlotte is on her feet.

'Have you seen the news?'

Two blank looks and matching shrugs.

'Himself's getting a massage. One of you get round to Tessa's place – he'll never pick up while he's on that couch.'

'What did we miss?'

In reply, Charlotte waves them to silence and points to the screen.

'I'll tell him.' Rick is out of the door, heading for the Fireblade.

Charlotte is on the phone again dialing Tessa Van Hagen's number for the third time.

IN TESSA'S KITCHEN, Pierre gives the phone an evil look. His sister never answer's while she's working; she insists it's not fair to clients. He dislikes telephones and would never normally presume, but this is the third time it's rung so he puts his bacon sandwich aside and gets up to answer it.

'Hello?'

'Is that Pierre?' Charlotte's voice, not to be dismissed. 'Put Taffin on. He needs to get over here fast.'

'He's not going to like it. And my sister will kill me. She's very strict about not being disturbed.'

'Just do it.'

Pierre winces at the tone, and again at the roar of a motorcycle outside.

'On your head be it.' Pierre tiptoes to the treatment room, taps on the door and delivers the message.

A moment later, Taffin, clad in a towel, is in the kitchen with the phone to his ear. He is about to say 'What's up' when his eye falls on the newspaper on the table.

MINISTER'S WIFE FOUND DEAD IN FAM-ILY HOME.

Janice Glennan, wife of Transport Minister Gordon Glennan, was found dead at the couple's country home yesterday morning following an anonymous call to local police.

Cause of death has not been established but Mrs Glennan is thought to have fallen down a steep flight of stairs, tragically resulting in a broken neck. There is no clue to the identity of the anonymous caller, who could prove key to the investigation.

Police are anxious to talk to Mrs Glennan's husband, Gordon Glennan, who has not been seen publicly, in his constituency or in Westminster, for over a week. The investigation continues…

ALL THE NATIONALS are running the story and Erica Lyle is hungry for details. 'What can you tell me, Dave?'

'Not a lot at the moment.' Sergeant Dave Walls is in no position to talk to his sister-in-law. 'This is too big. Sorry Sis, I can't comment.'

'Can you confirm cause of death?'

'I can't speculate. You'll have to wait for the post mortem result.'

'Come on Dave, the public's got a right to know. How long had she been dead when she was found?'

'Time of death, somewhere between midnight and six yesterday morning but that's not official and you didn't get it from me – don't push it, Sis.'

Moments later, Erica is in her car heading for Stoleworth Central. A high profile death on her patch is a major career opportunity and she resents having to jostle with the competition at the press briefing – but that's how it is. A *Sun* reporter beats her to the question: 'Is foul play suspected?' – and she keeps moving to catch the eye of DI Robertson, who has taken charge.

Robertson is an old hand, not easily drawn. 'At the moment we have no reason to treat this as anything other than a tragic accident. We're waiting for forensic results and the post mortem will no doubt tell us more.'

'Any leads on the anonymous caller?'

'The call was made from a mobile, pay-as-you-go – untraceable. We're hoping the caller will reveal him or herself in some other way. Yes...?'

Erica finally gets above the noise level. 'Her husband is a high-profile politician. Is there any clue to his whereabouts yet?'

'There's no information on that at this time.'

'Will you be interviewing him?'

'When contact is made, we shall of course be talking to him. That's all I can give you for now.' Robertson makes a move to leave.

Erica keeps bouncing for attention. 'Is Gordon Glennan a suspect?'

Robertson makes a calming gesture and addresses the room quietly. 'When cause of death has been established we'll know whether suspects are being sought. Until then, I'll ask you not to speculate on the circumstances of Mrs Glennan's death. That's all for now.'

THE WHITE LION IS HEAVING. Perry Butt, the veteran journalist, is holding court. Everyone has a theory but the old warhorse trumps them all.

'There are only two possibilities,' he announces above the babble at the bar. 'Either she accidentally fell down the stairs and broke her neck, or she was murdered. The press will want to keep everybody prattling about it as long as it sells copies, hoping, of course, that the police investigation will be inconclusive so the story can run and run. There's still mileage in the Lord Lucan story, I'll remind you – if anyone here can remember that.'

'Where's her husband, that's what I want to know.' Ivy Lewis voices what everyone is wondering. 'Doesn't anyone else think it's strange that he's not around at a time like this? His wife dies suddenly and he goes missing – come on, there's something not right there.'

'The paper said he hasn't shown up in London for a few days.' Harry Hawkins peruses the much-handled copy on the bar. 'He's a government minister – supposed to be in Whitehall doing whatever he does – which obviously isn't much.'

'Ten to one he made the anonymous phone call.' Meg wipes the bar with a passionate swirl of her cloth. 'Who else would have been in the house? He lives there.'

'The evidence points strongly in his direction –' Mostyn's face is troubled; a look of permanent youthful innocence has followed him into middle age, never more noticeable than when a point of ethics arises – 'but it doesn't constitute proof and we should be aware of that.'

'Yeah, bollocks.' Harry Hawkins expresses the general view.

All heads nod in unison. It was murder – whether premeditated or not is irrelevant – and that is the finding of the White Lion jury. Gordon Glennan killed his wife, rang the police in a fit of agonized conscience, changed his mind and made a run for it.

No one pays any attention to a man at the far end of the bar. Prominent jaw; black cheese cutter cap pulled down shading his face; easily ignored.

Dean Elton sips his beer and pretends to read the racing page.

'THIS ARRIVED BY MESSENGER.' Charlotte finds Taffin propped against the Mustang and hands him a brown A4 envelope.

'What have we got here?' He slits it open, pulls out a colour print and shows it to her.

'Very pretty. I believe that's a Cord, and don't it look smart in white?'

'It's a Cord 812.'

'You haven't said much today, young man.' Charlotte watches him closely. 'What's on your mind?'

'I've got to go away for a bit, girl.'

'How long's a bit?'

'As long as it takes. I'll be in touch as soon as I can.'

'What's going on in there?' She steps in closer; her face mirrored, double, in his dark lenses. 'I'm tired of your disappearing acts. Talk to me.'

'I'll tell you about it when I can.'

'Don't give me that. It's about that woman's death. You know something. Don't make me guess –' her eyes widen; she leans up and removes the dark glasses – 'You know where Gordon Glennan is, don't you.'

Taffin's stillness gives her the answer.

'Tell me this then, did he kill his wife?'

'No.'

'You sound very sure. How do you know?'

'He ain't got it in him. He's a man with problems but he ain't a murderer.'

'You know him that well, do you?'

'I know where he was when it happened because I put him there.'

Charlotte sighs, wanders away and comes back. 'Does Ed or Rick know about this?'

'No.'

'Only, I don't like the sound of what you're getting into. I'd be a whole lot happier if one or both of them was with you.'

'I can't involve them.'

'Alright, have it your way – be a hero.' Charlotte stares

into his face. 'I forgot to tell you, that old man rang – Bob, I think his name is.'

'What did he say?'

'Not a lot. He just likes someone to talk to – said he saw a car being delivered and thought you'd want to know about it.'

'Smart man.'

'Promise you'll call him or he'll think I didn't tell you.'

'I'll do that.' Taffin climbs into the Mustang and fires the engine up. 'If anyone asks I've gone to collect a car. Don't worry about a thing.'

TWENTY-EIGHT

DEAN ELTON SHAVES with a cutthroat razor. Given experience and a steady hand, the results are incomparably better than any flashy modern system. The cold steel demands a master's touch, a certainty that suits his temperament to perfection.

The practice of shaving gives him time to reflect. The last conversation with his boss left him with a nameless unease that is only now coming into focus. The problem is simple: the prospect of affluent leisure never featured in Elton's plans, which have always been vague, at best.

His job as Frey-Morton's chauffeur, bodyguard and enforcer was more to his taste than anything he had previously imagined and he hasn't yet come to terms with the idea of a new, unfamiliar pattern, however ideal it might sound.

Dean Elton is not, and never has been, a man of leisure. He thrives on action, needs to use his skills, and life without short-term objectives equals boredom. The present matter in hand suits his temperament better than the promise of five-star retirement.

Priorities then: first, find Gordon Glennan. The

politician has vanished but the bait of his wife's death ought to flush him out. Once the spotlight is on him again, he can be reached. All that's required is a hunter's patience, and Elton learnt that long ago in a variety of war zones.

He rates the odds of Glennan showing up at the couple's country home at fifty-fifty. On the one hand, the place will be under surveillance round the clock, so the Minister would be wise to stay away; on the other, it was the scene of his wife's death, which might trigger a reckless, emotional instinct in an already broken man.

In either case, Michael Wyatt has been detailed to keep a discreet watch on the place and if his clumsiness attracts police attention, Janice Glennan's murder will eventually be laid at his door anyway. No risk there.

So it's a waiting game. Elton contemplates his face in the shaving mirror and turns his mind to the second objective: destroying Taffin.

This will be a real pleasure but not a major challenge by comparison.

He knows how; he has no interest in why; and in this case, he knows where to look for his quarry.

GORDON GLENNAN looks up sharply from the chess board as Bob Sherman ponders his next move, lifts a deliberative finger, swoops with his queen's bishop to knock out Glennan's queen's knight and sits back.

'Did you hear a car?' Glennan peers glumly at the board, hardly daring to raise his voice.

'I did not.' Bob's concentration is focused on the game. 'It's terribly important not to let such minor details distract you. Check.'

'I wish I had the knack.' Glennan is dealing with the private turmoil of a public man cut off from all contact with the outside world.

There's no TV here and Bob's ancient radio resists all attempts to tune it to a recognizable station. He hasn't seen a paper in days. He is fairly sure Taffin relieved him of his own phone before leaving – presumably so he couldn't be traced through it. Added to that, he has no idea where he is and his companion, though entertaining company, lives in an Arthurian parallel universe.

But it *was* a car he heard: a gruff, throaty note that rose once and cut out.

In the yard, Taffin sits at the wheel of the Mustang listening to the silence. He has covered the distance from *Muscle Motors* in just over an hour. All the way here he has been reflecting on his last conversation with Charlotte. She divined what he hadn't told her and he reminds himself never to think of concealing anything from her in the future. Equally important, she unwittingly confirmed the link he suspected between Mister Adams, the mystery buyer, and Glennan.

The picture he received this morning showed more than a white Cord: it showed him the location.

First thing, make certain. He leaves the Mustang by the door to the main house, walks round to the barn and hauls the door open.

He never really doubted it. The Cord is parked with its blunt grille and curving wings facing the entrance, headlamps concealed, white coachwork, white sidewall tyres and chrome domed hubcaps gleaming like new. That is fat, fast and beautiful; he could love it.

Taffin allows himself a moment's appreciation, then drags the barn door closed and heads for the house.

Bob Sherman raises his head as the door opens to reveal an expanse of dark suit. He was anticipating mate in two moves before his opponent palpably lost interest in the game – something he can't forgive – but his knit brow clears as he recognizes the intruder.

'Mister Taffin – what a pleasure. Your friend plays a splendid game but lacks concentration. I have him, see?' he indicates the board, 'how would you judge his chances?'

'Not too good.' Taffin takes the old man's offered hand. 'I need a private word with him if you don't mind.'

'Not at all, if he concedes.'

'I concede. I haven't beaten him yet' Glennan gets up with a helpless shrug, follows Taffin out to the corridor and stares anxiously into the blank face.

'I'm relieved to see you. I've come to a decision –'

'Save it.' Taffin watches him quietly. 'I've got some bad news for you.'

'Oh Lord...' Glennan leans against the wall. 'You're going to tell me it's all out in the open – I don't even get to redeem myself by confession.'

'It's your wife.'

'I might have guessed.' an exasperated upward glance. 'What's she done? Sold the story to the gutter press I suppose – *"Disgraced Minister's wife tells all"* – that's about her level, greedy bitch.'

'She's dead.'

The words hang in the air for a beat while Glennan stares into Taffin's face, then sinks down to an awkward sitting position on the top step, gazing into the dark stairwell.

'How?'

'Looks like she fell down the stairs.' Taffin lowers himself to sit beside the Minister.

A heavy minute passes while Glennan stares into the abyss. 'What now?'

'That's for you to decide.'

'I suppose everybody's wondering where I am.'

'That's about the size of it.'

'I was going to say, I want to go on record with what I've done and – how did you put it? – take the bad guys down with me.'

CHARLOTTE NOTICED THE MAN in the black cap a few minutes ago and paid him no attention at first; just another punter browsing the stock on the forecourt. The Porsche Cayenne he arrived in is parked at the head of the lane.

She looks up as he comes into the office, closing the door behind him, and instinctively checks to see that her mobile is within easy reach. Big bloke; big jaw. That cap gives him the look of a bird of prey.

'Can I help you?'

'Where's the man?'

'That depends which man you're looking for.'

'Mister Taffin.'

'He's not here. Perhaps I can help.'

'When are you expecting him?'

'He may be a while.' Charlotte regrets the words as soon as they're out of her mouth. 'He went to collect a car. Shouldn't be long.'

'That's all I wanted to hear. I'll wait.'

He lets himself out and she watches through the window as he settles himself against the wall.

'SHE WOULDN'T JUST FALL DOWN THE STAIRS.' Glennan gazes into the shadows in the well of the old house. 'Something must have distracted her. Did she suffer?'

'I don't know any more than you do.' The floorboards complain as Taffin rises to his feet.

'What do the police say? Do they think I pushed her? Oh God, I'm a suspect.'

'Probably.'

'But I haven't been anywhere near her. I was in London, then you brought me here.'

'So what's the problem? I know you were here when it happened, so does Bob Sherman. There's your alibi.'

'So you believe I need an alibi. That must mean foul play is suspected.'

'Like I say, we can vouch for where you were.'

'I won't say I'm not relieved, but... with the greatest respect, will the police regard you as a reliable witness?'

'I ain't got a record, Minister – and no one's going to doubt Bob Sherman's word. You're an innocent man – get a grip.'

Glennan struggles to his feet. 'Not entirely innocent though, am I?'

'You've got stuff to answer for – no way out of that.'

'As you say, no way out – not now. I'd decided to face up to it anyway. Ironically, turning myself in for defrauding the public offers some degree of safety. I'll spend most of my time in interrogation rooms. Not an appealing thought, with the press clamoring for details, but I don't care for life as a fugitive. It's time to come out of hiding.'

'No point hanging around here then.' Taffin leads him into Bob's room and the phone rings in his pocket as he does so.

Charlotte's voice: 'Can you hurry it up?'

'I'm on my way.'

'There's a fella here asking for you. I said you'd gone to collect a car. He said he'd wait.'

'I'll be there as quick as I can.'

Taffin slips the phone back in his pocket and turns to Bob Sherman. 'We'll be leaving now. Thank you for your help.'

'Bon voyage then. One more thing –' the old man pushes the chess board aside, produces an envelope from his jacket pocket and hands it to Taffin – 'a small token of gratitude.'

'That's not necessary.'

'I insist. If you don't want to open it, give it to your good lady.'

'I'll do that.' Taffin takes the envelope, slips it in his pocket, shakes the old man's hand and turns to Gordon Glennan. 'Are you ready?'

'When you are.'

'There's a car here for me to collect so you'll have to follow in mine. Ever driven a Ford Mustang?'

'HOW MANY PHONES DO YOU NEED?' Charlotte cocks an eyebrow with her question. She is standing in the open office doorway watching Black Cap who is still leaning against the wall, one phone up to his ear, another clasped in his left hand.

He half turns. 'What?'

'A black one and a white one. You must be very organised.'

'How long have I got to wait?'

'He's on his way.'

'Why don't you call him and find out?'

'Because I'm not his nanny.' Charlotte drops all pretense at affability. 'No one's making you wait. Why don't you call back tomorrow?'

'Tomorrow's no good.'

'I'll get back to you.' Charlotte shuts the office door and goes to her desk. Through the window she watches Black Cap dial a number and speak briefly into his phone – the black phone, she notices.

She imagines he's closing a deal. The truth would surprise her: Dean Elton is calling the police.

GORDON GLENNAN sinks into the left-hand driving seat of the Mustang with some apprehension. He has never enjoyed driving. The cars he has owned have always been designed to cushion him from what goes on outside. This brute has a nose that suggests aggressive power and a steering wheel that feels too slim to cling to.

Taffin gave him a brief tour of the dashboard before shutting him in and now he is alone in an alien machine with a daunting journey ahead.

'Just keep me in sight,' Taffin told him. He has every intention of doing so.

THE CORD rumbles into life like an elderly athlete disturbed from sleep. Taffin makes a brief inspection of the interior, tests the pedal pressures and pauses to answer his phone. Charlotte's voice comes to him over the engine in a droning, uneven rush.

'What's up, girl?'

'That geezer's still here. Did you find what you're looking for?'

'Yeah. I'm sitting in it. It's a throwback from the nineteen-thirties.'

'Hurry it up. This bloke gives me the creeps.'

'Lock up and go home.'

'I can't leave the place unattended. Ed and Rick are out delivering the Dodge. They'll be back here soon so don't worry about me. How long will it take you to get here?'

'In this thing, anybody's guess. We're leaving now.'

'We?'

'Me and a client.'

Taffin eases the Cord forward, gives Glennan the thumbs up in passing and watches the Mustang jerk with the minister's first tentative efforts to get it rolling.

AT THE SAME TIME Michael Wyatt is wondering how much longer he will need to sit in this rented Nissan watching the Glennans' driveway.

Black Cap told him to keep that house in view and gave him a number to call if Gordon Glennan appeared. It's tedious work but it doesn't call for a lot of effort, so put up with it.

Wyatt shifts awkwardly in his seat. He has always resented authority but needs direction to function at all – a contradiction beyond his grasp that leaves him in a state of unrelieved, tacit belligerence. But he has found it pays to follow a leader; that has been the pattern of his life.

The Black Cap won his obedience in a split second through a cocktail of fear and respect by murdering his colleague in front of his eyes.

On top of that, Janice Glennan died in his presence with

Black Cap in attendance. He is still not sure what happened. He watched her fall down the stairs and looked immediately to Black Cap for guidance the moment he realised she was dead. He has given up trying to piece the sequence of events together.

There has been no sign of Gordon Glennan and Wyatt doesn't think there will be. Police activity has been going on all around him and he has got used to ignoring it, so he sits up smartly as a squad car slides to a halt across his front and another pulls up behind him.

Moments later he is in the back seat of the lead vehicle staring with passive resentment into the face of Sergeant Dave Walls.

An anonymous call to Stoleworth Central gave the number of his rented Nissan together with a description of the driver.

TWENTY-NINE

AFTER TEN MINUTES in the Cord, Taffin is longing for his Mustang.

The car slipped out of gear once before he was clear of the farm gates; the next few miles required a heavy touch while he got used to the steering. In spite of the power of the Lycoming V8, progress is ponderous, with an assortment of vibrations adding to the Cord's obstinate refusal to convey any kind of surface awareness.

Driving this antique, he decides, is more like an assault course than a pleasure and watching Glennan's attempts to keep up adds to the discomfort.

'Must be going soft,' he mutters, heaving the wheel through a series of tight bends.

So far, the effort has taken his mind off more pressing matters. Now, as he allows that slab of nose to lead him in a more or less straight line, he begins to speculate on how this drive will end.

He has no idea who he is going to meet, or why he has been singled out for a stranger's attention. All he knows for certain is that Charlotte is aware of a threat: the flat tone of her voice on the phone told him that.

The road unfolds before him, mile after mile. Every so often he slows to let the Mustang catch up.

DEAN ELTON leans against the outside wall of the office, clearing his mind of everything but the job in hand.

The gun that doesn't exist hangs heavy under his left armpit. He would have preferred a Glock 17 but this heavy Colt revolver was stowed away for him in the Porsche so he didn't argue: he doesn't expect to use it anyway. The white phone will take care of everything and then he'll be away, *Muscle Motors* will be history and the bitch in the office who looked at him slant-eyed will end up as a casualty. Collateral damage – a phrase Morton used in connection with Glennan's wife. Best do a thorough job.

While he's thinking this, Charlotte is scanning the forecourt yet again. Black Cap is still where she last saw him and she opens the door to give herself a wider view.

Her phone is in her hand and she would like to call Taffin again but remembers his views on people who use phones when they're driving and decides it can wait. Ed and Rick should be back any time now.

She is about to shut herself into the office when Black Cap turns to her.

'You're keeping an eye on me,' he remarks. 'You ought to be more trusting.'

Something in his tone causes her to freeze. 'I only trust people I know, and I don't trust all of them.'

'That's not very friendly.' Black Cap moves as if to stretch his shoulders and her phone is gone, snatched away faster than she could think.

Charlotte's eyes blazing. 'You can give that back right now.'

'Get inside.' He is facing her and she has a flash glimpse of the gun under his arm as he turns.

Charlotte stares at the man, feels her world slow down and backs away towards her desk.

Black Cap follows her in, rips the phone and computer connections out of the wall, goes back outside, closes the door and leans against it with his back to her.

Charlotte sits very still, perched on the edge of her desk. She glances at the rear window that looks out over the workshop: too small. It sticks and she doubts that she could squeeze herself through it. No way out there. She is imprisoned, cut off, unable to communicate with anyone, and the man outside is a killer – of that she is now certain.

Stay active – get Black Cap used to her moving – keep calm but be ready to make a break for it given the chance. She tidies her desk, puts tomorrow's worksheets in order ready for Ed and Rick, locks the filing cabinet, looks around for something to use as a weapon in emergency.

Nothing comes to hand. Defenseless. Bad feeling.

'Who needs two phones?'

Something inside her weakens.

No weapon? What were you thinking? Her eyes suddenly open wide. There's a gun in the safe a few feet from her. Taffin took it off the man he called the Tooth Fairy.

She gets up slowly, a smooth flow of movement.

Reach out, turn the knob, two clicks right, three left, two right, four left: Click. Ease the handle down. The heavy door opens under pressure.

Black Cap glancing briefly over his shoulder.

Charlotte reaching into the safe, hand searching, closing on the weapon.

The gun is in her hand, heavy, snub, grimly reassuring.

A closer look. She has never even held one before but assumes there is a safety-catch. A grooved button under her thumb. She presses it forward and flinches as the cylinder drops sideways. Not the safety-catch then, but a glance tells her Taffin left it loaded.

Close it up with a click and hope the weapon would work if she dared use it.

On her feet now, ambling to the door, hands behind her back.

TAFFIN GLANCES at his watch. Given a clear road he should be at *Muscle Motors* in about twenty minutes.

He needs to see Charlotte and make sure she's had the sense to lock the office door. He is hoping Ed and Rick are back at the workshop.

With a mounting sense of urgency to contend with, all he needs is a hold up in the high street of a small town. But here is a large woman in a high-visibility jacket holding a STOP sign.

The engine settles to a deep-seated grumble as he waits. A procession of school children screeches and clatters across the road, more queuing up ready to cross, some of the boys breaking away to cluster round this weird car, one or two trying to climb on the front wings.

Sharp commands from the woman. The kids reluctantly getting back in line. When the last of them is safely across, the woman allows a moment to pass before marching off after them.

The Cord slips out of gear again as it pulls away. An argument with the linkage, a grudging uptake of power, Taffin takes a deep breath as he leaves the town behind and slows down again waiting for the Mustang to appear in his mirror.

Open road stretching ahead again. The Cord clears its throat and surges on while Taffin allows himself to relax. A saying of Russell Chambers Gates calms him: *'Time passes at its own set pace regardless of our efforts to compete.'*

The huge motor home looms in his windscreen, square, impassable and slow. Low gear called for, refused a third time, and the Cord slows down in spite of the rumbling power.

The motor home continues on its way and is lost to view. Taffin steers the Cord onto the grass verge, wrestles to find a gear, feels the jerk as it engages and glances back, willing the Mustang to catch up.

CHARLOTTE stares at the broad back leaning against the office door.

The gun is a lump of cold metal in her hand, the muzzle mere inches from a jacket that encloses flesh, blood, bone, sinew, life. Every instinct works against destroying that – and with the back turned, you're powerless.

Even with a lethal weapon in your hand.

Close-shaven bristle on the back of the neck beneath the black cap. The man feeling her presence behind him by some ancient sense, turning round to look.

Charlotte staring at him through the pane of glass. Two-way eye contact. Elton facing her now, arms held out, a phone in each hand.

'Settle down, lady.'

'Let me out, now. There's laws against imprisoning people.'

'You're too tense. Tension's a killer.'

He should not have used the word. A flash of fury and Charlotte shatters the glass with a punch, gun in hand, aimed at the man's face.

'That's a dangerous toy,' Elton remarks, as the last shards cascade at his feet. 'What are you going to do with it?'

'What are you here for?'

'Just business.' He makes a weighing motion, one phone in each hand. 'Sit back and enjoy the moment.'

Charlotte braces herself, both hands on the gun. She has seen that on the movies. 'Put the phones down and walk away.'

'Or you'll shoot me?' Elton seems to look through her. 'Big decision. You have the power of life and death in your hands.'

'Just drop the phones.'

'Which one?' Elton brings his hands together, shuffles the phones and holds them out again – one black, one white. 'Life and death – which is which?' Another shuffle. 'Black or white? Life... or death?'

'I'm telling you, drop them right now.' Charlotte curls a finger round the trigger, wondering how much bluff is left in her.

Elton slips the black phone in his pocket and weighs the white one in his hand. 'Compromise.'

Charlotte feels her teeth gritted. Flash of memory – the speed of his hand when he took her phone. His calm voice has kept her attention and he has moved closer.

She takes a step back in anticipation. He throws the door open. A moment face to face with nothing between them, her arms still straight out gripping the gun. No bluff left.

'That won't save you.' Elton's face set like granite now. 'You couldn't pull that trigger to save your life.'

Charlotte's eyes suddenly wide open as a flash of white appears among the trees along the lane and the roar of an engine reaches them.

Elton turning to look, taking a step outside, the white phone in his raised left hand as the Cord heads up towards them.

'I'll be leaving now.' He throws the remark over his shoulder. 'Go say hello to Mister Taffin.'

And against instinct, Charlotte knows what has to happen. Eyes tight shut as her finger closes round the trigger. The gun jumping in her hand, the *Bang* mingling with the growl of the Cord's engine.

The bullet chips Elton's shoulder blade carrying off a gush of muscle and splinters of bone. Elton jerks and stumbles forward on one knee, left arm flicking out in crazy mime, white phone spinning away across hard ground.

Charlotte running wildly towards the approaching Cord. Taffin flinging the door open to greet her as she grabs his arm, hauling him from the car, mouthing frantic words, starting to run.

Elton rolling over searching for the phone, dragging himself towards it.

Taffin staring at the man on the ground who is now clambering to his feet, falling forward, righting himself, reaching for the phone.

The world slows down. Taffin turning away from the Cord, reaching for Charlotte, covering distance together.

As Elton fumbles for the phone with his right hand, straining against swelling agony in his left shoulder, staggering to his waiting Porsche, letting himself in, glancing behind to see two figures flinging themselves flat as he grips the phone, thumbs the numbers 812, fights the car into gear, pressing SEND as he accelerates away.

AS GORDON GLENNAN steers the Mustang into the lane leading to *Muscle Motors*, it seems to him that an already overloaded day has turned manic.

A car is driving straight at him, the driver preoccupied with something in his hand.

Glennan making a stab for the brake as the oncoming car swerves, slowing to miss him, the driver staring across the narrow space, Glennan's eyes wide as a gun flicks into view pointing at his head, a blare of sound, a surreal instant of leather-clad figures flashing between them, wiping away the vision of the gun.

A rush of wind and Glennan is left staring at the trees flanking the lane as the car that all but rammed him screams out to the main road and is gone.

ED PENTECOST has spent his day at high speed. An hour ago he delivered the restored Dodge Charger to the new owner, spent a little time discussing the car's characteristics, shook hands and handed over the keys.

Rick Bishop picked him up on the Fireblade and brought him back to *Muscle Motors*, taking advantage of an experienced pillion rider to lean into the bends on the way.

They were in sight of the red Mustang just as it turned into the lane and caught up with it at the exact moment it swerved to avoid an oncoming Porsche Cayenne that slowed, the driver apparently pointing out of his window.

Rick's only option was to aim for the narrow space between the two cars. The decision taken in a micro-second, a fleeting impact and now they're through, Rick braking hard as they reach the forecourt, the two of them stepping off the bike as it slides on, shielding themselves from the inferno blazing on the concrete apron in front of them.

A HUNDRED YARDS AWAY, farmer Peter Shaw fancied a break from mowing his field, parked the John Deer tractor, gang-mowers raised, and perched on a style to roll a cigarette. Rizzla paper between his fingers, a generous caterpillar of Golden Virginia spread out on the surface promising a peaceful interlude under a clear sky. He licks his lips, raises the paper and as he does so the tobacco vanishes, a blast of air rocks him backwards and a beat later, incredibly, he hears a clap of thunder.

At the same time, a field away, Marcia Griffin is surprised when her trusted Horse, Trigger, skitters to his left, stumbles and rights himself in time for her to take a firm hold and stay in the saddle.

The sound of thunder. A rich gob of smoke rises above the trees and gradually disperses.

CHARLOTTE rolls onto her back, the singing in her head blotting out the sound of boots approaching. Two helmeted heads swim into view, then Ed's face, close to hers.

She says, *'I can't hear a fucking thing,'* but the sound is lost to her.

She raises her arm, sees Rick mouthing *'Woah!'* but hears nothing as Ed gently removes the revolver from her outstretched hand.

She becomes aware of a weight across her chest. The weight lifts and she sees a black clad arm as Ed's attention shifts to the figure lying beside her.

Some time later she hears sirens as the buzz in her ears subsides; then blue lights swirl and she is being lifted and slid into an ambulance, conscious of another supine form beside her.

THIRTY

GORDON GLENNAN was found sitting at the wheel of the Mustang at the head of the lane, staring into the distance. The first officers on the scene recognized him immediately.

As night falls he takes a seat in an interview room at Stoleworth Central.

He has said little, other than to confirm his name. DI Robertson and DS Barker sit facing him. The interview begins slowly; Robertson is not a man to rush things and at this early stage he is more interested in Glennan's manner than anything he might tell them.

'You are Gordon Barnes Glennan, a Minister of Her Majesty's Government, correct?'

Glennan nods.

'For the tape please, Minister.'

'I am.'

'You understand that you're under caution. I have some hard questions to put to you and it's important that you answer them fully and openly. Clear?'

'Yes.'

'First, I must assume you're aware that your wife has died.'

Glennan nods. 'Yes.'

'Can you tell me where you were at the time of her death?'

'Not exactly, no. I've been keeping a low profile in the last few days. Mister Taffin knows where I was – he took me there. He can confirm that...'

An exchange of glances between the detectives.

Glennan continues: 'So can the old man who lives there. I was with him – we played chess.'

DS Barker watches Glennan's face. 'You don't seem very upset, for a man who's just lost his wife.'

'That's... not the case. Ours was not a close marriage. We didn't spend a lot of time together but I hoped we could be closer in the future.'

Robertson refers to his notes. 'Would the names Linklater Farm or Sherman mean anything to you?'

'I don't know about the farm but I believe the old man's name was Sherman. The place did look like a farm, now I think of it. That's where I've been, but I wouldn't know how to get there.'

'Why's that?' Barker puts the question.

'I was taken there.'

'By the owner of that American Ford you were driving?' Robertson sits back and glances at Barker.

'Yes.'

'That would be a Mister Taffin.'

'Yes.'

'And what is your relationship with Mister Taffin?'

'There isn't one really. He's shown me some kindness – some concern for my welfare – I don't know why. May I ask a question?'

'Go ahead.'

'My wife's death – was it accidental?'

'Not for me to say at present. Mrs Glennan's death is the subject of an ongoing investigation and we should have some more positive data before long.'

'Am I a suspect?'

'Let's concentrate on the present, Minister. Why were you on Mister Taffin's premises – Muscle Motors – earlier today?'

'Mister Taffin wanted me to follow him there – he'll confirm that.'

'What did you see when you arrived?'

'A lot happened in a short time.' Glennan shakes his head as if to clear it. 'There's a narrow lane up to the garage. Some maniac drove straight at me. He pointed a gun at my head. Then there was some sort of collision and he was gone.'

'He pointed a gun at you?'

'I'm pretty sure it was a gun.'

'This gun?' Robertson holds up an evidence bag containing the gun that doesn't exist. 'For the tape, I'm showing the suspect a Colt Python revolver.'

'It could be. I've seen one like it before.'

'Really? Where would that have been?'

'A former associate had one. He showed it to me.'

'Who was this *associate*?'

'I'd rather not say.'

'We'd rather you did, Minister. We'll come back to that. What happened after the maniac pointed the gun at you?'

'There was a bright flash beyond the trees and a hellish kind of blast, then a *clang* and a *crunch*, like metal falling to earth. I don't know... I'm still...'

'Alright,' Robertson gets up. 'That's all for now.'

'Where do we go from here?'

'We have to hand you on now. You'll be collected later this evening and taken to London for further questioning. Beyond that, I can't comment. Is there anything else you'd like to say – anything you want to ask us?'

'Where did you find that gun?'

'It was in the bushes near the car you were driving.' Robertson takes his seat again. 'Let's talk about your *associate* who had one like it. Don't be shy.'

CHARLOTTE is hearing perfectly now. The babble around her has resolved into snatches of conversation from which she gathers she has been lucky: a slice of car door, which must have spun in the air, embedded itself in the ground like a lance within a few feet of her body.

She also hears murmurs of concern for the man who was lying across her when the paramedics picked her up.

On this hard hospital bed she explores her limbs and finds them functional. Feeling coming back. Reality fighting its way to the front.

'How is he?' her voice comes sharply, as if belonging to somebody else.

A young woman's face close to hers. 'You're back with us then?'

'I said how is he.' Charlotte struggles to sit up, resisting hands that try to stop her.

'Just take it easy. The doctor will be along in a moment.'

'I don't need a bloody doctor, I want to know if my fella's alright. Where is he?'

'The man who came in with you? He's being looked after. You just settle down and get your strength back.'

But Charlotte is up, walking barefoot along the row of beds, shaking off hands that try to steady her.

A woman doctor hurries to her side – an authority figure with a stricter turn of phrase. Instructions are given and Charlotte is taken to a waiting area where Julia and Kate rise to meet her. Ed and Rick hover in the background. No one says much but she senses tension in the air.

'Will someone tell me what's going on?'

'They haven't told us much.' Julia guides her to a seat and sits down with her.

Hours pass. Kath watches the news on her iPad and all but Charlotte lean in to look. The announcer addresses camera from the forecourt of *Muscle Motors* where tape is stretched across an area where the smoldering carcass of a car is just visible.

No one listens to the commentary: '*...the wreckage was too hot to approach for some time and it's still not clear what caused the explosion that reduced a car to twisted wreckage on the forecourt of this specialist garage...*'

'I didn't like it.' Charlotte's voice, broken, despairing. 'I didn't like what he was getting into. I didn't like it from the beginning.'

Rick puts an arm around her, protective by instinct, but she shakes off any comfort.

'I always knew he'd go a step too far and now look.'

She flings a pointed finger at the television but the announcer has handed back to the station link, who continues with the face of Gordon Glennan on screen.

'*Missing Transport Minister Gordon Glennan is this*

evening helping Police with their enquiries into the death of his wife, after being apprehended by police attending the explosion in the previous report. Glennan, who until recently chaired the StarTrack enquiry, has not been seen publicly since the high speed rail project was abandoned. The question now is, how did the missing Minister come to be at the location of this afternoon's explosion?'

'Never mind that –' Charlotte shouts at the screen – 'find out who that fucker in the black cap was. He set off the fucking explosion. Why don't the cops ask Glennan about him – why don't they talk to me? Are they all fucking stupid?'

Mo and Shirley arrive to join the vigil. White-coated figures drift in and out and eventually word reaches them that the man they came in with – Mister... Taffin – is in surgery.

Finally a robed figure approaches them, searching their faces, wondering who to address. Charlotte stands up.

'You can talk to me.'

'Are you a relative?'

'Close enough.'

'I'm his brother –' Mo steps up and puts a hand on Charlotte's shoulder – 'but this lady is as good as family.'

The surgeon nods. 'He's lost a lot of blood. We've removed a sharp metal object from his side. If he had an appendix before, he hasn't got one now.'

'Bloody hell –' Charlotte has no time for details – 'you can fix him up though, can't you?'

'We're doing all we can.'

'What was the metal object?' Mo wants to know.

'It was a twisted fragment of something. Could have

been part of a piece of machinery. All I can say for certain is it was hot when it struck him – that's the best I can do.' He pauses for a moment. 'He's had surgery before, hasn't he? There's evidence of an old abdominal wound.'

'Some bastard stuck a knife in him once.' Charlotte looks the surgeon in the eye. 'He survived that alright, so a bit of hot metal won't bother him.'

The surgeon nods again: practiced sympathy. 'It's early days yet. He looks like a strong man so let's hope his metabolism will take over where surgery left off. The body has remarkable ways of repairing itself. In the meantime we'll be keeping an eye on him. There's nothing you can do here now.'

'We'll be back.' Mo steers Charlotte towards the exit. 'My brother's as tough as old boots.'

THIRTY-ONE

'YOUR NAME IS MARK TWILL TAFFIN?' DI Robertson and DS Barker take their seats beside the hospital bed.

'That's right.'

'In view of the unusual circumstances this will have to be conducted as a formal interview.' Robertson glances at Barker: a mute direction to take notes. 'I know you've had a rough time but this won't wait so I hope you're feeling up to it.'

'Go ahead.'

'Would you mind taking off the dark glasses?'

Taffin removes his glasses, revealing an equally expressionless gaze.

'Thank you.' Robertson looks the man over with interest. 'First, what can you tell me about the explosion that caused your injuries?'

'Not a lot. My partner didn't get hurt – that's all I care about.'

'You were both lucky.'

'Is that what you call it?'

'Your partner was discharged the following day. I understand you will be walking out of here any time now.'

Robertson sits back and folds his arms. 'So why don't you tell me why a car you were driving blew up?'

'I can't answer that.'

'Can't or won't? If I had to guess I'd say someone wanted you dead, Mister Taffin. I want to know who and why?'

'Same answer.'

'Alright, let's talk about your connection with Mister Gordon Glennan. He says you hid him for protection and made him follow you, in your car, to your premises in Lasherham. What was that about?'

'He was fed up with hiding. I said I'd bring him in.'

'Sounds like he put a lot of trust in you.'

'We're mates.'

'You're mates? Socially or business?'

'Gordon likes to talk. I don't mind listening.'

'What does this Government Minister talk to you about?'

'Private stuff.'

'This particular Government Minister has quite a lot of private stuff to explain. Can you shed any light on that?'

'He got into bad company – wanted a sympathetic ear.'

'That's interesting.' Robertson leans back in his seat. 'Why would he choose your ear?'

'You tell me.'

'No, you tell us.' Barker comes to life and subsides at a gesture from Robertson.

'It ain't my business.' Taffin's gaze settles on Robertson. 'The man came to me for help and I gave it to him.'

'Did he offer to pay you for your services?'

'No.'

'Sticking your neck out, weren't you? I can't decide if you were being heroic or just plain rash.'

'I ain't a hero.'

'Are you sure about that?' Barker huffs a laugh. 'They made a movie about you, didn't they?'

Taffin's gaze settles on him. 'I wouldn't know, squire.'

Robertson leans forward, excluding Barker. 'That was a rare, collectors' car you were driving. I don't know a lot about your business, Taffin, but I guess there are rivalries in it. What would a car like that be worth?'

'More than you and me make in a year.'

'I don't know what you make in a year Taffin, and my pay is a matter of public record. You're saying it's worth plenty.'

'That's right.'

'Who knew you would be driving it yesterday afternoon?'

Taffin sits back and folds his arms. 'That's the best question you've asked all day, squire.'

TAFFIN LOOKS UP to see Charlotte pushing a wheelchair with his dark suit draped over it. Mo and Shirley are with her.

'What's that?' Taffin jerks a thumb at the wheelchair.

'Your transport for this afternoon, Young Man. Let's get you dressed, I'm getting you out of here.'

'I ain't getting in that.'

'You'll do as you're told. I've had your suit cleaned so you'll be decent.' She holds up a bulky white envelope. 'I found this in the inside pocket.'

Taffin swings is legs over the edge of the bed, wincing. 'The old man gave me that – old Bob Sherman.'

'You haven't opened it.'

'Something for services rendered, he said. I told him he doesn't owe us anything so he said, give it to your good lady. You must have made an impression.'

'I've only spoken to him on the phone. He's a nice old fella.' Charlotte slits open the envelope, pulls out a fold of paper and reads. 'Oh my goodness – he *is* a nice old fella.' She sinks down on the side of the bed and hands him the letter:

Dear Mister Taffin,

I write to acknowledge the kindness and courtesy you and your colleagues have shown to me during the brief time since we first became acquainted.

At the time we met, I was being propositioned, on a regular basis, by strangers who assured me that it was in my best interests to sign certain assets on my property over to them, for a consideration. These assets, I imagine, were to include my late Uncle Austin's collection of motor cars.

As I believe I mentioned during one of our conversations, this collection is of no interest to me; in fact, I was hardly aware of its existence until these people started making a fuss.

I believe, though, that a collection of motors such as this might well be of interest to you. Having no deserving relatives to leave it to, I have no hesitation in offering it to you, in its entirety, with any related paperwork you may find, to dispose of as you see fit.

I hope I have made my feelings clear on the matter of legal documents and my aversion to signing anything drafted in their incomprehensible jargon. However, I am happy to make an exception in this case and will willingly sign any further papers that may be necessary to make this gift binding.

In the hope that this signed document makes my wishes clear, I remain yours,

Sincerely,
Robert Sherman.

PS Feel free to drop in any time you're passing this way!

'YOU CAN'T BEAT LOCAL KNOWLEDGE.' Perry Butt has a stack of the last two weeks' national dailies beside him and is in a mood to lecture anyone who'll listen. He whacks the latest copy of *The Stoleworth Observer* down on the bar. 'This girl's been keeping her eyes and ears open and look where it's got her.' He nudges the stack of the week's national dailies at his elbow and swivels on his stool, glass raised, to face the White Lion's regulars. 'Young Erica Lyle – home-grown talent. *Salut.*'

'She's a pushy little devil,' Harry Hawkins remarks. 'I remember her as a cocky teenager.'

'Blue hair she had, at one time –' Ivy Lewis leans over and reads from the nearest copy:

MAN CHARGED WITH JANICE GLENNAN MURDER

Police today charged former steel fixer, Michael James Wyatt, with the murder of Mrs. Janice Glennan, who was found dead at her Lasherham home having apparently tripped and fallen down the stairs. A Post Mortem revealed that Mrs Glennan, wife of disgraced Transport Minister Gordon Glennan, died from a single blow to the back of the neck and the fatal injury was inconsistent with a fall.

Police are still seeking the caller behind an anonymous tip-off that led to Wyatt's arrest. Wyatt admitted to being inside Mrs Glennan's house at the time of her death but insists that it was an accomplice in the break-in, whose name he could not supply, who killed Mrs. Glennan.

According to Wyatt, his accomplice drove a Porsche Cayenne, but he was unable to supply any more detail. Wyatt was remanded in custody pending trial…

Ashley Gunn moves up to the bar. 'That's Gordon Glennan off the hook, right there. You all reckoned it was him, didn't you?'

'It was always a dangerous assumption.' Mostyn studies his half of bitter. 'Gordon Glennan was miles away when his wife was murdered but he's got problems of an entirely different nature.'

'Who says he didn't pay someone to get rid of her?' Ivy Lewis offers the question with round-eyed innocence.

'No way.' Ashley Gunn sweeps the idea aside. 'He's the politician everybody loves to hate, but a good friend of mine, who knows him better than any of us, says he hasn't got it in him.'

'That would be Taffin.' Ivy's face softens. 'He confirmed Glennan was somewhere else at the time – and if he can vouch for Glennan's character, that's good enough for me.'

'Perhaps the Minister just fell in with bad company –' Perry Butt brandishes a later front page. 'Save your sympathy – the truth is, he was an elected representative who abused public trust. Here's more from the redoubtable Miss Lyle. Now tell me this doesn't do your heart good.'

GLENNAN FACES STARTRACK FRAUD IN-QUIRY
The defunct high-speed rail loop project, StarTrack, was plagued by early mismanagement that left it open to exploitation by ruthless speculators, according to a Home Office source.

> *Transport Minister Gordon Glennan, who chaired the Select Committee monitoring StarTrack's progress, now faces questions on how the project was directed and why the proposed route continually changed, causing untold distress to thousands of householders, who had to stand by helpless while property values plunged.*

'Yesss!' Harry Hawkins rubs his hands together and grabs another national daily. 'And how about this...'

> ## DISGRACED MINISTER REVEALS LAND GRAB CONSPIRACY
> *Gordon Glennan, former Chair of the StarTrack Advisory Committee, admits he collaborated with an unnamed entrepreneur to defraud property owners along several routes proposed for the aborted StarTrack plan. The objective was to depress property values to make cheap land available for development.*
>
> *Glennan, briefly a suspect following the death of his wife, Janice Glennan, now faces further questions and will be required to name names in connection with the StarTrack fiasco.*

'Just like we all thought.' Debi Royce sweeps the assembled company with an iron stare.

'And now we know who the unnamed entrepreneur was.' Perry Butt holds up this morning's front page and they all crowd round to read:

> ## BILLIONAIRE RECLUSE SOUGHT IN STARTRACK INVESTINGATION
> *Police in sixteen countries are today seeking property magnate Daniel Frey-Morton, named by disgraced Minister Gordon Glennan as the driving force behind*

the StarTrack conspiracy, which aimed to drive down property values to favour speculators. Thousands of householders would have suffered loss of their principal assets had the plan succeeded.

Frey-Morton lives and works in hotels when on shore, or on one of his three yachts, one of which is thought to be worth $200 million. He is known to have left the United Kingdom some weeks ago and his present whereabouts are unknown.

Assets of several subsidiary companies comprising Frey-Morton's business empire have been frozen until he is available to answer charges.

'And there you have it.' Perry Butt lowers the paper. 'That's what I call reporting. Don't let the bastards off the hook until you're sure you've got the whole story – not just the scraps they want to give you – all of it. You can't beat local knowledge – it can lead you anywhere.'

DEAN ELTON understood his wound perfectly. It was not his first and he had seen many like it. The effort of high-speed driving kept the blood flowing but at sunset he judged that enough time had elapsed and pulled into a field to rest. Here he mopped himself with the clothes he was wearing, changed into combat fatigues from his travelling kit and cleaned up the car.

The following day he left the Porsche in a car park near the Southampton docks, checked into an address he had been given and waited for a launch that would take him across the Channel.

With unlimited funds, the world was open to him. Now, ten thousand miles away, his wound properly tended, he is lying on a king-size bed in air-conditioned luxury wondering which of Singapore's bars and nightspots will get his patronage tonight. CBS News is burbling in the background. Elton pays no attention; he leaves the TV on to break up the silence.

Sooner or later, boredom is going to get to him and he knows it. Mercenary soldiers are always in demand somewhere in the world and he can't believe there's any way Mister Morton could find out.

He frowns. Mister Morton's information network is phenomenal: he would find out. Dean Elton had best learn to cope with the boredom or starve.

A knock on the door. A pause, then another, more urgent. Elton swings his legs off the bed, covers the distance in four strides and opens the door.

The Hotel Manager, whose badge identifies him as Jeffry Chung, stands before him.

'Ah, Mister Elton, I am sorry to disturb you.'

'Well, you've done that, so what do you want?'

'It's very embarrassing. I have to ask you to settle your hotel account.'

'That's not necessary, my credit is good. The hotel management knows that.'

Jeffry Chung remains as still as one of the sculptures in his own foyer. 'I'm afraid that's not so, Mister Elton – not any more. I must ask you to settle your account before you leave the hotel.'

Dean Elton turns his back on the man, flicking the door closed as he does so, and is immediately confronted by Daniel Frey-Morton's face on screen as the commentator's voice picks up the story:

'...*all assets in Frey-Morton's companies frozen until further notice pending investigation of his affaires in Europe and the United States...*'

Some time later, Elton presents his credit card at the hotel check-out desk.

'I'm sorry Mister Elton, your card has been declined.'

'Try it again.'

He has three cards; all are declined. Finally he turns to Jeffry Chung, hands spread out. 'What can you do for me, Jeffry?'

'I can order you a taxi, Mister Elton. That's the best I can do.'

THIRTY-TWO

ALICE BECKER wasn't expecting visitors this morning. She pauses in the act of raking leaves in her front garden to watch the red Ford Mustang nosing in through her narrow gate.

'Mister Taffin, how nice to see you.'

'I can get someone to help you with that.' Taffin climbs out and glances round the garden.

'No need. It's my therapy. When the Post Office is sold I won't have much else to occupy my time. Until then, I rake leaves to take my mind off things.'

'No offers yet?'

'Nothing serious.'

'I have a proposition for you – a serious one.' Alice watches Taffin as he heads for the front door and wonders what a man who wears intimidating dark suits, whose shoulders swing like a wrestler's, with a slightly bow-legged walk, could possibly have to offer her.

She follows him, opens the door and leads him into the kitchen.

'Tea?'

'Always a cup of tea, Mrs. Becker. That's the way to seal a deal.'

ON A BRISK AUTUMN MORNING, Erica Lyle catches sight of Perry Butt in the High Street and follows him into the White Lion.

'I've been wanting to talk to you, Mister Butt.'

'Then do so, Miss Lyle – or is it Ms?'

'I don't really give a stuff, you can call me what you like.'

'And people most definitely will in the profession you have chosen. I'll call you Erica, and ask Meg here to supply me with a large gin and just a splash of Angostura. Have you ever tried pink gin?'

'This will be my first... Perry.'

'Good girl.' The old journalist nods. 'And why would you want to talk to a dinosaur like me?'

'Part of my education, let's say. Have you been reading my stuff?'

'Very impressive. You have tenacity and nerve.'

'I appreciate that. Nerve is what I want to talk to you about. I've had a sniff of local news and I don't know who else to consult.'

'Do you want to concern yourself with a local story?'

'Local knowledge got me where I am.'

Meg has poured two pink gins and set them on the bar. 'Is this with you, Mister Butt?'

'Good grief.' Perry Butt fishes in his pocket until Erica comes up with the cash, then raises his glass and clinks with her. '*Slainte mhaith*. Yes – local knowledge – you can't beat it.'

'Someone's bought the Post Office and is busily stocking it with the entire contents of the old Tollgate Bookshop. That's quaint, but there's obviously a minor philanthropist in the background. Any ideas?'

'Are you asking me to spread rumours?'

'I'm asking for your instincts.'

'True humility.' Butt relishes his gin and peers at Erica through the glass. 'Tell me, where do you think you're headed?'

'Right to the top.'

'And where would that be?'

'Managing Editor of a national daily. Any advice?'

'Yes –' Butt's gaze wanders to the middle distance as he recites: '*To learn the age old lesson day by day, it is not in the bright arrival planned, but in the dreams men dream along the way they find The golden Road to Samarkand.*' He knocks back the rest of his gin. 'To this day I've no idea who said it, and I can still hardly quote it without cracking up – but for what it's worth, it's the secret.'

'So who should I talk to?'

'Taffin.'

The two fall silent for a moment. Meg pours them each another drink. Finally Erica nods.

'I was afraid you might say that.'

CHARLOTTE looks up from her computer as Erica Lyle walks into the office.

Two transporters loaded with classic cars from Bob Sherman's barn are due any minute. Kath has taken delivery of a van full of equipment for inter-active displays and is now in the new main building working out where to position them. Julia is around somewhere photographing every stage of the development for future reference. And now there's a reporter on the doorstep. No problem: the press is welcome any time.

'Are you the lady who called earlier?'

'That's right. I was told Mister Taffin was here. I'd like to talk to him.'

'Good luck with that. Getting more than two words out of him entitles you to a mystery prize. He's out there somewhere on the building site, love. Why don't I walk you round?'

They walk out together. Erica says, 'I hardly recognized the place. Everything's new. Is this going to be your new show room?'

'It's going to be a classic motor museum, love – state-of-the-art –people will flock here to see it. You're a journalist, tell the world.'

'It'll be a pleasure. Are you Mrs. Taffin?'

'We're not that formal, love.'

'You don't mind me asking?'

'That's your job. What do you want to ask Himself about?'

'I don't know where to start. He watched over Gordon Glennan for a while – gave him an alibi and seemed to be the man in his corner during the trial. I'm curious to know why he'd do that.'

'He had his reasons.'

'Is it true he visits Glennan in prison?'

'Now and again.'

'Why would he do that?'

'Glennan asked him to. Himself made a promise and that's one of the few things he sees as binding.'

They walk past a massive polished wooden sculpture of cogwheels and chains. Erica glances back.

'What's that?'

'That's the centerpiece for the new forecourt. It's a commissioned original by Graham Lester. I hope you're impressed.'

'I don't know the name.'

'He's a sculptor. He studied the burnt out skeleton of the car that blew up – a Cord – and then produced that amazing bit of sculpture based on what he saw. Then he designed a whole new look for us, including the sign you'll soon see over the entrance.'

They walk on towards a structure of steel and glass where a new sign is being raised by pulleys to hang over the double glass doors. Erica stands back to read: THE BOB SHERMAN MOTOR MUSEUM.

'Who's Bob Sherman?'

'A friend.'

'Must be a very good friend.'

'You'll have to ask Himself. Here he is.'

Taffin turns to watch them approach. Dark suit, dark glasses, hands in pockets.

Charlotte says, 'I'll leave you with him,' and wanders back to the office.

Erica shows open hands. 'Look, no notebook.'

Taffin studies her quietly. 'Good for you.'

'I've been training my memory. There's a lot I want to ask you.'

'Help yourself.'

'Do you mind if we talk about Gordon Glennan first? He's not a popular man. A lot of people would like to see him strung up but you stood by him. Why?'

'He asked for help.'

'You must have believed he didn't kill his wife.'

'I know he didn't.'

'Why do you visit him in prison?'

'He don't get a lot of visitors.'

'Apart from lawyers, I imagine. What do you talk about?'

'He needs to unburden to someone. He tells me stuff.'

'Has he told you anything about his billionaire friend, Daniel Frey-Morton?'

Taffin glances up at the steel beams that form the roof of this new structure and wanders across the floor of what will soon be the museum. His right leg betrays a slight limp as he turns to face her.

'You're a journalist, you know about Frey-Morton.'

'They caught up with him in Buenos Aires last week. The Americans want him for tax evasion. You know that's how they got Al Capone?'

The hint of a smile brushes Taffin's face. 'You don't need me to tell you that. What do you really want to ask me about?'

Erica takes a deep breath and stares him in the face. 'You think I'm going to ask about that movie again, don't you? Well, I might. I still don't know if you believe it's about you or not.'

He shrugs. 'I'm not the person to ask.'

'Alright, let's move on. Would I be right in saying it was you who acquired the Post Office building, insisted on keeping the service running and transferred the Tollgate Bookshop stock there, so it's all central to the village? Would you have a problem if I printed that?'

Taffin shrugs. 'No.'

'What gave you the idea?'

'Charlotte suggested it.'

'The lady I just met?'

'That's right.'

Taffin steps outside to watch a massive transporter loaded with classic automobiles making its way up the lane. Rick Bishop jumps out of the cab on the passenger side and signals the driver into position. Ed Pentecost appears from the workshop to supervise unloading.

Erica follows Taffin out and stands beside him.

'Is this the famous collection?'

'Part of it.'

Another fully loaded transporter has turned into the lane and is making its way towards them.

'Will it all fit in here?'

'Some have been sold to collectors. How do you think we're paying for all this?'

'That makes sense. Bob Sherman – who is he and how did you meet him?'

'Through business.'

'And he became your benefactor?'

'He's a generous man – a friend.'

'You seem to have a lot of friends these days. That wasn't always the case, was it?'

'Times change.'

'There are people who still think you had a hand in derailing StarTrack – you'll forgive the pun. Is there any truth in it, given your association with Gordon Glennan?'

'No.'

'Aren't you flattered that people believe it?'

'Someone should put them straight.'

'Well,' Erica flicks blonde hair from her forehead, 'here's what I really want to ask – and I'm asking as a human being, not as a reporter – why is it that people seem instinctively to trust you with their problems?'

'Ask them.'

'But you can understand why people are curious. How does anyone abduct a Minister of the Crown, survive a car bombing, come through a major police investigation untainted and end up building a museum. My readers would love to know how it's done. Any advice?'

'Yeah.' Taffin turns to face her. 'Be lucky.'